THE GODLESS

* available from Severn House

THE GODLESS

Paul Doherty

CRÈME de la CRIME

This first world edition published 2018
in Great Britain and 2019 in the USA by
Crème de la Crime an imprint of
SEVERN HOUSE PUBLISHERS LTD of
Eardley House, 4 Uxbridge Street, London W8 7SY.
Trade paperback edition first published
in Great Britain and the USA 2019 by
SEVERN HOUSE PUBLISHERS LTD.

British Library Cataloguing in Publication Data
A CIP catalogue record for this title is available from the British Library.

ISBN-13: 978-1-78029-110-9 (cased)
ISBN-13: 978-1-78029-591-6 (trade paper)
ISBN-13: 978-1-4483-0185-0 (e-book)

Typeset by Palimpsest Book Production Ltd.,
Falkirk, Stirlingshire, Scotland.

In memory of our beloved parents and grandparents.
Forced to flee Poland in 1939 so that we could live in freedom.

Dziekujemy Marek, Ela, Alexandra, Tomek Kubiakowski

HISTORICAL NOTE

B y the autumn of 1381 England had recovered from the Peasants' Revolt which had erupted in the late spring of that year. The rebel leaders were either dead or in hiding. The Crown, under the regency of John of Gaunt, uncle of the boy-king Richard II, had exerted his authority. London was now pacified, at least on the surface, though the vibrant and frenetic life of the city swirled on as usual. English wealth depended on the export of wool, but fortunes had also been made during the long, bloody war with France. Now the days of plundering were over. The soldiers had returned and many donned the mask of respectability. However, as the chroniclers point out, ancient sins constantly lurk beneath the surface, ever ready to break through. The violence of the English armies, particularly in Normandy, had not been forgotten. There were scores to be settled, injuries to be acknowledged and blood to be paid for.

PROLOGUE

Normandy, Late Summer 1363
Canes Belli: *the Dogs of War*

Madeline de Clisson, châtelaine of the fortified manor which proclaimed her family name, tensed as she heard the owl, deep in the trees outside, hoot yet again.

'Twice,' she murmured to herself.

She waited fearful as she heard the night birds' mournful repetition. Madeline lay sprawled on the broad, four-poster bed in her chamber on the first gallery of the château. She had pushed back the thick drapes; now she rose and pulled open the shutters across her bedroom window. The long summer was proving to be extremely hot. Night had fallen but the darkness brought no relief from the implacable heat. Madeline just wished it was morning. She longed to hear the thrush's pure fluting and feel the breeze before it died. Perhaps, when dawn broke, she'd leave the château and go down past the windmill to where the stream broadened. It would be so pleasant to lie down amongst the light-yellow primrose along the banks, or sit in the hollow amongst the wood sorrel. Nevertheless, dawn was hours away and the night stretched like a dark, lonely pathway in front of her. Madeline caught her breath as the owl hooted again.

'Four times,' she whispered, 'oh Lord God!'

Garbed only in her nightshift, Madeline leaned forward, staring into the darkness. Old Joachim, her principal manservant, believed a storm would burst and clear the humours. Madeline, leaning against the windowsill, hoped so, yet that hooting did not help, it deeply disturbed her. True, the night was close and clammy but she felt an unresolved unease which curdled her stomach and agitated her mind. Something was wrong but she could not determine what it was.

She glanced up at the starlit sky. Perhaps it was just the weather and the morning would clear all anxiety from her soul, soothe her nerves and prepare her for a fresh day. Nevertheless, that hooting! She recalled ancient Gertrude, who sat in the inglenook of the hearth in the great kitchen downstairs. The old woman would squat on a stool, chomping her gums as she lectured the other servants about this or that. Gertrude regarded herself as an authority on owls. She maintained that the dark, softly floating night bird was a prophet of desolation and destruction. How, if you heard an owl hoot more than twice in the space of an hour, then some dire messenger from hell would be creeping towards your threshold. Yet, how could that be? Château Clisson was well protected, lying deep in the dense forest of eastern Normandy, well away from the mayhem now spreading like a thick pool of blood across northern France. The English, the tail-wearing Goddams, were now in full retreat. Du Guesclin, that ugly yet brilliant Master of Arms, had united the armies of France. They were pushing the English back to the coast and, hopefully, across the Narrow Seas to their own kingdom, where they could lurk and lick the grievous wounds inflicted by the victorious French.

'Go home in your ships,' Du Guesclin had ordered the English, 'or we will send you home in your coffins.'

Madeline closed her eyes and prayed for her father's welfare. Lord Pierre had taken every able-bodied man from his estates to join the Golden Lilies of the French King. Lord Pierre had written how truly bitter the struggle had become along the River Seine and the banks on either side. Du Guesclin's troops, shields locked, swords and spears flickering out like dragon tongues, were pushing hard. Some French commanders even dreamed they might seize and recapture the great fortress of Calais.

Madeline just wished her father would return. At Clisson, they were relatively untouched by the war; yet, even here, the effects of the savage struggle were sometimes felt. In the main, only women and old men remained, and what defence were these against the horrors which sometimes prowled the forests of Normandy?

Madeline breathed in deeply, savouring the rich smells from the thickly clustered copses which surrounded the château. She was pleased her father had sent messengers. Three Scottish merce- naries, who had served with the French host, had emerged from the woods just as the sun began to set, twilight time, the hour of the bat. All three were garbed in brown and green jerkin and hose, their possessions clinking in sacks tied across their shoulders. They sauntered through the gate but stopped all courteous outside the main porch waiting for Madeline and her maid Béatrice to greet them. They gratefully accepted the stoups of watered ale and platters of crusty bread served by old Joachim with the other servants looking on.

'You are most welcome.' Madeline had gone down the steps to greet the three visitors, who immediately knelt as if she was of the blood royal. They bowed their heads, putting the tankards and platters on the pebble-crammed path beside them.

'That is not necessary,' Madeline had teased. 'I am a simple young lady, not some *grande dame* of the court. So please, get up.'

She had spoken slowly, as she noticed all three men seemed to have difficulty understanding her, as she did the thick, harsh-toned speech of their leader.

'Please,' Madeline lifted her hands, 'do get up. Gentlemen, who are you? Where are you from? What do you want here?'

'My Lady,' the man in the centre replied, 'we are here to greet you.' His lips curled into a smile. Madeline stared hard. Like his two companions, the speaker had a hood pulled over his head whilst his face was thickly bearded and moustached. Madeline noticed they all wore warbelts with sword and dagger pushed into their sheaths, whilst their apparent leader, the man who did the talking, had a small hand-held arbalest dangling from a clasp on his warbelt. The man bowed again and fished in his wallet.

'My Lady, you are gracious. We bring you messages from your father, the Lord Pierre.'

Madeline clapped her hands in joy as she beamed at these most welcome of couriers.

'I am sorry, my Lady,' the man's stumbling French was almost difficult to understand, 'as I've told you. We are Scottish mercenaries. Our kingdom and France, as you may well know, are close allies against the Goddams. We have journeyed from the main royal camp outside Rouen and are travelling southwest in the hope of joining the great chevauchée into Gascony. We asked for licences to leave as well as information about the roads. Your father, who works in the royal chancery, heard of us and sent this message.'

The man stepped forward and handed Madeline a scroll of parchment, clean and white despite the journey, and neatly tied with a blood-red ribbon. Madeline hastily undid the scroll and read the message scrawled in a clerkly hand. The letter declared how her father Lord Pierre was in good health and excellent spirits, and that he was now amongst the King's most chosen councillors. Lord Pierre added that he did not know when he would return, but entrusted this message, along with his love, to his one and only beloved daughter. In a hastily written postscript, Lord Pierre added that his three messengers, Scotsmen, Samuel Moleskin, Matthew Hornsby and John Falaise, could be trusted. The letter, as usual, was not signed, but sealed in green wax which boasted the Clisson coat of arms, a flowering palm tree recalling the family's involvement in Outremer hundreds of years earlier.

Madeline, delighted to read such news, had ushered her guests into the main hall. Joachim, Béatrice and Gertrude had served them a pottage of pheasant, spiced and sprinkled with the freshest herbs, as well as goblets of the finest Alsace. The young châtelaine had joined her guests at table. Moleskin, their leader, was affable, but the other two just sat staring morosely. Madeline quietly wondered if one of them, Hornsby, was madcap, fey-witted. The conversation turned desultory. The messengers repeated their assurances that Lord Pierre was, as he had written, in the best of health. In truth, Madeline had been distracted by that letter; there was something amiss but she could not place it. Nevertheless, her guests were pleasant enough. The conversation eventually turned to the war. Béatrice recalled stories she had heard about an English free company: a cohort of mercenaries who manned the war barge *Le Sans Dieu* – 'The Godless' – under a hideous leader, the Oriflamme, a mocking reference to the sacred war banner of the kings of France kept in its own special shrine behind the high altar at St Denis. Béatrice had breathlessly recounted what she had learned from local villagers, as well as their old curate, Father Ricard, who served the solitary woodland chapel of St Hubert. Béatrice, using her hands, described the abomination; how this demon incarnate wore a fiery red wig, his face covered by a white mask, his body garbed in a woman's grey gown. The Oriflamme's followers were no better, being cursed as the 'Flames of Hell' for their ambuscades, attacks and raids along the banks of the Seine. Béatrice commented how these malignants must also be part of the great English retreat, and she prayed that they would be caught and given just punishment.

Madeline's visitors hardly commented on Béatrice's account, just sitting eating and drinking, nodding or murmuring in agreement at what she said. Madeline's unease had only deepened. She felt uncomfortable but she could not decide why. Eventually the meal had ended. At first, Madeline had been inclined to allow her unexpected guests to lodge in the château. However, by the time the supper was over, she had decided to allocate them comfortable paillasses in one of the outhouses within the inner courtyard. All three visitors seemed satisfied with that.

Madeline broke from her reverie, aroused by what she thought was a scream followed by other unexpected, muffled noises. Madeline closed the shutters, pleased that certain kinsmen were due to visit her very early the next morning. She'd certainly feel more comfortable when they arrived. Her gaze was caught by a lanternhorn gleaming on the small chancery table. She glanced at a piece of parchment, part of an indenture sealed by her father regarding certain livestock grazing in the great meadow. Madeline, despite the heat, abruptly felt a cold, clammy fear. She now realized what was wrong with the message brought by Moleskin. The letter was sealed in green wax with the family coat of arms, but that was only used to confirm documents here at the château. Any letter sent by her father would be stamped with red wax bearing the mark of his personal signet ring. Madeline swallowed hard. Lord Pierre was a highly skilled clerk, a prominent official in the King's Secret Chancery at the Louvre. Perhaps the mistake was due to the war or the confines of the camp?

Madeline heard a stifled cry from below, followed by a creaking, then a shuffling sound as if furniture was being moved. She seized a robe and wrapped it around her. She left the bedchamber and cautiously made her way down the oaken staircase, gleaming in the golden glow of the night lights deep in their wall niches. The door to the hall was closed but Madeline glimpsed slivers of light around its edges. She made her way down and pushed the door open. She went in and stopped in horror. Béatrice, her maid, stripped completely naked, was hanging by her wrists from a ceiling beam, a gag thrust into her mouth. Béatrice's lovely snow-white body twisted and turned in the fluttering candlelight. She was alive but the terror in her glazed eyes pleaded with her mistress. On the floor behind Béatrice, placed side by side like slabs of meat on a flesher's stall, lay the corpses of old Joachim, Gertrude and others, throats cut, the floor glistening with their drying blood.

Madeline found she could hardly breathe. She jumped and turned as the door slammed shut behind her. She wanted to cry out but the shock of the abomination before her was too much to bear. All the horrors of hell had swept up to seize her. Three grotesques now guarded the door: each was garbed in a woman's grey robe, white masks over their faces and on their heads; thick, fiery red wigs. Madeline could take no more. She felt herself falling and collapsed to the floor in a dead faint . . .

Five days later, just before sunset, Gaspard, spit-boy at The Heron, an ancient forest tavern, decided to hide. Gaspard knew he would be missed for a while but, there again, visitors were few nowadays. The Heron stood on a woodland trackway which snaked through the trees towards the main highway leading to English-held Calais. Only the occasional trader or merchant would stop, eager to seek lodgings or warm food. However, as the summer had proved to be long and hot, visitors would only pause for a drink before swiftly moving on. Consequently, Gaspard's work was very light and he didn't want to be found other tasks. Gaspard loved the tavern. The Heron, with its thickly thatched roof, its plaster and wood walls built on hard stone, provided ideal hiding places in which Gaspard could lurk, hiding from Madame Agnes who managed the hostelry. Agnes's husband was often absent, taking the produce of the tavern and the surrounding forest – rabbits, quail, hens and chickens – to the many small markets along the Calais road. Gaspard particularly loved the cellars of the old house, with their low-hung ceilings and narrow lanes winding between huge black casks and vats.

On that late summer afternoon, Gaspard decided that he had worked long and hard enough. He had sat for hours in the inglenook, turning the spit, basting the meats hanging there with ladles of herb-rich gravy. The hams were now cooked and placed in white nets to hang from the ceiling beams so they could be cured even further. Agnes and her cook Lavalle would come searching for him but, until then, Gaspard decided he would hide and feast on the strips of roast meat and the thick slab of creamy cheese he'd filched from the buttery. Gaspard positioned himself in his favourite place, on top of a huge cellar cask. Once settled there, Gaspard could, through a rusty grille placed where the wall met the floor, view the entire taproom with its tables, tubs and benches. Above all, Gaspard could keep under constant scrutiny the long serving table where Madame Agnes and her cook would serve drinks and food to customers – not that there were many. Gaspard squinted through the grille. Agnes and Lavalle were gossiping to two wandering chapmen who'd stumbled into the tavern, protesting at the heat and demanding tankards of cold ale. Both men, now satisfied, were sitting on a wall bench, regaling minehostess with stories about their travels. Gaspard listened intently then started as the door to the tavern crashed open. Three friars, garbed in grey gowns, hoods pulled close, strode into the taproom. Their leader, the man in the centre, sketched a blessing in the direction of the serving table and moved to sit in a window embrasure overlooking the herb garden. Agnes and Lavalle became all solicitous, eager to serve these newcomers, especially when the leading friar put a clinking purse on the table before him.

'Madame,' the man declared, his voice low and guttural, 'we are wandering mendicants intent on preaching along the great road to Calais. Perhaps we can help the Goddams to hasten even faster to their boats.' The friar's voice was low but carrying, he spoke Norman French haltingly, stumbling over certain words; his two companions remained quiet. Like their leader, they had pulled back their hoods to reveal thick, matted hair, bushy moustaches and beards. Gaspard narrowed his eyes as he stared through the grille. Most friars shaved both their head and face, yet there were so many orders and a number of mendicants visited The Heron on their pilgrimage to this shrine or that.

'Madame?' The leading friar supped from the tankard Mistress Agnes had served.

'Yes, Father?'

'We have left a sumpter pony outside. We would be grateful for its stabling.'

Agnes gestured at one of the chapmen to assist and hurried out of the taproom. Gaspard felt guilty. He really should help, and was about to climb down from the cask when the three friars abruptly stood up. One of them hastened to the door, closed it and brought down the beam to keep it locked. The second chapman sprang to his feet but the leading friar suddenly produced a hand-held arbalest, primed and ready. He released the catch and the barbed bolt shattered the chapman's face. Lavalle the cook could only stand, fingers fluttering to her cheeks; she was about to scream when one of these terrifying visitors came up swiftly behind her, putting an arm around her throat and pressing the tip of a dagger just beneath her chin. Gaspard, heart beating, could hardly breathe. The violence had been so sudden and abrupt, the chapman had collapsed in a pool of blood pouring from the horrid wound in his face. Lavalle could only clatter her sandalled feet against the floor. The leading friar crossed to the door, pulled up the beam then stood back. The door opened. Madame Agnes came in, the chapman trailing behind her.

'Father, there is no sumpter pony?'

'Of course not,' the friar grated, and pointed the arbalest, primed with a fresh bolt, at the chapman. He tried to turn and flee but the sharp quarrel shattered the back of his head. He staggered against the wall then collapsed to the floor. One of the attackers, dagger out, pulled Madame Agnes towards him, forcing her to kneel. Lavalle was pushed into the centre of the taproom and two of the assailants began to strip her. Once finished, they bound her hands with rope collected from the stables. They threw one end of the cord over a ceiling beam and hoisted Lavalle up to hang like some piece of meat. They then turned on Agnes and did the same to her. The two women dangled beside each other, so shocked they could only mutter and moan at the indignities inflicted on them. One of the tormentors left and returned with a sack. He emptied the contents out on the floor; each then picked up a fiery red horsehair wig, put it on their heads with white masks across their faces. Gaspard could not understand what was happening, though he realized this ancient tavern now housed three demons bent – not so much on plunder – but the horrific abuse of these two women. Their leader, once he was garbed in his grotesque costume, bowed mockingly before the two captive women.

'My name is Brother Samuel, Samuel Moleskin, and my two friends are Walter Desant and Alexander Cromer. Ladies, you are here to entertain us.'

Gaspard could not watch the horror unfold. Getting down from the cask, he crawled into a dark-filled corner, hands across his ears, as he tried not to listen to the blood-chilling screams from the taproom above him.

PART ONE

The Thames: November 1381
Tenebrae facta: *Darkness fell*

R eginald Dorset, master of the royal cog *The Knave of Hearts*, stared up at the clouds hanging so gloweringly over the Thames. Faint daylight remained, but soon it would be completely dark. Dorset just hoped that the thickening mist and the fast-flowing river would be protection enough as he, his ship and its precious cargo made its way out into the Narrow Seas. Dorset prayed for fair winds and calm weather in his journey to English-held Calais on the Normandy coast. Thibault, John of Gaunt's Master of Secrets, had paid him well for this expedition. He'd also insisted that Dorset take a solemn oath over an exquisitely bound bible in the Chapel of St Edward the Confessor at Westminster. Thibault had watched him intently; Dorset knew that England might be ruled by John of Gaunt, the self-proclaimed regent on behalf of his young nephew Richard, but Thibault was the real power behind the throne.

The Master of Secrets had impressed upon Dorset how vital his journey was, and Dorset had solemnly vowed to do all in his power to protect and guard the gold as well as the black cannon powder intended for the garrison at Calais. Both precious cargoes were to be safely delivered and stored in the great treasure arca deep in the bowels of Hammes Castle, a formidable fortress which controlled the approaches to Calais, that English enclave situated so strategically, pointing like a dagger at the heart of France and all its power. The Valois King and his ministers, gathered in conclave in the Chamber of Secrets at the centre of the Louvre in Paris, dreamed of retaking Calais, of completely removing this threat from its coastline. In their eyes, English-held Calais was an open sore on the body politic of France, a pernicious canker full of rottenness. Of course it was no secret that as long as the English held Calais, they had a doorway into

France: the war lords of England could lead swiftly moving chevauchées deep into the French countryside, threatening its principal cities, plundering to their heart's content. Dorset knew all this. After all, he had served in Normandy and recognized only too well how important Calais really was. Dorset had been a member of a mercenary free company 'The Godless', who took their name from the war barge they'd served on. Dorset repressed a shiver. He must not think of those days, not now! He had other problems to confront. Instead, he went back to that exclusive jewel of a chapel where Thibault had hoarsely whispered how the garrison of Calais needed to be paid, its captain given the necessary to buy fresh supplies in preparation for any outbreak of war between England and France. The precious gold coin that *The Knave of Hearts* carried, would achieve all this. Dorset was also warned that the powder barrels for the garrison's cannons, culverins and bombards were to be safely lodged in the dry cellars of Hammes Castle and elsewhere. Dorset had taken the oath recognizing only too well the price he'd pay for failure. He would lose his ship and be given no further preferments: nothing from the royal treasury; no patronage from the lords of the council.

'Steady now,' the tiller-man bellowed from the stern.

'And how say you?' Dorset called to the watchers in the prow. 'What can you see?'

'Sandbanks,' they shouted back. 'We approach sandbanks. Gently does it.'

'Gently does it.' Dorset repeated the refrain as he walked over to the taffrail and stared through the gathering murk. He felt the cog swerve beneath him as the mainsail creaked and twisted, the shouts of the mariners pulling at the cords and ropes so the ship could turn, catch the breeze and so move further to port. The real threat were the sandbanks: desolate islands thrusting up through the surface of the river; dark, sinister humps which gave the impression of some monster emerging from the deep. Dorset narrowed his eyes, fingers falling to the hilt of his dagger. These sandbanks were highly dangerous even on a summer's day, a real hazard to the unwary. Places of shadow where pirates lurked and hid their narrow skiffs, ready to pounce on some slow-moving merchant barge or herring boat weighed down by its catch, but not tonight. *The Knave of Hearts* was a royal war cog; even the most foolhardy pirate would think twice before attacking it. Dorset smiled sourly as he glimpsed the corpses impaled on stakes along the sandbanks they were now passing. He gagged as he caught the foul stench of the decaying, rotting corpses of five outlaws. These malefactors had been caught plundering along the Thames, and so had suffered the full rigour and penalty for piracy; being stripped naked and impaled through the anus as a stark warning to other would-be marauders.

The Knave of Hearts shuddered as the full surge of the river thrust it forward. The darkness was deepening. Occasionally a hunting gull would shriek and float like a ghost over the ship. Strange, eerie sounds echoed across the water. The cog seemed to reply with its creaking timbers, the screech of rope and the clatter of the crew as they managed both the wheel and the sail. Dorset moved away from the taffrail, staring around to make sure all was well. He glanced across at the entrance to the hold where the treasure, locked away in a hand-held coffer, was guarded by two Cheshire archers. A cry from the prow sent him hurrying forward. The watchmen were pointing to a great barge with a high stern and jutting poop. A macabre, sinister-looking vessel, its black painted hull gleaming in the light of lanterns hanging along each side. The barge rowers could be clearly seen, hooded figures bending over the oars which rose and fell in close precision. Dorset peered through the mist. The barge abruptly changed tack, swinging further away to give *The Knave of Hearts* full clearance. A horn sounded from the barge, followed by the hollow blast of a trumpet, the usual sounds of river craft proclaiming their presence as well as exchanging fraternal greetings with another boat or ship. Dorset raised a hand and one of the watchmen in the prow of the cog answered the calls with a low, heavy wail of a river horn. The barge drew closer. Dorset recognized the shadowy figure sitting on a majestic throne-like chair in the stern.

'God bless you, sir,' the master shouted. 'God bless you and your good work.' The figure sitting enthroned, all cloaked and cowled, simply lifted a hand in reply.

'The Fisher of Men,' Dorset whispered to his henchman Bramley, who now joined him at the rail. 'He combs the river for corpses and takes them to his own private chapel, The Chapel of the Drowned, on a deserted quayside near La Réole. He is paid by the city council. He dresses the corpses for burial and lays them out so family and friends can come to inspect and claim the remains of someone the river has taken; be it accident, suicide or murder.'

Dorset peered at Bramley. Ever since they'd set sail, his henchman had seemed very nervous, ill at ease. Was something bothering him? Had he left his wife in good friendship, or had there been trouble at home? Bramley certainly seemed distracted, pacing up and down the cog, going down into the hold to inspect all was well – and was it? Bramley had not yet taken in the bum-barge, the ship's boat, a sturdy skiff travelling behind the cog on a thick hempen rope tied to the stern.

'I've heard about the Fisher,' Bramley answered quickly, glancing away as if he couldn't hold Dorset's gaze, straining his neck to get a clear view of the death barge as it passed. 'I wonder if he has collected any corpses, or will they harrow in vain tonight? I did glimpse the fish-boy.'

'Ichthus,' Dorset murmured. 'He looks like a fish. He has no hair, not even on his eyelids. He has a mouth like a cod and the smallest nose I have ever seen. He's an ugly creature, yet he can swim like a porpoise, and seems to have no fear of the river. One of the few who do not. As for me,' Dorset watched as the barge disappeared into the mist, 'I have never lost my fears of these waters.' He added in a whisper: 'Treacherous they are, and dangerous even on a clear day in June.'

Bramley nodded his agreement and turned away to shout orders to the cog's sacristan to light more lanterns and make sure their flames burned fiercely. Dorset sighed and moved back to stand beneath the mast. *The Knave of Hearts* was now running fast, making full use of the swollen turbulence of the Thames. The northeasterly breeze was growing stronger, and the cog strained in a screech of wood, cordage and flapping canvas. Dorset braced himself against the movement of the ship as it rose and fell before twisting from side to side. He glanced up; the sky was now clearing. The moon and stars hung low. Dorset smiled to himself. Soon they would be out in the Narrow Seas. A flicker of light caught his eye and he glanced to starboard. Bonfires burned merrily along the rise of the riverbank, a host of leaping flames which illuminated the three-branched gibbets, four in all, each arm of the gallows exhibiting a corpse, a stark warning of how dangerous the river could be. Dorset needed no such reminder. The Thames was truly dangerous; it was a highway to and from the heart of London, a river which could shift in mood as it swept up and down to the estuary. Once clear of the city, the banks on either side – with their closely crowded copses of trees; oak, elm and weeping willow – seemed to hedge the ancient river: an arras of greenery to conceal the inlets and narrow harbours fashioned out over the passage of the years. These riverside forests or woods were ideal places of concealment, a haunt for those plotting sudden attack and ambuscade.

Dorset's mind went back to another river, the Seine, which cut through Normandy. 'The tributary of war', as some of his former companions called it; a fitting description: control of the Seine, and the banks either side, had been fiercely contested by the armies of England and France.

As if he could read his master's mind, Bramley left the taffrail and, staggering against the abrupt jerking of the cog, moved across to grasp a sail rope and stand as close as he could to his captain. 'Nights like this,' Bramley breathed, 'do you remember them, Master Dorset? That war barge, our white masks, the fiery red wigs, the sheer terror we inflicted on the French, who called us the Flames of Hell.'

'And we were,' Dorset replied, clinging more tightly to the mast rope as the cog now battled against the full swell of the river. 'We were the Flames of Hell. We created a fire of fear along either bank of the Seine. What we did . . .' Dorset's voice faltered.

'You regret it?'

'Of course I do,' Dorset snapped. 'And don't you? I have tried to make reparation. I ask a priest for a blessing on every voyage I make, including this one. You know that. You brought him on board.' Dorset crossed himself. 'I have been on pilgrimage along the sacred way to Compostela, Jerusalem, Rome, as well as to the shrines at Walsingham and Canterbury. Yet the ghosts of those I slaughtered still throng about me with their hideous groans and gruesome wounds.'

Dorset startled as a gull swished low and disappeared into the gathering gloom. He took a deep breath. 'You've heard the news?' Dorset demanded. Bramley just stared back. 'The French have arrived in London; well, they have been there for weeks. They have a task which should concern us.'

'Master?'

'They want the seizure of the Oriflamme and his henchmen. The years have passed. Peace now reigns between England and France, but those at the Louvre have unfinished business. They do not hunt the likes of us, thank God, but our former leader, his henchman and the keeper of the tavern, La Chèvre Dansante, The Dancing Goat . . . Crimes were committed by both sides,' Dorset continued. 'However, according to Master Thibault, the French want the Oriflamme arrested because of his particularly atrocious attack on an innocent French noblewoman just before the end of the war. You remember when we had to fall back to the coast? We had little choice? Either go home by ship or be sent home in our coffins. Anyway, this French noblewoman has powerful kin who now sit close to the seat of power at the Louvre. They believe the Oriflamme could still be lurking in England and want him seized. Naturally I am nervous. I recall those days of blood, and I worry. Awake or asleep, the past still haunts me.'

'I am the same, but we were young, master. The blood ran hot . . .'

'Other people's blood,' Dorset whispered back. 'Innocent blood, Bramley! Women and children. You must remember the villages consumed in a sea of dancing flame and billowing smoke. The barges we plundered. The crews we slaughtered. The fires we lit.' He paused.

'And our leader, the Oriflamme, as he called himself,' Bramley replied, 'we never discovered who he really was. We would just receive the summons and our war host would muster.'

'He came from the Lord Satan himself.' Dorset shifted his grasp and stared around. Night had fallen. The river had grown more swollen, fast running, as if desperate to reach the estuary and so embrace the sea. Dorset checked that the ship's lanterns in both prow and stern were burning fiercely, whilst the cabin boys, standing on the prow or high in the falcon nest at the top of the great mast, were awake and vigilant. Such watchers were chosen because they had the keenest eyesight, ever ready to shout against some approaching danger. They also carried horns and hollow trumpets to proclaim a warning to any other craft. Bramley murmured something about checking the treasure, as well as prepare to lessen sail as they approached Sodom and Gomorrah, the names of two enormous sandbanks which thrust themselves up from the river in a tangle of briar, gorse and other hardy plants. Both sandbanks were great humps, highly dangerous because sometimes they shifted, pushing sand, soil, silt and gravel into the river. A true hazard for the unwary and inexperienced mariner.

Dorset, now lost in memories about those days of fire along the Seine, half listened to his crew's shouts and cries, the crack and snap of his ship battling the surging current. *The Knave of Hearts* began to slow, pitching and tossing on the river swell. Dorset, peering through the dark, moved across to the taffrail. He glimpsed the beacon lights placed along the sandbanks. *The Knave of Hearts* was now sidling its way through the swirling water. Dorset gripped the taffrail. He heard bumps against the side of the stern where the bum-barge trailed. He peered over the side. He felt something was wrong but he could not account for his unease. A sound made him turn. Dorset glimpsed two corpses sprawled on the deck and gazed in horror at the nightmare figure which was emerging abruptly from the dark. Hell's own messenger had arrived! Memories started. For a few heartbeats, Dorset wondered if this was some horrid vision from the past. Had vengeance come to claim him? Surely this vision from the flames of Hell was punishment for past sins . . .?

The Fisher of Men slouched fast asleep in his great throne-like chair on the prow of his barge. They had combed the river, but found it deserted by both the living and the dead. The only ship they had passed was the war cog, *The Knave of Hearts*. The Fisher of Men had decided that it was time to rest and, with a chafing dish on a cushion in his lap, he had fallen asleep to dream about his warrior days under a burning sun, fighting in Outremer for the glory of God and the advancement of Holy Mother Church. In his dream, the Fisher could almost feel the cloying warmth of both sun and desert. He relaxed, sinking deeper, when he was roughly awakened. He opened his eyes; his henchman Ichthus was shaking him by the shoulders, pointing back downriver, making signs in the glare of the lanternhorn placed on the deck beside him. The Fisher watched intently until he fully understood what Ichthus was describing.

'My friend you are claiming to have heard a sound like thunder and seen the brightness of a flash of lightning?'

Ichthus nodded in reply, his fish-like face breaking into a grin. Using his long fingers, he begged his master to turn the barge around. The Fisher peered into the murk behind him. He was tempted to ignore his henchman's request, but Ichthus was very rarely wrong. The Fisher of Men got to his feet, bellowing at Hackum, leader of the Seraphim, as the crew were called, that they should rest on their oars. The order was passed down and the barge ceased its thrust through the water, rising and falling on the swell, buffeted and pushed by the icy, cold river wind.

'Turn the barge around,' the Fisher ordered, 'we will go back. Ichthus, watch to port. I will look to starboard.'

The barge turned. The Seraphim, bending over their oars, forced the great barge back along the way they had tacked. The Fisher stared into the darkness. Ichthus stood at the rail opposite, watching the waters, ready to detect anything amiss. The Fisher was inclined to dismiss Ichthus's declaration as a mistake, when he glimpsed a piece of wood, still slightly smoking, clatter into the side of the barge before it drifted away. Ichthus made those strange sounds in his throat and the Fisher glanced over; his henchman had seen the same. The barge ploughed on, its prow cutting the swirling mist; then both fog and night seemed to disappear. The mist parted. The Fisher stared in astonishment at the blazing mass of timbers being swept backwards and forwards by the river. He glimpsed part of a sail, a shattered mast, strips of cordage and planks along which flames still danced above the cold water.

'In heaven's name,' he whispered, '*The Knave of Hearts* – or what it used to be.'

The Fisher heard one of the Seraphim call out, so he crossed to stand beside Ichthus. There was a man in the water, drifting towards the light of the lantern hanging on the side of the barge. The Fisher rapped out orders. Long poles with hooks were brought and the Seraphim skilfully pulled both man and the plank he was clinging to closer, until they could reach down and pluck him out of the water. They laid him gently along the gangway between the rowing benches, Hackum ordering the Seraphim to man the oars and keep their barge as steady as possible. The Fisher crouched down and stared at this survivor. He cleaned the dirt and water from the man's face and gently turned his head, noticing the grievous wound, a deep cleft in the man's skull.

'In heaven's name,' the Fisher breathed, 'it's Reginald Dorset, master of *The Knave of Hearts*!'

He asked for the lantern to be brought closer, took the small wineskin from a hook on his belt, and tried to force it between Dorset's lips, though he sensed the master was past all help, his life-blood trickling out of both nose and mouth. Dorset's eyelids fluttered as he coughed on the wine. He made to speak but then his body began to shake; the man was clearly dying. The Fisher leaned closer.

'What happened?' he whispered in Dorset's ear. 'In heaven's name, tell me. Was it an accident?'

'The snares of death have me,' Dorset gasped back. 'Ghosts from the past.' He flailed a hand and grasped the Fisher's wrist just above the gauntlet. 'You never ever escape your sins,' Dorset muttered. 'Do you understand, never! Hell's own messenger appeared on my ship, a red-haired demon, garbed like a woman with a painted white face. He's been waiting. Now he has come to take my soul, as he has all the souls who sailed with me.'

'Hush now man.' The Fisher prised Dorset's tight grip from his wrist. 'We will take you back to Queenhithe. A good leech or physician . . .' The Fisher tried not to look at the deep cleft in the man's skull as he attempted to comfort the dying Dorset with a lie, 'A leech, a skilled physician,' he repeated, 'will tend to your wounds.'

'I need a priest,' Dorset blurted back. 'I want a priest to shrive my soul as I am bound for judgement.'

'In which case,' the Fisher replied, 'let us recite the Mercy Psalm. "Have mercy on me oh God," he intoned, "in your great kindness. In your infinite compassion . . ."'

The Fisher continued to move from verse to verse, but he was only halfway through, reaching the line 'in guilt was I conceived, a sinner I was born', when Dorset began to tremble and shake in his death throes. The Fisher hastily sketched a cross on the dying man's cheek, then held his hand as Reginald Dorset, master of the King's cog, slipped into death.

Once he was certain the man was dead, the Fisher rose to his feet, telling the Seraphim to sail round the paltry wreckage and keep their eyes keen for any more survivors, or indeed anything from the doomed cog. They spent hours doing so, but the Fisher and his crew failed to detect anything except shards of burning wood, their flames dying as the river washed over them. The Fisher could only stand on the prow, staring into the dark, and wonder how a war cog like *The Knave of Hearts*, could be obliterated as if fire had erupted from the bowels of hell to engulf the entire ship.

The grotesque known as the Oriflamme walked along the stinking, dirty passageway of the derelict house on the corner of Slops Alley. Dawn was about to break, the first light appearing against the darkness. The Oriflamme measured his steps carefully. He felt tired after his return from the Thames, but he needed to think, to reflect. He tried to curb the rage seething within him. He had been tricked and duped but, in his tangled mind, the game was not yet over. He walked along the narrow, paved gallery, garbed in his nightmare costume; the red wig pulled tight over his head, a white mask hiding his face, and a woman's grey gown disguising his body. He carried an arbalest just in case, though he knew few people would come to this ruined house which, most deservedly, had the horrid reputation of being haunted by malevolent ghosts.

'And you are correct,' the Oriflamme agreed as he entered the shabby, derelict solar and stared up at the beams, 'it is truly ghost-ridden.' He lifted the lanternhorn he carried and glimpsed the shards of rope, still clinging to the wood, where he had fastened the nooses. He recalled that day, the sheer enjoyment of watching those two bitches choke to death. They had so much to answer for! The Oriflamme crouched, still staring up at the rafters, ears keen for any sound. He closed his eyes and recalled those glorious days in Normandy. He'd thought such times were finished but they were not. He opened his eyes, staring through the gaps of his mask and felt a fresh stab of rage. The French were in London. There were rumours about why they were here and whom they were hunting. He now regretted his mistake. He should have cut that châtelaine's throat; with one swift slash she would have been silenced forever. But now what could he do? He'd taken his revenge and would do so again, though he'd be careful. De Clisson had been a mistake and so had *The Knave of Hearts*. He'd been misled and duped.

The Oriflamme heard a sound and stiffened. Was there someone else in this haunted house? He had not told anyone to meet him here. Again the sound from one of the chambers upstairs. The Oriflamme rose to his feet. The arbalest he carried was primed. He left the solar, ignoring the squeak and scurry of the rats and other vermin. Softly he climbed the stairs. The sound was now distinct. The place was cloaked in darkness, yet he knew every inch of this damnable house. He paused at the top of the stairs and listened. He was correct. Snoring, snuffling sounds came from the chamber to the right, its door hanging crookedly on battered hinges. The Oriflamme slipped across the dusty gallery and into the room. He glimpsed a shape in the far corner; someone struggling to rise. The Oriflamme, lithe as a cat, hurried across and crouched down. Despite the poor light, he made out the wizened features of a beggar woman.

'Who are you?' the old crone whispered hoarsely.

The Oriflamme did not reply. Instead, he rose to his feet and pulled back the battered shutter across one of the windows. The darkness thinned and he studied the old crone, now standing, shoulders hunched, hands hanging down by her side.

'I came here,' she whined, 'I came here because I used to clean here.'

'Of course you did.' The Oriflamme murmured. 'Brunhild, aren't you? You are Flemish? You worked for the wicked harridans who managed this house? Free with your hands. You used sharp-quilled brushes to smack the poor children. Do you remember Brunhilda?'

The old woman took a step forward. 'Cold I was.' She moaned. 'Always cold. Very few people come here so I thought I'd take some warmth. Who are you? Why are you dressed like that? It brings back memories.' She staggered back as the Oriflamme raised the arbalest.

'I should hang you,' he muttered, 'but the hour is passing and a new day awaits. I have certain business to attend to. Important matters to be settled. However, I will send you to a warmer place.'

Lifting the arbalest a little higher, the Oriflamme pointed it directly and released the catch, watching the barbed quarrel hiss through the air to catch the old woman deep in her throat. She crumpled to the floor as the blood gushed out. The Oriflamme watched her shake and tremble before turning her over with the toe of his boot. He peered down at her glassy, dead stare. 'One small comfort,' he whispered, 'at least the night has not been totally without profit. Now I have that other business . . .' The Oriflamme primed the crossbow with a fresh bolt, left the chamber and hastened downstairs. He went up and down the passageways checking other rooms – the squalid kitchen, the filth-ridden buttery – before returning to the solar and the basket he'd hidden away there. He opened this and stared at the severed heads of the two men he'd killed the previous day. 'So it's time for you to go,' he murmured. He picked the basket up and walked back through the kitchen, out into the derelict overgrown garden at the back of the house. The entire place reeked of the midden heap, a rank stench from the great, open sewer at the far end of the garden, which cut across the alleyway beyond. The Oriflamme emptied the basket then kicked both heads, as if they were pieces of dirt, into the mouth of the sewer, forcing them further down with a pole he'd found lying close by. Once satisfied, the Oriflamme threw the basket into the darkness. He wiped his hands on his grey gown and stared up at the lightening sky. 'Ah well,' he whispered, 'it's time to return.'

Athelstan, Dominican parish priest of St Erconwald's in Southwark, braced himself for another day as he sat staring at his parish council. Sometimes Athelstan believed he served this parish because of his many sins, yet in truth he loved the people seated before him. A real paradox, as he had confessed to his good friend and companion, Sir John Cranston, Lord High Coroner of London. Athelstan firmly believed that he was in for a memorable day. He could sense that in the heart of his being. He'd glimpsed mischief in the faces of his flock and wondered what was about to be revealed. He had risen early that briefly beautiful but chilly morning. He had recited a prayer, crossed himself, washed and shaved at the lavarium, then dressed in his Dominican robes. He had gone out into the dark and opened the church, before returning to the priest's house to feed both himself and his constant dining companion, the great, one-eyed tomcat Bonaventure, who had adopted Athelstan as his lifelong friend. After breaking his fast, Athelstan had returned to the sanctuary of his church and, with Bonaventure crouching beside him, had softly chanted matins and lauds. Once finished, the friar had prepared to celebrate his Jesus Mass. The church bell had tolled its summons and his parishioners duly assembled yet, even as they trooped through the door, Athelstan felt trouble was brewing. During the Mass, the parishioners remained in a tight knot around Watkin the dung-seller, leader of the parish council, and his not so loyal henchman, the narrow-faced Pike the Ditcher. Both of these worthies flanked Joscelyn the one-armed former river pirate, now the honest minehost of The Piebald tavern. This rather majestic hostelry stood close to the church and, in Athelstan's view, was the fermenting pot of a whole host of mischief in the parish. Mischief! Mischief! The friar grimaced, that's what he could sense. A pot of mischief was being swiftly brewed and brought to the boil.

Athelstan had prepared himself against the approaching tumult by concentrating on his Mass and the sacrifice of Christ's body and blood. The parishioners had celebrated the Eucharist, listened to the readings and bowed their heads for the final blessing. Now the liturgy was over, the parish council had gathered to do business. Watkin and his coven squatted on benches either side of Athelstan, who sat enthroned in the ornately carved celebrant's chair. The door to the rood screen behind the friar had been deliberately left open. Athelstan wanted to remind his parishioners that they were in God's holy place, and across the sanctuary winked the pyx light burning to signify Christ's bodily presence amongst them.

Athelstan sighed, blessed himself, and intoned the 'Veni Creator Spiritus'. Once finished, he forced a smile as he stared at his parishioners, who simply gazed back. They were wary of this gentle little friar with his nut-brown face, full mouth and

large soft eyes. They truly loved their priest. He had proved
himself to be a true pastor who cared for his flock, not just the
fleece. A man who revelled in their lives. True, he had his strange,
eccentric ways. A friar who climbed to the top of their church
tower to study the stars. Yet, at the same time, he was a priest
who would spend nights by a parishioner's sickbed. Athelstan
was a cleric who quietly mocked himself and lived the true life
of a poor brother.

Nevertheless, there was another Athelstan. The Dominican
who was Sir John Cranston's chancery clerk. He accompanied
the larger-than-life Cranston on all his forays to unmask and trap
those sons and daughters of Cain. Murderers and assassins who
struck others down, then tried to hide from the consequences of
their hideous sin. The parish council had heard of their little
priest's exploits, as they had learnt about his fiery temper, when
a red mist would descend and Athelstan would give vent to the
anger boiling within him. Occasionally, though very rarely, they
had glimpsed the same here in St Erconwald's. They were always
vigilant about that. As Watkin had once declared, 'If you unleash
the tempest, we must face the storm.' On that cold November
morning, with the church turning warm in the glow of the braziers,
the parishioners wondered how their priest would accept their
latest revelation.

'Well!' Athelstan decided to break the silence. He raised a
hand. 'Our parish council is now in session. Oh, by the way.'
Athelstan pointed towards Cecily the courtesan, who sat all
pert and coy next to her equally voluptuous sister Clarissa. 'I am
aware of your concerns,' Athelstan reassured her, 'but now is not
the time. We have other matters.'

'But the corpses?' Cecily wailed. 'Stripped naked, cruelly
stabbed, and those wigs all flaming red. It's disgusting. We sisters
of the night—'

'Listen to Father,' Mauger the bell clerk thundered. Parish
clerk and keeper of the purse, Mauger nursed a deep dislike for
Cecily and her sister. Athelstan secretly suspected that the bell
clerk had made advances to both these ladies of the twilight and
been rejected. Two women who spent most of their time, or so
Mauger would have him believe, lying down in the cemetery more
often than many a corpse. Others now joined in the argument

being waged over whether Cecily should be allowed to speak or not. Athelstan stood up and clapped his hands until he had the silence he demanded.

'Let there be order,' he declared. 'Now,' the friar pointed at Mauger, 'what is the first item of business on the council scroll?'

'Roughkin,' Mauger snapped, still glaring at Cecily. 'Roughkin,' he repeated. 'Once taverner in this parish, former owner of the The Piebald, mortuary-keeper to our former priest who is now the permanent resident of plot 306 in God's Acre outside.' Mauger's declaration caused general amusement and Athelstan heaved a sigh of relief as the tension lessened.

'And so what now?' Athelstan demanded.

Mauger sat down as Watkin, shuffling his muddy boots, rose to his feet, fat thumbs stuck in the broad dung-collectors' guild belt strapped around his bulging stomach. Face flushed, lips jutting, he stepped forward.

'Senlac,' Watkin rasped. 'Senlac, Roughkin's son, arrived in our parish three days after All Hallows. He lodged all friendly at the The Piebald, which made us suspicious.'

'Why?' Athelstan demanded.

'Because, Brother, he also lodges in Catskill Street, which lies within this parish.'

'So he took up residence here, though he is not a gospel greeter?'

'In a word, yes, Father. Apparently Senlac was a former soldier in the Earl of Arundel's array, but who gives a damn about his past? Senlac has now returned from his travels abroad.'

'And so?'

'Well, Father. Shortly after he lodged at the The Piebald, we became most curious when Senlac was glimpsed walking the tavern examining little crevices and hidden places.'

'So he was searching for something?'

'Yes.' Joscelyn now lumbered to his feet to stand beside the dung-collector. He opened his shabby belt wallet, took out and held up a square of stained parchment. 'He was secretly looking for this.'

'What is it?'

Joscelyn glanced over his shoulder at his fellow parishioners then leaned forward. 'Father, I need to speak to you in private, but . . .'

Watkin nodded in support so Athelstan, his curiosity now pricked, beckoned both men forward.

'What is all this?' he demanded.

'Well,' Watkin now shoved Joscelyn aside, 'Roughkin once owned the The Piebald. He probably did a good trade amongst those going on pilgrimage to pray before the blessed bones of Becket as well as those travelling to the eastern ports and towns in Kent.'

'I know all about the roads leading east,' Athelstan replied drily.

'I know you do, Father,' Watkin replied loudly. 'But listen! Roughkin was also gravedigger here at St Erconwald's, and keeper of the old death house.'

'My home now.' Godbless the beggar, clutching the lead of his pet goat Thaddeus the Younger, clambered to his feet. Athelstan glanced at the old beggar man with his bald head, wispy moustache and beard, and recalled how Benedicta had become increasingly concerned about Godbless. Generally quiet, a soul who kept himself to himself, Godbless had become strangely excited and agitated of late.

'God bless you, Father,' the beggar man shouted. 'And you too, my brothers and sisters in Christ. God bless us all, but the old death house is mine now, my cottage. Me and Thaddeus look after the dead. We keep constant vigil at night. We lock our door and allow no one in but we peer through the cracks in the shutters. Oh yes, when the blackness gathers, all sorts of dark shapes appear amongst the tombs. We see them and drive them off. Father, you gave the house to me for that reason.'

'Hush now,' Athelstan gently gestured at the beggar man to take his seat next to Moleskin. Athelstan studied the boatman curiously. Usually Moleskin was vociferous and noisy but now he slumped morose and withdrawn. Athelstan glanced away as Godbless once again sprang to his feet, ready to proclaim his ownership of the old mortuary. 'Don't worry Godbless,' Athelstan declared, raising a hand, 'the old death house in God's Acre is yours in perpetuity.'

'God bless you Father and—'

'That's enough,' Athelstan pointed at Watkin. 'Continue.'

'Well, Roughkin was tavern master, gravedigger and guardian

of the death house for the priest before you, Father. Now, he truly was a wicked wretch.'

'Don't you have anything,' Athelstan raised his voice, staring at his parish council, 'don't you ever have anything good to say about my poor predecessor?' Silence greeted his question. 'Yes?' he demanded. 'Surely for once you can say something charitable?'

'Well, the one before him was much worse,' Pike growled to guffaws of laughter.

'Watkin?'

'Father, Roughkin and his priest were two cheeks of the same dirty arse. Both of them loved money, especially Roughkin. He was a hoarder and a miser. Rumour had it that he'd amassed a treasure which he hid away in God's Acre.'

'Or the The Piebald,' Joscelyn shouted. 'I have searched high and low yet there is bugger-all in the cellars except rats.'

'But now you have found something?' Athelstan fought to hide his impatience.

'Oh yes we have, as we shall show you!'

'And what does Senlac think of all this?'

'Oh he is sulking in the taproom at the The Piebald.'

'In which case, let us go there.'

Athelstan turned to Mauger. 'The other business can wait.'

'Why the hurry, Father?' the bell clerk asked. 'Why must we go to the The Piebald?'

'I, not we.'

'Very good, Father, but why now?'

Athelstan sat down in his chair. 'My apologies,' he said, striking his breast. 'Forgive my impatience but,' he spread his hands, 'I can see you are all deeply interested in this matter. A map chart or something has been discovered, yes? But,' Athelstan smiled thinly, 'this has not been shared amongst you all?' Athelstan studied his parish council. He could sense their deep impatience over the matter in hand. They were not in the least interested in any of the usual items, in particular the continued painting of the church walls. The author of these – the Hangman of Rochester – just sat, eyes half closed. The hangman had been held over the font as a child and been baptized Giles of Sempringham; he had been given his new title because of his skill as a hangman. The executioner, however, did not seem at all keen in demanding time to describe his new creations. Instead, he sat head down, clawing his long, straw-coloured hair, twisting its ends into knots. He glanced up and gazed expectantly at his parish priest, his large, dark eyes like pieces of coal in his snow-white face.

'Your paintings?' Athelstan teased. 'Are we to discuss them?'

The friar pointed to an unfinished fresco on a nearby pillar. 'You have Samson trapped by Delilah but you haven't described what happens next.'

'We know what happens next.' The hangman's voice was hardly above a whisper. 'There will be time enough for them but not for the treasure, our treasure,' he added pointedly.

'Ah,' Athelstan relaxed, glancing sharply at Mauger. 'I now know why this is our only item of business. Treasure found buried in the cemetery of God's Acre belongs to the parish that owns the cemetery. Canon law says this is the case, but a cemetery is also God's Acre and canon law argues further that anyone who actually finds such treasure can claim it as their own. The codex is very clear on this. Mauger, I wager you are more than aware of these clauses, hence the present haste to organize a thorough search.' Athelstan gazed at his parishioners and shook his head in mock sorrow. 'You are my beloveds but you are also like children racing from one thing to another.'

'Hungry children, Father,' Imelda, the sharp-faced wife of Pike the Ditcher retorted. 'Father, if there is treasure in God's Acre, it's ours. We need all the money we can get to feed ourselves and our children.'

Athelstan again struck his breast. 'Mea culpa,' he declared. 'My fault. Of course,' he sighed. 'Such news will spread, that St Erconwald's might conceal a pot of gold.'

'True, true Father,' Watkin shouted. 'And all the cunning men in Southwark and beyond will swarm like bees over a flower . . .'

'Or flies over a turd,' Pike growled, turning to his fellow parishioners. 'We should set up guard, strict watch over our cemetery, God's Acre.'

'So be careful,' Mauger taunted, pointing at Cecily and her sister.

Athelstan rose swiftly to his feet and the growing clamour subsided. He glanced at Cecily and Clarissa. The friar felt sorry

for both young women as they gazed fearfully back, so he promised they could speak then turned to address the council.

'I will go with Joscelyn, Pike and Watkin to visit the The
Piebald, where we shall investigate this matter more closely.'
Athelstan held up a hand. 'Be prudent in what you do. There is
no real need to set up a guard over the graves; our cemetery is
too big. It's nothing more than rambling, common land with
sturdy gorse, rank weeds, hard soil, ancient trees, mounds and
little pits. I cannot envisage would-be treasure hunters stumbling
around these in the dead of night. Indeed, to set up a guard would
only deepen interest. What say you?'

The parish council quickly agreed.

'Very well,' Athelstan gestured at Cecily to come forward and
speak. The courtesan rose and approached the lectern. As usual,
Cecily ignored the whispers of the womenfolk and the lewd
suggestions mumbled beneath their breath by the likes of
Crispin the Carpenter and Ranulf the rat-catcher. The latter sat
cradling the cage containing his two ferrets, Ferox and Audax,
fast asleep after hunting their quarry in the new death house just
before Mass. Both Crispin and Ranulf were sniggering behind
their hands; they abruptly stopped as Ursula the pig-woman, her
great sow lying stretched out beside her, rose threateningly, fists
clenched. Athelstan called for order and gestured at Cecily
standing at the lectern. She gripped its sides staring beseechingly
across at her parish priest.

'Father,' she began, 'over the last few weeks a number of our
sisters of the night have been cruelly butchered; their bodies
stripped, throats slit, their corpses set adrift in a skiff along the
Thames, their heads crowned with fiery-red wigs.'

'But isn't that the headdress of whores?' Mauger taunted.

'Silence!' Athelstan glared at his bell clerk. 'And I mean
silence. Cecily?'

'It's the coldness of it all,' she wailed. 'Stripped naked, throat
slashed, the red wig is a cruel mockery. My sisters have now
approached me. They seek the help of the parishes along the
riverside. But, above all, Father, they want your assistance and
that of Sir John Cranston.'

Athelstan rose and walked over. He gently stroked Cecily's
arm, then turned as the corpse door leading into the cemetery

opened. Benedicta the widow-woman came in, her beautiful olive-skin face wreathed in concern.

'Benedicta?' Athelstan called.

'Father,' she hurried up the nave, gesturing at the other parishioners, 'I apologize for being late.' Benedicta's lovely eyes filled with tears. 'But there was a commotion down near the approaches to the bridge.' She patted the courtesan on the shoulder. 'Cecily has already told me about her fears.' Benedicta turned to address the council. 'They've found another corpse! A woman, naked as she was born, hands tied, her throat slit, a flaming red wig pushed over her head. All this before she was set adrift on the Thames. This has caused more than a stir. The dead woman was a favourite of a city alderman, a confidant of Master Thibault.'

'So,' Athelstan murmured, 'such a murder tweaks the tail of the powerful.' He smiled bleakly at Cecily. 'I am more than sure my Lord High Coroner will be summoned to deal with this. Now,' Athelstan added briskly, picking up his cloak draped over the arm of the celebrant's chair, 'Mauger, see that everything is put back in its proper place. Cecily, Clarissa, light tapers in the lady chapel, and pray for the Virgin's protection. Go on,' he urged, 'there is no need to give a coin. Joscelyn, Watkin, Pike and my lady Benedicta, let us visit that second church of this parish, The Piebald tavern.'

They left St Erconwald's by the main door. Athelstan flinched at the bitterly cold breeze as his parishioners pushed by him down the steps. Athelstan stayed, staring out over the great concourse stretching before his church. The gathering place, as he had quietly confided to Benedicta, of all the weird and wonderful, who always dallied here before making their way down to London Bridge or the Southwark quayside, not to mention those journeying in the opposite direction towards the twisting roads of Kent. A throng of chapmen always assembled to do business with these travellers. Itinerant cooks had already pushed barrows into place, their grills and stoves all aflame to roast the putrid meat they'd bought from the offal sellers. The air reeked with the rank odours of the cooking viands and the tang of spices used to disguise both smell and taste. Hotpot sellers offered mulled wine, boiled milk and other drinks to lessen the chill. A group of mummers had set up a makeshift stage to enact Herod's pursuit of the Three Kings: a sharp reminder to Athelstan that Advent and Christmas were fast approaching. Athelstan quietly promised himself that the parish would be ready for these great feasts. He also wondered when he would next meet Sir John Cranston. Was the coroner busy already? Was he involved in investigating the horrific explosion which destroyed a royal cog only a few days ago? The news had swept the parish, though there were few details. The cog in question, *The Knave of Hearts*, had left Queenhithe, heading for the estuary, when both ship and crew were totally destroyed by a mysterious explosion. The friar had tried to discover more, but the destruction remained a real mystery, whilst he had to face more pressing concerns.

Athelstan recalled his meeting with the parish council. He glanced towards God's Acre; thankfully its great lychgate was closed. However, on either side of this clustered a number of cowled figures. One of these had climbed onto the wall, staring across the sea of gorse and coarse grass. Watkin espied him and roared at the trespasser to get down, which he hurriedly did. Both the climber and his companions moved swiftly away as Crispin and Ranulf escorted Godbless with his ever-present pet goat through the gate to the beggar man's cottage.

Athelstan also noticed others had gathered close to the cemetery: a fire-eater; a self-proclaimed magician with his bag of tricks, troubadours and minstrels, itinerant quacks and other cunning men, a moving mass of colour and raucous noise. Athelstan, threading ave beads through his fingers, watched intently. He wondered how many of these were genuinely resting and how many had simply been attracted by the whispered stories of the hidden treasure at St Erconwald's. A self-proclaimed story-teller had placed his box at the foot of the steps and began to describe the latest news, which included how a royal cog had been utterly destroyed on the Thames, devastated completely by roaring sheets of flame which had devoured both ship and crew.

Athelstan ignored him, more concerned with his own problems, yet quietly marvelling at how matters had abruptly changed during this tumultuous year. Months ago, before the Great Revolt of the early summer, this concourse, the parish cemetery and The Piebald tavern had been a veritable hot-bed of intrigue as the Great Tumult, as it was now called, boiled to its bloody, violent climax. The secret peasant organization the Great Community of the Realm, its leaders the Upright Men, and their fierce street warriors the Earthworms, regarded St Erconwald's parish, and The Piebald tavern in particular, as ideal places to plot and plan their great insurrection. In the end, the rebels had been crushed like grapes in a wine-press, their dreams perishing in a welter of violence as the blood of the common man lapped the streets of London. Now it was over, the Lords of the Soil had fully assured themselves that the last flickers of that savage conflagration had been extinguished for good. Indeed, since the end of the revolt, Athelstan had offered one Mass after the other in thanksgiving that St Erconwald's had escaped relatively unscathed from the retribution of men such as Gaunt and Master Thibault. In some wards across London, taverns which had fallen under suspicion, had been pillaged, burnt and razed to the ground; their owners, together with servants, hanged on makeshift gibbets outside. Thankfully not here! Joscelyn and the likes of Watkin and Pike had been saved from such ferocious culling.

'Father?'

Athelstan broke from his reverie and stared down at Crispin the Carpenter.

'We have chased off those rogues. Now, do I have your permission to buy materials for your garden? Hubert the hedgehog requires a new house?'

'Of course,' Athelstan replied. 'And I need an even stouter fence, a sturdy palisade, against Ursula's sow ravaging my herb plot and vegetable garden. So yes, buy what you need. Have a word with Mauger.'

'Father?'

Benedicta, who had stayed in the church to comfort Cecily and Clarissa, now came out, her dark-blue hood and cloak pulled so close she looked like a nun. Athelstan smiled at this beautiful woman whom he secretly loved.

'Benedicta, what is it?'

She nodded at Joscelyn and his two escorts, who stood waiting at the foot of the steps. 'Father,' she whispered, 'you should go and, trust me, this is going to be interesting.'

They walked down, pushing their way through the crowd, across the concourse and along the alleyway, a filthy runnel at the best of time, with an open sewer which reeked to high heaven. However, this morning the pungent smells swirled not so strong, the air being laced with heavy fragrances from Merrylegs' cook shop. The bakers within were producing trays of pastries, their tasty soft crusts crammed with spiced mince and stewed fruits. Merrylegs and his host of helpers, all members of his family, gathered at the open hatch and doorway, as well as parading up and down the alley offering their delicacies for sale 'at a much-reduced price.' Athelstan sketched a blessing in their direction and followed Joscelyn and the others through the cavernous doorway of The Piebald and into its low-beamed taproom, a place of delicious smells, strong wines, freshly baked bread and roasting pork.

Joscelyn insisted on serving morning ales and a batch of soft manchets from Merrylegs' cook shop. He then ushered Athelstan to the high table behind a trellised screen at the far end of the taproom. Apparently, this was a place of honour. Athelstan murmured his thanks and gratefully accepted the tankard of ale and platter of sliced bread smeared with butter and honey. Once seated, Watkin, Pike and Joscelyn immediately began to discuss the possibility of finding Roughkin's wealth. Benedicta went across to have a word with Joscelyn's pretty-faced wife. Athelstan was tempted to ask her to search around for anything significant but decided that would be futile. If treasure was hidden away in this tavern, it would be in some secret, greatly disguised enclave, be it in the walls or beneath the floor. Instead, he decided to get the measure of this place and asked Joscelyn's permission to walk around 'his splendid tavern'.

Athelstan finished his ale and bread, then left his parishioners to their own devices. He had been in The Piebald on a number of occasions but always kept, albeit very courteously, from delving too closely into the secret life of this hostelry. Here rebellion and revolt had been plotted. Treasons committed. Crimes which could have led to the most gruesome execution on the scaffolds of Newgate or Smithfield. Moreover, Joscelyn was a former river pirate already under suspicion, a man who had narrowly missed the gallows dance, losing his arm in some violent river affray. Joscelyn, along with his two fellow sinners Watkin and Pike, was steeped in mischief, attracted to it like Bonaventure to a bowl of

cream. The Piebald was a veritable kitchen where all kinds of wily
stratagems were brought slowly to the boil, be it receiving stolen
goods or smuggling wine, precious cloths and other luxuries.

As he walked, Athelstan noticed with wry amusement how
the Hangman or Rochester had been hired by the taverner to
decorate the light-pink plaster walls, recently refurbished. The
Hangman had been busy, not with carefully lined frescoes as
in the parish church, but swiftly executed drawings, outlined in
charcoal, revelling in the world of drink and meats. One painting
in particular caught Athelstan's attention. The fresco depicted
Satan's own banquet in the Long Hall of Hell. The Prince of
Darkness, skin glowing red, a crown of pearls on his golden
hair, sat enthroned, with fire lapping all around him. The Lord
Satan presided over a great supper attended by all his henchmen,
Beelzebub and the rest of the great dukes of the underworld,
the Riders of the Shadowlands, the Guardians of the Gates. A
host of minor demons with purple-red skins, eyes glowing like
embers, their faces those of bat-eared monkeys or ferocious
hunting dogs, feasted below their masters. They all drank from
goblets glowing like braziers and supped on platters piled high
with black, smoking meats. Athelstan peered closer, fascinated
by the detail, when he felt a hand on his shoulder and turned
to face the furrowed face of a stranger, a man who looked well
past his fortieth summer. A former soldier, Athelstan guessed,
glimpsing the cuts and wounds to the side of his face, the shorn
hair, the leathery skin and watchful eyes.

'You are . . .?' Athelstan stepped closer.

'Senlac, Roughkin's son.' The man pointed back down the
passageway. 'A slattern told me what was happening here.'

'You are a parishioner but you do not come to Mass?'

'If you had seen what I have seen, priest, you wouldn't believe
in the good Lord or his mercy.'

'That's why we need both,' Athelstan retorted, stretching out
his hand for Senlac to clasp. 'But at least we have met. You have
served abroad in the King's array?'

'Aye.'

'And you have come home to claim your father's wealth? Was
he a miser, a hoarder? Did he have a pot of gold which he hid
away?'

Senlac leaned against the passage wall, a look of sadness softening his harsh face. 'My mother died when I was a boy. I miss her more than I can say. My father had grasping, grubby ways. He ruled this tavern as a despot would his kingdom. He was free with his punches, slaps and kicks. A man who buried the dead in your cemetery, Father, and never gave them another thought or a pattered prayer.' Senlac wiped his mouth on the back of his wrist. 'But to answer your question, my father was paid by his priest. He also had his mortuary fees from parishioners and, of course, there was revenue from this tavern.' Senlac pulled a face. 'Money enough yet . . .'

'Yet what?'

'There were times, priest, when my father seemed very wealthy, his purse heavy with silver coin to buy the best wine and food, as well as to purchase whores for both his taproom and bedchamber. I could never fathom the true source for such wealth. Anyway . . .' Senlac pushed himself away from the wall and stood as if listening intently to the sounds drifting from the taproom. He turned back to Athelstan.

'I hated my father,' he hissed. 'I was glad to run away. I was picked up by the commissioners of the array and became a hobelar as well as a skilled bowman. I have seen the days, priest. I have fought the length and breadth of Normandy. In the end, like the rest, I became sick of the filthy food and even filthier whores.' Senlac's face abruptly suffused with hate, a look of deep revulsion and Athelstan wondered what nightmares gripped this man's soul. 'So I came home. I recalled my father's wealth, his secrecy, his love of intrigue. On a number of occasions he mentioned a treasure chart, a confused, jumbled reference to angels staring down at treasure in the earth, but I couldn't understand a word of it—'

'Nor do I,' Athelstan interrupted.

'I am sorry, priest, but that's what my father mumbled on a few occasions when deep in his cups; there again, my father said many strange things. He hated to sleep here. On occasion he would awake screaming, claiming demons and other evil spirits were haunting him.' Senlac shrugged. 'But that was the drink. God knows what he really meant. Yes, he may have hidden treasure away but it might be just one of his nasty tricks. Anyway,

I came here to find out.' Senlac paused as Joscelyn, Watkin and Pike lurched from the taproom. Even from where he stood, Athelstan smelt the heavy ale fumes on their breath. 'I'd best go,' Senlac said and disappeared, flitting like a stealthy shadow back up the passageway.

'So you have met our guest?'

Joscelyn, swaying slightly on his feet, peered through the poor light. 'I know Senlac's angry. Angry with himself. He alerted us to what he was looking for. He didn't find it but we have.'

'What?' Athelstan demanded.

Joscelyn tapped the side of his fat, sweaty nose. He beckoned the friar to follow him up to a dimly lit gallery, then up another set of loose stairs to a passageway. The gallery was gloomy and cold, lit only by the flickering glow of tallow candles under their caps. A place of deep darkness, with only slivers of light around which shadows curled and twisted. Athelstan shivered. He had attended a number of exorcisms and now he experienced that same nameless dread which afflicted him on such occasions. A mysterious terror, a real feeling that he'd left ordinary human experience and entered into a domain of spiritual darkness. As he walked along the gallery, Joscelyn shuffling before him, Watkin and Pike trailing behind, Athelstan sensed that he'd entered a truly evil place. Something really wicked had happened here, unforgiven, mouldering mortal sin which demanded to be confronted and resolved. In a word, this tavern had the stink of Hell about it and Athelstan wondered why?

They reached a chamber at the end of the gallery. Joscelyn unlocked the door, murmuring how he always kept it locked, and ushered Athelstan in. The taverner apologized for the dark as he stumbled around, opening the shutters across the narrow window and lighting a lanternhorn placed in the centre of a shabby chancery table. The room was dingy, with tawdry sticks of furniture, some stools, a bench, an unwashed jakes' pot and two battered coffers. Joscelyn pointed to a hole, deep in the plaster above the chancery table.

'There was a crucifix there, the Cross of San Damiano. When we searched the tavern, I wondered about that cross, bearing in mind that Roughkin couldn't give a fig about God or man. So I took the cross down; a piece of plaster had been inserted and cunningly fixed to cover the cavity behind it. This is what I found.' Joscelyn drew the same square of parchment from his wallet that he had produced in the church.

'Let me see this.'

Joscelyn reluctantly handed it over. Athelstan, with his three parishioners crowding around him, sat down on a rickety chair before the chancery table. He studied the parchment stained with streaks of dirt yet, rubbing its texture between his fingers, Athelstan concluded that Roughkin had used the best vellum for this mysterious chart. The friar carefully unfolded it, spreading it out on the table. The chart was a complete square of about nine to ten inches along each side. The ink was clear and distinct, as were the different words and symbols. He studied the message carefully written in dog Latin at the top of the manuscript. *'Angeli spectant thesaurum terrae* – Angels stare down at earth's treasure.' Athelstan paused over the translation before moving to the drawing beneath this cryptic message, a collection of roughly etched ovals containing small rectangles. In some of these rectangles was a small triangle.

'Only God knows what this means,' he murmured.

'It's God's Acre,' Joscelyn declared. 'It must be. The rectangles must be tombstones or graves.'

'And the triangles?' Athelstan glanced up at him.

'Perhaps special gravestones which hide the treasure?'

'And you've tried to compare this,' Athelstan smiled at his three parishioners, 'with St Erconwald's cemetery? You have, haven't you? Don't lie to your priest.'

'We have, Father,' Watkin confessed. 'Believe me, we've walked our cemetery and spent more time with the dead than the living.' The dung-collector tapped the chart that Athelstan held. 'We had to. God's Acre is an oval: there are grave slabs, but nothing similar to this drawing.'

'We think the angels mentioned are those carved on the side of the church tower,' Joscelyn offered. 'But . . .' His voice trailed away.

Athelstan continued to study the chart. He also suspected it was a map of St Erconwald's cemetery. Were the ovals burial pits and the rectangles gravestones? But why did some have triangles in the centre?

'So you have compared this chart to our cemetery but discovered nothing?'

'Yes, Father,' they all chorused.

Athelstan folded the chart and, ignoring the muted protests from his parishioners, slipped the square of vellum into his belt wallet. 'Look. It will be safe with me,' Athelstan reassured his companions. 'I shall lock it away in the parish arca in our sacristy. I need to study it carefully. Moreover, if people get to know, as they surely will, that you no longer hold the chart, all to the good. But first,' Athelstan sat back in the shabby chancery chair, 'we have to think and reflect. I do not know what happened in the past. There is no chronicle of St Erconwald's. None of the previous priests kept records or muniments, not even a blood book; well, nothing you can boast about. Manuscripts were destroyed or taken away. In some cases, no record was made. You know that. So,' he heaved a sigh, 'what did happen here during Roughkin's tenure? Do you know? Are there any personal memories which could help?'

The three parishioners just stared back. Athelstan rose, walked to the window, and stared down at the cobbled stable yard. Benedicta was sitting on the wall of the small tavern well, deep in conversation with Joscelyn's wife and others who helped her manage the kitchen.

'Well?' He turned and came back to sit in the chancery chair. 'Joscelyn, can you help?'

The taverner lifted his head sheepishly. 'Years ago,' he admitted, then winked at his associates who looked equally embarrassed, 'fifteen to twenty years ago,' he repeated, 'we all ran wild.'

'We were true roaring boys,' Watkin interjected, 'Some more than others. We didn't give a bee's turd about our priest or his church. Indeed, the priest was a bigger sinner than any of us. We didn't go to Mass – not that he often celebrated one.' Watkin wiped his mouth. 'Now, as for Roughkin . . .' He coughed, clearing his throat, and stretched. Athelstan tried not to flinch at the gusty stench of sweat mingled with that of the dung and rubbish that Watkin cleared. 'Roughkin was cold and distant. A man who went bearded, hooded and visored, as if trying to hide his face. He married very young. They had a son, Senlac: you've met him. Then, about twenty years ago or more, it all changed. Senlac ran off to the wars. A short while later, Roughkin disappeared.'

'And his wife?'

'Oh, she'd died some years previous.'

'And so Roughkin disappeared?'

'Without a trace, Father.'

'Many say,' Pike blurted out, 'well, they say Roughkin may have been murdered. Just a rumour, that his corpse lies buried in God's Acre, or he was drowned in the river.'

'Why should someone murder him?'

'Father, Roughkin lived in the shadows, I mean deep in the shadows. It was only a matter of time before these shadows turned on him.'

'So,' Athelstan recapped, 'Roughkin and Senlac disappear. The wife has died; all that's left is this tavern. Yes?'

'Not very prosperous at the time: the haunt of those who lurk along the river, it enjoyed a malignant reputation. I believe Roughkin made more money from mortuary fees, as well as digging and tending the graves.'

'And his reputation as a miser, a hoarder?'

'It was very well deserved. Roughkin had a mean soul. As you know, Father, many taverners give the poor the remnants of any food, be it rancid or not. Roughkin never did. A silent, sinister shadow of a man. A true wolf.'

'Then what?'

'Well,' Joscelyn replied, 'he left The Piebald a poor place. I tell you this, Father, no silver or gold was ever found but, as for the rest, what the tax collectors call the moveables – furniture, chests, clothing and kitchen equipment – remained; not that they amounted to much.'

'And who owned it next?'

'Oh, it passed from hand to hand. Usually rented by those who wished to boast about being minehost of a bustling, prosperous tavern.' Joscelyn shook his head. 'That never happened. The Piebald had acquired a chilling reputation as a place of darkness. The gossips even claimed it was haunted by its former owner Roughkin.'

'And you changed all that?' Athelstan playfully poked Joscelyn in the chest.

The former river pirate grinned and raised his good arm. 'Well, life changed for me,' the taverner declared. 'I boarded a Hainault cog, greedy for its cargo, and a Genoese mercenary put paid to my fighting days. I'd managed to save a little gold and silver, so I sued for a royal pardon during the Time of Mercy leading up to the birth of our boy-king.' Joscelyn pulled a face. 'I bought this tavern and, I think, I made it an important part of our parish, Father.'

'Yes, you certainly have,' Athelstan laughed. 'It's more visited than our sanctuary chapel ever is!' The friar paused. 'Oh, by the way, did Roughkin ever clash with the law?'

'No.' Watkin shook his head. 'When it came to Roughkin, it was more of a question of being much suspected but nothing proved. Anyway,' Watkin gave a gap-toothed grin, 'your good friend the Lord High Coroner would know more about that.'

'Jack Cranston?'

'The very same,' Watkin agreed. 'Big, merry Jack, though his face was not as red as it is now nor his hair and beard so snow-white.'

'And?'

'At the time Sir John was chief bailiff of the Bridge and its approaches. As you can imagine, he became the veritable scourge of the malefactors, confidence tricksters, and all the cunning men who ply their trade along the waterway. Sir Jack often came to St Erconwald's, sniffing out mischief as keenly as Ranulf's ferrets would a rat.'

'Well, well, well.' Athelstan stood up as he heard his name being called from the stable yard. He rose, crossed to the narrow window and peered down. Benedicta stood staring up at him; beside her was Tiptoft, Sir John Cranston's courier, immediately recognizable, being garbed completely in Lincoln green, his red hair spiked with nard, his pallid-white face all wreathed in concern. Tiptoft's presence could only mean one thing: Sir John Cranston, 'Merry Jack', was summoning Athelstan to some heinous crime.

PART TWO

Cottereau: *(Medieval French) Mercenary*

Meg Tumblekin, called that for reasons only known to herself, was a young whore and a very pretty one. Pert and confident, she plied her trade along Queenhithe ward, a frequent visitor to the many taverns and alehouses which served that quayside, especially The Leviathan in St Olave's parish. Meg hoped to do good business that day. If she was fortunate, some merchant or the captain of a visiting cog would hire her and they would meet in a narrow tavern chamber where they could make merry and sport on the bed. If she pleased them, she would be given something to eat and drink as well as good coin for her ministrations.

Meg prayed that would happen as she paused at the mouth of a needle-thin alleyway leading down to the quayside. The morning was dark, murky, made even more so by the thick river mist which rose, coiled and twisted around the buildings. Meg stopped and shivered. For some reason she was reluctant to go on. She felt a presence, as if she was being secretly followed and watched. A lonely gull came in low and shrieked above her. Meg, all startled, recalled childhood stories about lost souls struggling through a fog-bound purgatory searching for a path to heaven. Meg slowly made her way down the runnel. The walls on either side were blind: no windows, no gaps, no enclaves or doorways to shelter either beggar or footpad. Halfway along the alley she paused as she caught the fishy tang of the quayside. In truth Meg was frightened of the river, and tavern chatter had only deepened her fear. Stories about a war cog *The Knave of Hearts* being totally destroyed, along with its crew and precious cargo. People had seen the ship leave Queenhithe but it never reached the watchtowers close to the mouth of the estuary. Those on guard there had not seen it, only distant sheets of fire and flame which marked the cog's destruction. The devastation had been complete, without explanation or reason for it. Nothing! Tavern gossip claimed that demon-ghosts which haunt the lonely reaches of the Thames had swept up from Hell and wiped the cog and all it contained off the face of God's earth. Other stories were more chilling, more threatening. How prostitutes, riverside whores like herself, had been abducted, brutally slaughtered, stripped and set adrift in some narrow skiff, their heads festooned with the cheapest horsehair wigs dyed a deep blood red. Meg reached the end of the alleyway and almost screamed at the cowled figure who emerged from the swirling mist.

'Meg Tumblekin?'

The whore relaxed at the soft voice, the lower part of the stranger's face not covered by the cowl was smooth. The touch on her hand, soft and warm. 'Meg you must be going to The Leviathan? You are well known there and very welcome. You have a fine reputation, Mistress, that you tumble most prettily. They say you can tease the most jaded appetite. How your skin is soft and sweet-smelling. Now that's what I like.'

Meg, her cloak now thrown back, put hands on her hips and struck a provocative pose.

'Come.' The stranger stretched out a mittened hand, which Meg clasped. 'First,' the stranger leaned down, 'first,' the voice repeated, 'I need to collect a present for Minehost Mistress Alice at The Leviathan; a tun of the best Bordeaux, a small barrel left by my friends who do not wish to pay the custom due.' The stranger, grasping Meg's hand, hurried from the mouth of the alleyway and across the mist-strewn quayside. Muffled sounds echoed eerily. Shapes loomed up then disappeared. Meg, feeling deeply excited at such an accosting, watched her step, as the battered cobbles were littered with the offal left after the fishermen had sorted their early morning catch. She would be glad to get away from here. Despite the thick, cloying mist, the stench of brine, salt, tar and rotting fish was almost overpowering. For a few heartbeats Meg imagined some warm, comfortable chamber at The Leviathan, with a jug of Bordeaux on the table and platters of piping hot meat.

They reached a narrow flight of steps leading down to the waterside. The stranger waved Meg on before him. Clinging to the tarred help-rope, the whore carefully went down. She reached the bottom, turned and smiled. Meg's pretty head went back, exposing her swan-like neck and throat to the serrated dagger that the stranger thrust deep into her flesh: he gashed the snow-white skin, slicing deep, rupturing the blood in a matter of heartbeats. The assassin, unaware that he too was being watched, peered closer. He watched the woman die, gargling and choking on her own blood as the life light faded in her eyes. Meg slumped to the ground. The murderer moved swiftly. Meg was stripped naked, her clothing flung into the river, which was lapping hungrily against the narrow quayside ledge. A red wig was pulled over the dead woman's head, her corpse tipped into a narrow skiff boat, one of those river craft used by anyone who had the courage to travel along the banks of the Thames. The skiff was pulled closer, Meg's corpse carefully positioned in it. Once satisfied, and humming a tune, the assassin pushed the boat out to be caught by the river swell. The skiff bobbed for a while then floated away, disappearing into the rolling bank of mist.

Athelstan made himself comfortable in the canopied stern of Moleskin's new barge, *The Glory of Southwark*, rowed by the bargeman's constant companions. These helpmates rejoiced in the names of the four archangels, Michael, Raphael, Gabriel and Azuriel. All the crew had dressed well for the bitterly cold crossing, their woollen hoods pulled close, leather jerkins and hose stiffened with pitch and tar. They bent over the oars, kept in order by Gabriel, who began to chant a song, deliberately chosen because of Athelstan, about a fresh young maid and a friar as hot and lecherous as a sparrow. They stopped their singing in surprise when Athelstan joined in, his powerful voice initiating the second ditty about a meeting between the friar and his leman in some green-wooded dale. The four archangels abruptly changed their song as they left Southwark steps and braced themselves against the surging tide. Athelstan leaned forward and peered round the canopy; the river was mist-hung, swollen and forbidding. Lanternhorns winked through the murk. Horns and trumpets brayed across the water, signals from other craft desperate to avoid any mishap in such a harsh season. Athelstan leaned back and took out his ave beads. He was about to intone the 'Pater Noster', when Moleskin, 'The Great Navigator of the river', as he styled himself, sat down on the bench opposite his parish priest. Athelstan sketched a blessing. Moleskin pushed back his cowl, blessed himself, and stared sadly at his priest, as morose he had been from the moment they had met earlier in the day.

'What is the matter, Moleskin? You look as if you have lost a pound and found a farthing. You have been so since I first glimpsed you at the Jesus Mass. Is trade bad? Are you earning good coin? Has this weather affected you badly?' Athelstan gestured at the river, even as the barge pitched and swung from side to side. A horn shrieked. Raphael screamed a warning and *The Glory of Southwark* lurched to the side, moving swiftly to avoid a narrow cockle boat.

'Well?' Athelstan was keen to chat with Moleskin, even if it was only to divert his attention from the turbulent, fast-running river. 'Well?' Athelstan insisted. 'Is it trade?'

'No, Father, it's the past. It's . . .' Moleskin, hands on knees, leaned forward. 'The past, Father. Always the past! You have given sermons about how what you do in your youth can, like some viper, slide through your life and lurk, waiting to strike. This viper is choked with the poison of your sins and will eventually spit a deadly venom into your soul. Memories return; they bring a deep unresolved guilt of sins not truly forgiven or atoned for.'

'In heaven's name,' Athelstan, astonished, wiped the river spray from his face, 'you have truly turned philosophical, Moleskin. Indeed,' Athelstan smiled, 'deeply spiritual and reflective.'

'I was a scholar once, Father. I attended school in the transepts of St Paul. Good with my Horn Book, I was. I even spent a year at the halls of Oxford.' He shrugged. 'Then I threw it all away when the old King's commissioners of array visited the university. They wanted to raise a troop of scholars, promising us glory and ransoms in France. And so they did and I was one of them.'

Moleskin stared down at his mud-stained boots. Athelstan closed his eyes. In his youth, the bargeman had turned and followed a path thronged by other young men, including himself. The friar felt the same feelings of guilt. He had run away to war, encouraging his beloved brother to accompany him. In the end, there was no glory, no ransoms, just bitter hard fighting in the

towns, villages, meadows and fields of France. Days without food
or water. Freezing nights, when he would sleep with one eye
open, weapons clutched in his hands. Stinking latrines, makeshift
refuges and, for the wounded, the ministrations of men more
skilled in butchering meat than healing wounds. The chevauchée
had proved to be a veritable descent into hell. His brother had
been killed and Athelstan had brought his corpse back for burial
in a Carmelite church, close by the pilgrim road to Canterbury.
Athelstan had then returned home to give his parents the dire
news and the agony had only deepened. Both his father and
mother were utterly distraught and, Athelstan would believe this
until his own dying day, their hearts were broken by a searing
grief which sent both of them to an early grave.

'Father? Father?'

Athelstan opened his eyes. Moleskin was staring at him
beseechingly.

'I am sorry, Father, were you asleep?'

'Oh no, far from it, Moleskin. I was thinking about what
you said. Anyway,' the friar added briskly, 'what has caused this
change of mood?'

'The corpses, Father. Those whores who had their throats
slashed, bodies stripped, a red wig pulled over their heads, before
being despatched along the river in some skiff.'

'And?'

'Memories, Father, of the past; of *Le Sans Dieu*, a war barge
I served on along the Seine. The barge was well named. "The
Godless"! We were all Godless! What has sharpened my memo-
ries is that we dressed in the same garb as those dead whores.'

'What?'

'We dressed like whores in garish gowns, our faces painted
white or hidden behind masks of the same colour. Red wigs
adorned our heads, but we weren't whores. On no. We were
killers, slaughterers, Father. Men of war; men of blood. We terrified the French to the very marrow of their souls. They called
us "The Flames of Hell". We were led by a captain, a master of
array, who proclaimed himself "The Oriflamme". A mocking
reference to the sacred banner of the French, kept in its tabernacle
behind the high altar at St Denis. But that was the past.' Moleskin
turned and spat over the side of the boat. He was about to continue

when his son, popularly known as Brass-Nose, who acted as poop-boy, blew hard on his hunting horn, shouting at the oarsmen to swing to port. The mist parted. Athelstan glimpsed the north bank of the Thames as *The Glory of Southwark* turned to aim like an arrow towards the desolate, deserted quayside, just past La Réole. Athelstan caught the ever-pervasive stench of the river: salt, brine, fish, and the rank smell of the filth swilled in by the different sewers of the city. The friar readied himself, pulling his cloak more tightly around him and making sure his leather chancery satchel was firmly buckled. Tiptoft, before he'd left St Erconwald's on other business of the Lord High Coroner's, had informed Athelstan that Sir John would be waiting for him in the Chapel of the Drowned Men, the abode of the Fisher of Men. Athelstan had visited this place on many occasions; a magnificently refurbished mansion, the former property of a long-dead former merchant overlooking the derelict quayside.

Moleskin guided his barge into its berth and helped his parish priest up the greasy, narrow steps, where the Fisher of Men's gargoyle-like retainers were waiting. Athelstan knew them well; a group of deformed, misshapen dwarves, rejected by society but warmly welcomed by their master. The Fisher provided them with comfortable lodgings in his mansion in return for their work on his magnificent death barge, as well as in the timber long hall, which served as his mortuary and chapel. Here lay the exposed, mortal remains of those who had died on the river due to accident, suicide or, as in many cases, murder.

The Seraphim, as the Fisher called his henchmen, warmly greeted the friar. They knelt down, heads bowed, hands outstretched, as Athelstan came onto the quayside. The friar, touched by their profound humility, intoned a solemn blessing, and the hooded heads bowed even further as they chanted the '*Deo gratias* – thanks be to God'. Once Athelstan had finished, the Seraphim crowded around him. Two of them clutched his hands, others tugged on his cloak, whilst Hackum, a red-faced dwarf with no nose, jumped up and down in front of Athelstan, begging the friar to carry his chancery satchel. The excitement of his escort was almost tangible. Athelstan heaved a sigh of relief when they entered the mortuary chapel, lit by candles and lanterns, its plastered walls decorated with scenes from the scriptures. All the frescoes had one theme in common: God's use of the sea and the mysteries of the deep, for his own secret purposes, be it the story of Jonah, or the Final Resurrection, when all earth's waters would give up their dead. Athelstan was fascinated by this lurid painting, which depicted the rising souls as ghostly tongues of flame. The hall's low ceiling and the constantly shifting light made this a truly ghostly place, with its two long lines of mortuary tables; each had its own grisly burden covered by a black burial pall edged with silver. A candle flickered on each end, head and foot. Beneath the tables, pots of soaked herbs exuded sweet fragrances against the pungent stench of the river, as well as the rank odour from the corpses. On the far end wall hung a huge crucifix; the tortured figure of Christ seemed to rise like a swimmer from the deep, a scene of turbulent waters and grotesque monsters. Athelstan bowed to this, sketched a blessing towards the row of mortuary tables, and followed his escort along the hall into a well-furnished chancery chamber.

Sir John Cranston, resplendent in a tawny sarcenet, knee-length jerkin, was waiting for him. The coroner sat opposite the Fisher of Men, slouching as if hadn't a care in the world in a majestic high-backed chair. Both men rose to greet the friar. A stool and small table were arranged, hands clasped, instructions issued to the Seraphim. During this exchange of courtly niceties, Athelstan swiftly studied his two companions. Cranston looked the very picture of health in his silver-trimmed sarcenet jerkin, bottle-green hose and cordovan riding boots, on which spurs tinkled and jingled. The coroner's belt, cloak and beaver hat, together with his gauntlets, were draped over a coffer. Merry Jack's rubicund, white bewhiskered face exuded bonhomie, and his constant touching of his well-trimmed hair, moustache and beard showed how the coroner must have been visited by the barber in the small washroom of Sir John's house. The Fisher of Men was a complete contrast, being tall, thin, with a narrow, bony face which was closely shaved, as was his dome-like head. Severe, even grim looking, the Fisher of Men's harshness was emphasized by dark, deep-set eyes and thin bloodless lips, although when he smiled, there was a genuine warmth. Garbed in black leather from head to toe, the Fisher enjoyed an eerie reputation as the Harrower of Corpses, patrolling the river with his Seraphim, led

by his fish-like principal henchman Ichthus, who now stood still
as a statue behind his master's chair. Athelstan had never met
any soul who so closely resembled a fish as Ichthus. He had a
cod-like mouth, he was hairless in every aspect, whilst both
fingers and toes were webbed together. In truth, he looked like
a porpoise, and could swim as swiftly as one. The Fisher of Men
leaned forward and tapped Athelstan on the knee.

'You are well, Father?' he asked. 'I can see you are in one
of your reveries?' The Fisher gestured in the direction of the
mortuary. 'Sir John, shall we show our Good Brother the reason
for your visit here?'

Cranston nodded, plucked at Athelstan's sleeve, and both rose,
following the Fisher into the mortuary. Cranston hung back.
He tapped the friar on the shoulder, whispering greetings to his
'beloved companion', who worked so skilfully with his sharp
eyes and even keener wits. The coroner asked after Athelstan's
health, and then hoarsely whispered how the Lady Maude, his
twin sons the poppets, and all of Cranston's household were in
good spirits and fine fettle. He fell silent when the Fisher of Men
reached a corpse table and pulled back the pall.

Athelstan's heart lurched as he stared at the grisly remains
exposed there, the cadaver of a young woman. In life, she may
have been pretty, but her gruesome death marred all this: her
corpse lay sprawled, head slightly turned, completely naked. A
bruise had blossomed on her right shoulder but the cause of death
was clearly the jagged cut across her throat. Athelstan reckoned
she must have died swiftly, yet the shock of death was obvious
in her glassy-eyed stare and gaping mouth. What was strikingly
macabre was the thick red horsehair wig pulled down over her
head, a mockery of the poor woman in both life and death.

'Rohesia of the Crossroads,' Cranston murmured. 'A comely
young whore who plied her trade in Queenhithe as well as near
the Great Conduit in Cheapside. She was found . . . well,' he
gestured at the Fisher, 'tell him.'

'Two days ago,' the Fisher's voice was harsh with a tinge of
a foreign accent. Athelstan recalled the stories about this
enigmatic individual. How he might have been a leper knight in
Outremer. Miraculously cured, the Fisher had journeyed back to
London to dedicate himself to this gruesome trade.

'Ah well, Brother,' the Fisher of Men continued, 'you know how it is. We were floating off Dowgate when we glimpsed the skiff, as we have others, drifting on the tide. A narrow cockle boat, and inside it . . .' he gestured at the corpse.

'How many of these have you found?' Athelstan asked.

'At least five,' Cranston murmured. 'Yes, about five over the last two months. All had their throats slashed, corpses stripped, a ghastly wig pulled over their heads before being set adrift in a cockle boat.' He paused. 'As you know, Brother, such craft can be found either side of the river. They are donated by city merchants for those who want to travel from one quayside to the next. I concede there may well have been other such corpse boats; these may have capsized or become caught in the thick weeds in one of the many inlets down to the estuary. Believe me, Brother, once you have broken free of the city, you could hide a flotilla of cogs in the dense undergrowth and dense copses which fringe either bank.'

Athelstan stared at the corpse and muttered a prayer. He stretched down and, using his thumb, anointed the dead woman's forehead before blessing her. He tapped his chancery satchel. 'I will anoint her before I go. Recite a psalm that her poor soul be brought into the light.' Athelstan crossed himself. 'I believe a further corpse has already been discovered, but that is a matter for you, Sir John. May God bless such poor victims.'

'And you will bless us too Father?' the Fisher of Men demanded. 'You know the Seraphim deeply appreciate that.'

'I promise you my most solemn blessing,' Athelstan smiled. 'Then we will sing the "Ave Maris Stella" – "Hail Star of the Sea" in honour of the Virgin. But,' Athelstan continued briskly, turning to the coroner who stood glaring morosely down at the corpse, 'tell me,' the friar demanded, 'why is the Lord High Coroner of London investigating the deaths of poor whores? Not that you shouldn't but . . .'

'You are correct, little monk.'

'Friar, Sir John.'

'Whatever.' The coroner sniffed. Taking the miraculous wine-skin from beneath his cloak, Cranston pulled out the stopper and took a generous mouthful before offering it to Athelstan and the Fisher of Men.

'Rohesia of the Crossroads,' Cranston smacked his lips; he was about to take a second gulp when he caught Athelstan's glare and hastily pushed back the stopper, 'Rohesia worked for "The Way of all Flesh", the Lady Alianora Devereux, who, though she dresses like a nun, is the greatest whore mistress in the city and manages a number of – how can I describe them . . .?'

'Brothels,' the Fisher of Men interjected.

'Houses of delight,' Cranston replied. 'Now The Way of all Flesh has many patrons in both city and court. Some of these enjoyed Rohesia's ministrations. She was very popular, hence the outcry at her murder and that of other daughters of joy.'

'But there's more?' Athelstan retorted. 'There is always something else?'

'And there is,' Cranston agreed. He heaved a deep sigh and stared at the Fisher of Men. 'You must know something of this, and if you learn anything fresh from me, you must keep it *sub rosa*.'

'Of course.'

'Not here,' Cranston said. He glanced pointedly over his shoulder at the Seraphim clustered in the doorway: Hackum, Corpse-Shifter, Sham-Soul and the rest. The Fisher of Men agreed and they returned to the chancery chamber, the Fisher closing the door behind him before offering cups of the most delicious Bordeaux. Athelstan gratefully sipped at his, wondering about Joscelyn and his other parishioners, eager to indulge in what was now being gleefully described 'as the great treasure hunt of St Erconwald's'. He also recalled Senlac, Roughkin's son. There was something about the man which deeply troubled Athelstan, certainly a mummer who hid behind masks. Before leaving the parish, the friar had secretly instructed Crim the altar boy, along with his friend Harold Hairlip, to keep a sharp watch on their visitor. Athelstan also hoped that both boys would remember to look in on Philomel, Athelstan's old warhorse. Earlier in the year, Athelstan had become alarmed at how thin-ribbed the ancient destrier looked, so he had sent his old companion off to graze during the summer and autumn seasons in meadow land south of the city. Philomel had returned, and Athelstan was pleased at how plump and sleek his old friend had grown. Athelstan startled as Cranston gulped from his goblet and set it firmly down on the pewter platter.

'This is what I want to say,' Cranston declared, 'it is pertinent to what we have just seen. About a week ago, just before the Feast of All Hallows, an English war cog, *The Knave of Hearts*, slipped its moorings at Queenhithe and made its way downriver towards the estuary. The cog was to signal with its lanternhorn and dip its sails as it reached the entrance to the Narrow Seas before tacking south towards Calais. The signal houses had been warned to watch out for it, but the war cog never left the estuary.'

'I have heard something about this . . .'

'Yes, my little friar. Somewhere between Queenhithe and the mouth of the Thames, a royal war cog, its cargo and crew, apart from one survivor, were annihilated by a horrific explosion. The hold of the war cog allegedly contained not only a hand-held casket of freshly minted gold and silver coin, but barrels of black powder for the cannons and culverins of the Calais garrison.'

'I saw *The Knave of Hearts*,' the Fisher of Men mournfully interjected, 'close to Sodom and Gomorrah.'

'Pardon?' Athelstan queried.

'Huge, treacherous sandbanks in the middle of the river,' the Fisher of Men replied. 'They have brought death and destruction to many craft. I should know,' he added grimly, 'I have fished a number of their victims out of the water.'

'And when you passed the cog?'

'Brother, all seemed orderly enough. Its sails were billowing; I glimpsed watchmen in the poop, stern and falcon's nest. We were making our way upriver, back to the city. I remember a bank of sea fog, dense and cloying, rolled in. Ichthus,' the Fisher nodded to the door where his henchman stood on guard, 'he claimed to hear an explosion and, despite the mist, a brilliant flash of fire and scorching flame. At first, I thought he was mistaken, but he was convinced of what he had heard and seen so I turned my barge around and made our way back. Of course, Ichthus was correct. *The Knave of Hearts* was just a blazing, floating wreck. There must have also been some oil on board, which would feed the flame, as would the ship's wood-work and cordage.'

'And survivors?'

'At first, none that we could see. Most of those on board would have been shredded like soft meat on a skillet.'

'And how many were the crew?'

'About twelve mariners, including the master and two Cheshire archers bound for the Calais garrison,' Cranston explained. 'Trusted men. Nobody else was allowed on board.'

'Nobody?'

'Nobody, Brother. Now, it could have been a horrific accident except,' the coroner pointed at the Fisher.

'We plucked a body out of the water,' the Harrower of the Dead replied. 'Reginald Dorset, master of the war cog, was found floating, clutching a timber. We pulled him on board our barge. There was little we could do for him; he was dying from a savage head wound. We forced wine between his lips and made him as comfortable as possible, but Dorset didn't seem to be aware of what was happening. He gabbled nonsense about phantoms and nightmares. How the underworld had spat filth into the darkness, vengeful spirits mottled in flesh had appeared on his war cog.' The Fisher of Men leaned forward. 'But, listen, Brother, you deal with matters spiritual. Dorset said something very eerie. He talked of a demon dressed like a woman with a painted white face, its head adorned with a wig, fiery-red like the flames of Hell.'

'Which is,' Cranston intervened, 'something similar to those poor whores, their throats cut, their corpses mocked with hideous red wigs.'

Athelstan shook his head and crossed himself. 'Is there a connection?' he asked.

'I cannot say but, to go back to the cog, if its destruction was deliberate murder, then the assassin must have escaped, surely? Though it is a mystery as to how he could do all that. As for motive? Well, it must have been the theft of the royal treasure, the gold and silver held in that hand-held coffer.' Cranston chewed the corner of his lip. 'The real mystery is how the assassin escaped and, I concede, there may have been more than one, yet the cog was totally destroyed. The Thames is treacherous, it's the dead of winter, the water is icy cold, the surge of the river violent, and a deep, cloying mist wouldn't have helped. So, to return to the assassin, he must have fled by boat.'

'The cog's bum-barge was found floating empty a few days later,' the Fisher of Men declared. 'Nothing suspicious was found in it. The assassin might have used it to escape. When I passed the war cog, the bum-boat was trailing behind, fastened by ropes with clasps to the stern.'

'Is that usual?' Athelstan asked.

'Yes,' the Fisher of Men pulled a face. 'Many masters do not haul such boats aboard until they have passed all the sandbanks. The boat can be very useful in freeing obstacles such as the heavy thick gorse which often trails from such sandbanks coiling out to scrape off the ship's side. So yes, Brother, what I saw was nothing out of the ordinary. And yes, the assassin may have used it to escape and transport the plunder.'

'What plunder?' Cranston laughed drily.

'Sir John?'

'There was no treasure! As you know, Master Thibault has a weasel mind and the cunning of a fox. He made great play about *The Knave of Hearts* taking gold and silver to Calais. It never went. At least not on board ship.'

'Sir John?'

'Brother,' Cranston held up a hand, 'I only discovered the truth yesterday. The treasury coffer on board *The Knave of Hearts* held nothing but rubbish, as the assassin would have soon discovered. No, the gold was taken by sumpter pony and put on board another cog with an escort of two more. *The Knave of Hearts* was simply a cat's paw, a ploy to divert any would-be robber. Even Master Dorset was not privy to the secret.'

'Of course, *The Knave of Hearts* had no escort?'

'That was all part of the pretence, news about its cargo being too important to share with another crew. Anyway, the gold and silver are now safely lodged in an arca at Hammes Castle.'

'And the cannon powder?'

'Oh that was on board, stored in its hold. Cannon powder is valuable but not precious. Moreover, it's hard to steal; the barrels are heavy and cumbersome.'

'So,' Athelstan scratched his chin, 'we have a ship leaving Queenhithe; it sails downriver towards the estuary. We must accept that Master Dorset was actually attacked, hence the wound to his head; it means that the assassin showed his hand. He somehow got down to that ship's hold, silenced the guards and any other members of the crew. He stole what he thought was the treasure, lit a long fuse to ignite the black powder, and then left the ship, having brutally attacked its master. Somehow he managed to get himself and that coffer into a boat, perhaps the cog's own bum-barge. He then rows away. The flame on the fuse races towards the powder and *The Knave of Hearts* is no more: that, Sir John, appears to be what happened. What I can't understand is how the assassin got on board in the first place, do what he did and apparently escape, if he did escape; though I suspect this evil-hearted murderer would save his own skin. In the end, however, Dorset and all those other poor souls were mercilessly slaughtered. God have mercy on them.'

'Master Thibault wants their killer or killers caught and hanged for all to see.'

'Yes, yes,' Athelstan murmured, 'there may be more than one assassin.'

'Whatever, Thibault is insistent that those responsible suffer the full punishment for treason, to be hanged, drawn and quartered. Brother Athelstan,' Cranston toasted the friar with his goblet, 'the hunt is about to begin. Dorset's soul cries for justice, Thibault wants vengeance. Once again, little friar, we enter the maze of murder, to pursue the children of Cain to the very death.'

'As long as it's not yours,' the Fisher of Men told them, 'for whoever destroyed that ship and all those men truly is a godless assassin.'

'Godless!' Athelstan exclaimed. 'What a coincidence! Moleskin on his journey across here claims to have fought on a barge, *Le Sans Dieu*, along the Seine in Normandy during the war with France. I gather from our bargeman that the memories of his time as a soldier are not at all pleasant.'

'And I suggest he is correct,' Cranston agreed. 'Ah yes, "The Godless". The coroner ran a finger around the rim of his goblet before pointing at the Fisher. 'You have heard of it?'

'I certainly have! Anyone who works along the river,' the Harrower smiled thinly, 'or at least those of our generation, has heard about "The Godless". Indeed, I understand that Dorset, master of *The Knave of Hearts*, was also a member of its crew along with his henchman Bramley.'

Athelstan straightened up in his chair, his interest now quickened.

'Strange,' he whispered, 'how this red-wigged shape from Hell appears to have risen from its pit to plague these waters. Yes, Sir John?'

'Red-wigged shape of Hell is an apt description.' The coroner rose from his seat and went to inspect the hour candle on its capped stand in the corner. 'We must leave soon,' he declared. 'We have a meeting with those who served on "The Godless". I have news for them fresh from France. I need to tell them.' He smiled over his shoulder. 'And that includes Master Moleskin. My friend,' Cranston came to stand over the Fisher, 'I also bring good coin for you from the Guildhall . . .'

'In which case,' Athelstan rose, clutching his chancery satchel, 'I shall administer the last rites for poor Rohesia.' The friar, accompanied by the Seraphim, returned to the death house. He took out the phials of sacred oil and holy water and sketched a cross on the dead woman's forehead. Once completed, he intoned the prayers for the faithful departed. The Seraphim, acting in as orderly a manner as any choir, recited the responses as Athelstan had schooled them to do during previous visits. Afterwards, the friar walked that macabre chamber. The Hangman of Rochester, St Erconwald's own painter, had been hired by the Fisher to decorate the walls of the mortuary. Many of the scenes played on the theme *Timor Mortis* – the Fear of Death. Garishly drawn skeletons sprawled across coffins, stood on gravestones or danced frenetically around a dying man. Demons with the faces of rats, badgers, pigs and cats, all garbed in full armour, solemnly carried a funeral bier towards a yawning furnace, its flames leaping up in hungry expectation. The brilliant red paint the hangman had used reminded Athelstan of those macabre wigs fastened over the heads of dead whores. The friar blessed himself and thanked the gargoyles for their company. At their request, kneeling before him, he bestowed his most solemn blessing on the Seraphim and intoned the first two verses of the 'Ave Maris Stella'. The Seraphim were delighted and, with their good wishes ringing in his ears, the friar returned to Sir John.

The coroner had finished his business so they made their farewells and left, hurrying along the narrow runnels and thread-like alleys leading into Queenhithe ward. Despite the weather, the streets were busy, clogged with stalls, carts, barrows and

horse-pulled sledges. Athelstan always experienced a spasm of
passing fear whenever he had to push his way through the noisy,
colourful throng of the city crowds. He kept very close to Sir
John who, hand on the hilt of his sword, surged through the busy
streets like a war cog in full sail. The coroner was soon recognized by the denizens from the mumpers' castles, the tribe of
thieves who perpetrated their mischief across the city: naps, foists,
cunning men, pickpockets, forgers and pimps; these glimpsed
the coroner and disappeared like snow before the sun. The street-
lurkers sank back into the shadows. The whores and lady-boys
withdrew into the dark.

A lunatic, set free to beg and plead for alms, danced before
them; a leaping, macabre figure in his brightly coloured rags.
Cranston threw him a penny. The lunatic expertly caught this
and promptly danced away into an alehouse. Now and again,
the coroner was greeted with catcalls and insults. Cranston
ignored these, marching on. He whispered to Athelstan to be
careful and keep a wary eye on the windows above them, from
where jakes' pots and stool pans were emptied, a rain of filth
cascading down into the street, its deep sewer already choked
with every kind of slop.

Athelstan, walking in Cranston's shadow, calmed himself
down, staring around at the different sights: the beadles leading
a line of bedraggled peace-breakers down to the stocks, thews
and pillories. Three other city officials, 'bum-snatchers', as they
were lewdly called, had caught two ancient whores plying their
trade where they shouldn't. The bailiffs had stripped them of
their ragged skirts and were now beating the ancient crones'
sagging buttocks with a leather strap, whilst their aged pimp had
to balance a piss-pot on his head, the punishment of all three
being proclaimed to the mocking wail of bagpipes and the
incessant beat of a drum.

The noise was now strident. Shouts and cries. The screams of
half-naked children dancing around the midden heaps or chasing
a cat, which raced along the street with a rat dangling from its
jaws. Funeral processions were assembling. Wedding parties
thronged in alehouses. A gang of mummers tried to attract an
audience with their grisly depiction of the martyrdom of St Agnes.
Smells billowed backwards and forwards, the delicate sweetness

of the pastry shops mingling with the rank odour of cheap fat sizzling in pans and skillets set over moveable stoves. Cranston murmured that it was also execution day outside Newgate, over Tyburn Stream as well as on the great gallows at Smithfield. The execution carts, with all the paraphernalia of gruesome death – axe, noose and cleaver – hanging over their sides, were slowly making their way along the streets. The gibbet men who accompanied the carts, hooded and visored, guided their great black dray horses, pushing away those who clustered close seeking information about the condemned. The executioners pointed behind them to the heralds who followed the carts and tried to proclaim the list of felons to die that day.

Athelstan sketched a blessing in the direction of the executioners and followed Cranston into an alleyway which cut down to the quayside. The coroner paused outside a tavern on the corner of a runnel. He pointed up at the huge, garish sign which displayed a gigantic sea monster and, above this, the title The Leviathan.

'The great prowler of the seas,' Cranston whispered. 'This is the home and hostelry of a sept, a division of the Worshipful Guild of Barge- and Watermen.' The coroner and friar entered the dimly lit taproom; a high-beamed chamber, clean and well swept, the floor covered with coarse matting rather than the usual mess of rushes. Tables, stools and overturned barrels stood around the taproom; the three windows overlooking the enclosed garden were shuttered, though the piercing breeze made the flames of a host of candles and tapers flutter wildly. At the far end of the taproom stood the brewers stall, where ale, beer or wine were served. Athelstan sniffed, revelling in the sweet cooking smells. He glanced up at the hams, flitches of bacon and other meats hanging in their nets to be cured by the smoke from the great hearth built into the sidewall of the taproom.

'Can I help you?' A woman appeared out of the doorway to the kitchen. She walked quickly across, wiping her hands on a napkin, which she then tucked into the broad leather belt around her slim waist. A young-looking woman with a long, thin, pallid face, made pretty by the large smiling eyes and pert rosebud lips. 'You must be Sir John Cranston?' She turned, her smile widening. 'And this must be the illustrious Brother Athelstan?'

'Flattery is like a perfume,' Athelstan quipped back, 'to be smelt but never drunk.'

The woman laughed, adjusting the veil which covered her dark, lustrous hair. She again wiped her hands, but this time on her grey gown, gathered at the neck and falling to hang just above soft leather boots. She sketched a mocking curtsey before gesturing at her visitors to follow her through a steam-filled kitchen into the adjoining buttery; a narrow chamber dominated by the long table around which four men, one of them a priest, had gathered. The woman introduced herself as Mistress Alice Brun and invited the others, who sat morosely glaring at her, to do the same. Greetings and courtesies were reluctantly exchanged, interrupted by the arrival of Moleskin who burst into the buttery, gabbling his apologies and excuses.

'I am sorry,' he spluttered, 'I was delayed. Sir John, your messenger Tiptoft—'

'Ordered you to be here,' Cranston finished his sentence. 'So, Master Moleskin, take your seat.'

Mistress Alice served morning ales and small wedges of freshly baked bread. The taverner talked breathlessly as she scurried backwards and forwards. She assured Cranston that she had followed his instructions and closed her tavern to all except the guildsmen gathered about the table. Athelstan, sitting next to Sir John Cranston, cradled his chancery satchel as he stared around at the bargemen. Moleskin seemed to be their leader, though Athelstan was impressed by the quiet manner of the guild chaplain, Father Ambrose, a serene-faced cleric, his greying hair cut in the conical tonsure, his black robe simple, with no ornamentation except for the white bands around the collar and cuffs. A man sure of himself, Athelstan concluded, content in his own skin. Apparently Father Ambrose had once been a bargeman. He had served in France but, on his return, entered the church and was appointed as priest of nearby St Olave's, as well as acting as chancery clerk to the guild. The priest sat relaxed, his writing satchel expertly tied on the table beside him. The rest of the sept were fairly nondescript, in many ways like Moleskin, with their hard faces, skin chapped by the rain and wind. All of them were well past their fortieth summer. Athelstan noted their names: Alexander Cromer, Walter

Desant, John Falaise and Matthew Hornsby. Mistress Alice was also one of them; a recent widow, her husband Luke Brun dead and buried within the last month. Alice now owned The Leviathan; she worked as taverner and had taken her husband's place amongst the guildsmen.

Athelstan sat still and silent whilst the chatter and gossip continued. The bargemen acted as if nothing was wrong, though the friar could sense the tensions seething beneath the surface. At last Cranston leaned forward and rapped the top of the table.

'My lady,' he bowed at Mistress Alice, 'gentlemen, we have a path to follow, one which will lead us back into the past. So let us be honest, blunt and stark with the truth.' Cranston paused. 'You know, I know, we all know about the prostitutes who have been murdered, their naked corpses set adrift on some skiff, their heads adorned with cheap, fiery red wigs. You must have also heard about the destruction of *The Knave of Hearts*, a war cog shattered to fragments, its crew annihilated, their souls sent unprepared to judgement. Now you may not know this but,' Cranston shrugged, 'there again, gossip and rumour sweep the Thames like a strong breeze. To cut to the quick. Reginald Dorset, master of *The Knave of Hearts*, died gabbling about some red-wigged apparition who appeared on his ship.' Cranston paused at the cries of exclamation his revelation provoked. 'And so we come,' the coroner continued, 'to something we probably all know. All of you are members of the Worshipful Guild of Barge- and Watermen, but in your youth, each and every one of you, apart from you, Mistress Alice, served on a war barge, *Le Sans Dieu* – "The Godless", fighting the Valois and their armies the length and breadth of the Seine. The French called you the "Flames of Hell". You certainly inflicted devastation along that river, waging war sharp and cruel against the enemy.'

'Many others did,' Cromer spoke up. 'And we only did what the old King, his son and the other great lords told us to.'

'Oh yes,' Cranston agreed, 'but you did it with relish.'

'Terrible things.' Falaise spoke up. He spread his hands. 'We must all face the truth. We perpetrated hideous acts, so much so that I doubt if men like us can be redeemed, saved even by Christ's blood.'

'My husband thought the same,' Alice said quietly. She smiled tearfully at Cranston and Athelstan. 'He died a month ago of a wasting sickness. He truly believed God was punishing him for his sins.'

'God doesn't punish us,' Athelstan replied, 'our sins do.'

'Well said, Friar,' Father Ambrose declared, crossing himself. 'But let me add, true the Flames of Hell waged war, most of us garbed in grey gowns with white masks on our faces and red wigs on our heads. Oh yes,' he tapped the top of the table, 'we were under the influence of the Oriflamme, who assumed command of our war barge.' He pulled a face. 'Or at least when we wanted him to.' The priest lifted a hand. 'However, I must make it very clear that I never went on certain expeditions, even though I became skilled in the French tongue and the Oriflamme asked me to.'

'Ah yes, the Oriflamme.' Cranston stared around. 'Your leader?'

'Yes and no,' Falaise, his thin face all set and sour, retorted. 'We elected our leader. We were a free company and we adopted the articles of war regarding fighting and plundering. Isn't that true? We fought, we looted and we shared out our booty. True?' Falaise pointed at Moleskin, who sat all solemn, his plump, bewhiskered face chapped raw by the river breezes, his narrow, close-set eyes screwed up in concentration.

'That's true,' Moleskin nodded vigorously. 'That's true,' he repeated. 'Every three months we voted for our captain of war.' He smiled and displayed a row of yellow, peg-like teeth. 'In fact I was often elected.'

'And?'

'Well, Sir John, you know how it is.'

'No, no Moleskin I don't, that's why I am asking you. I fought as a knight in the retinue of the Black Prince, as well as that of John of Gaunt, self-styled regent to our golden boy, Richard, the Black Prince's son.' The coroner's words came in a rush, so passionate they even surprised Athelstan. 'I was a knight,' Cranston continued, 'a warrior. I attacked the French in open battle or along castle walls. I did not—'

'Plunder like we did?' Desant, his flat face red with anger, small mouth twisted into a sneer, he showed no fear of the coroner as he glared back. Cranston did not react and Athelstan smiled to himself. The coroner liked nothing better than to provoke his opponent, as angry retorts could often be most valuable in searching for the truth.

'Sir John,' Desant continued, 'you may well have been the perfect knight. We also did sterling work ambushing enemy supply wagons, laying waste their villages, seizing their crops.'

'Oh, I know what Sir John means.' Hornsby, a little mouse of a man, though one with strangely long, muscular arms, spoke up. The boatman smoothed his moustache with his fingers then scratched at an angry pimple on the end of his snub nose. 'We were,' Hornsby said slowly, 'the Flames of Hell. We did things we should not have. And why? Because we fell into the hands of a real demon incarnate, the Oriflamme.'

'How?' Cranston asked.

'We manned a war barge. We were mercenaries, a free company,' Moleskin declared. 'We sheltered in a tavern, an *auberge*, La Chèvre Dansante – The Dancing Goat.' We camped there, ate, drank and divided our plunder. Then, one bright summer's day, the Oriflamme appeared. He strode into the tavern—'

'Disguised?' Athelstan asked.

'Oh yes,' Moleskin replied. 'He wore a fiery red wig, curled and thickened, hanging down to his shoulders, a white mask covering his face with holes and slits for eyes, mouth and nose.'

'And his dress?'

'Why, Brother Athelstan, you have said it. He wore a dress, a woman's dress, grey coloured, hanging from neck to ankle.'

'He must have been dismissed as ridiculous. Surely?' Cranston asked. 'Mocked and taunted?'

'Two of our company tried that,' Desant intervened. 'We saw it all, didn't we friends?'

'Except me,' Ambrose declared. 'Remember, I joined your company after the Oriflamme appeared.'

'But most of you met the Oriflamme that day?' Athelstan stared around. 'What happened then?'

'It was early morning, Father,' Falaise replied, 'I remember it so well.' He breathed. 'A hideous apparition. A man garbed like a whore, he and his henchman.'

'Henchman?' Cranston demanded.

'A veritable shadow,' Moleskin murmured, 'dressed the same,

a mute who never spoke. He accompanied the Oriflamme, but
not always. He served with his master in two or three of our
expeditions into the countryside and that was all. We later asked
the Oriflamme where he had gone? He just laughed, more of a
sneer. He said he'd sent his henchman to lead another group, but
we wondered if he'd killed him. Believe me Brother, the
Oriflamme liked nothing better. He was a true blood-drinker.'

'You were about to tell us what happened when you first met?'

'On that first morning, Sir John?'

'Oh yes!'

Moleskin glanced around and shrugged. 'Two of our company
burst out laughing. They ridiculed the Oriflamme's appearance,
stupid bastards! They were still sottish, mawmsy, after a night's
fierce drinking. Anyway, they got to their feet and continued
mocking both our visitors; that was a terrible mistake. The Oriflamme asked them to desist. They refused. Knives were
drawn.' Moleskin snapped his fingers. 'Sir John, I have seen
true dagger men at work. The Oriflamme was the most skilled.
He drew both sword and knife. Oh yes, he wore a warbelt
around his waist. So swift,' Moleskin closed his eyes, lost in his
memories, 'the Oriflamme was like a dancer; both those men
died within a few heartbeats.'

'Like lightning,' Falaise added, 'which appears in the east and
strikes in the west. Faster than a falcon plunging or any bird
on the wing. We didn't do anything. We were not stupid. Those
comrades had broken the rules of our free company. They had
offered violence with no provocation or reason. They had drawn
their weapons first and the Oriflamme simply defended himself,
didn't he?'

Moleskin murmured his agreement as he rocked himself
backwards and forwards against the table. He opened his eyes
and stared at Cranston.

'What happened then?' the coroner demanded.

'The corpses were removed,' Moleskin retorted. 'The Oriflamme
paid good silver for drinks to be served, then asked to speak to
the entire company, and so he did. He promised to lead us on
profitable expeditions and, believe me Sir John, he was true to
his word. The Oriflamme seemed to know which churches,
villages and châteaux were vulnerable to attack. He was fluent

in French and he knew the Normandy countryside as if he was born and bred there.' Moleskin blew his cheeks out. 'He soon won our confidence. It was he who gave our war barge its name: blasphemous but true. God certainly wasn't with us, the Oriflamme certainly was. He would appear once every ten days or so with fresh plans and plots. We were young, headstrong, the blood ran hot. We followed,' Moleskin added bitterly, 'like dogs would their master. We even copied the Oriflamme's appearance: women's dress, white face masks and those hideous red wigs. We became a truly frightening apparition, which swept through the Normandy countryside. We sailed our barge, closing in at nightfall, attacking at first light. We met some opposition, but the Oriflamme was a true fighter, a brave leader and a skilled swordsman. More importantly for us, he was extremely generous when it came to sharing out the plunder. He seemed to prefer killing to wealth.'

'Before the Oriflamme arrived,' Hornsby spoke up, 'we only plundered. We stole from the French peasants and townspeople, but we let them be.'

'The Oriflamme changed all that.' Cromer leaned forward, jabbing a finger at his companions. 'We let him emerge as the demon he was, one of Satan's angels, a true lord of Hell.'

'Why so?' Athelstan demanded.

'He liked nothing more,' Moleskin replied, 'than to humiliate and kill any nubile woman who fell into his hands. He would abuse them and we'd find the poor wench hanging from a beam or branch with a red wig thrust down over her head.'

'We tried to protest,' Desant murmured, 'but,' he swallowed hard and glanced around, 'let us be honest, he terrified all of us.'

'Did you ever ask him why, the reason for the slaughter, the mockery, the red wig?'

'Once I did,' Moleskin replied. 'The Oriflamme claimed he was exorcizing ghosts from the deep dark cellars of his own damned soul.'

'And so what happened?' Cranston asked.

'He disappeared,' Ambrose declared. 'I joined the company of *Le Sans Dieu*,' the priest glanced around disdainfully, 'I refused to join any expedition led by the Oriflamme. In the end, he disappeared, and we were happy to be rid of him. We'd had a glut of his wickedness. Sick to the heart we were.' The priest paused as Mistress Alice stretched across and squeezed his hand. Athelstan caught the look of deep tenderness in her eyes; a passing glance, though one not missed by the priest, who smiled back.

'My husband,' Alice withdrew her hand, 'my late husband cursed the Oriflamme to his dying day.' She dabbed her eyes, and again Athelstan caught her swift glance of tenderness at the priest. Athelstan smiled to himself and mentally beat his breast as he recalled his own deep affection, even love, for the beautiful Benedicta – so who was he to judge?

'The Oriflamme was truly terrifying,' Moleskin continued. 'He seemed to be able to read our minds. If he sensed trouble was brewing in the company, he could sniff it out, isolate the grumblers and dissenters.'

'And?'

'He would kill them. Lawful execution, he termed it, in accordance with the articles of war. No one dared challenge him. As we have said, he gave our war barge its name and he ordered us to wear the same hideous garb as himself.'

'And then he disappeared?'

'Yes, Sir John, he did. Eventually the tide turned,' Falaise explained. 'French troops flooded into Normandy. Flotillas of French war barges crammed with soldiers and armed with culverin, cannon and slingshot appeared along the Seine. Our old King was falling into senility, his eldest son the Black Prince sick to the point of death, our generals young and inept. So we all came home. God knows where the Oriflamme or his henchmen, including the taverner – the one who owned The Dancing Goat – went. They just disappeared. We didn't care. We desperately wanted to be back in London, safe and sound.'

'Once home,' Ambrose declared, 'each to their own. I decided to enter the church, being accepted for ordination by the Bishop of London. Once a priest, I petitioned for the parish of St Olave's, a small ancient church, a mere walk from here.'

'It's now the chapel, the meeting house of the Queenhithe sept of the Worshipful Guild of Barge- and Watermen,' Mistress Alice declared proudly.

'A happy place,' Ambrose spread his hands. He drew a set of ave beads from his wallet, 'I love my work, I—'

'The Dancing Goat,' Cranston brusquely declared, cutting across the priest whose serene expression swiftly soured as he glared at the coroner.

'What about it?' the priest snapped.

'Its tavern master?'

'Oh, Jacques Mornay.'

'Yes, Master Moleskin. Tell me about him.'

The bargeman rubbed his hands. He glared blearily at his companions before turning back to the coroner. 'Jacques Mornay,' he began, 'otherwise known as the Goat, a true devil of a soul, he always accompanied the Oriflamme's expeditions into the Normandy countryside. A hideous-looking man, his head and face almost hidden by long hair and bushy moustache and beard. He was as cruel and as vicious as his master.' Moleskin took a sip from his blackjack. 'Some claimed his wits were turned, but he proved to be a nasty creature with evil heart and foul lusts. He hid his face as he did his soul.'

The company now sat silent. Athelstan repressed a shiver. Old sins, ancient crimes never disappeared, they simply bided their time and waited for harvest to come to fruition. Malignant roots with malevolent fruits and poisonous flowers. So it was with these prosperous guildsmen, trusted barge masters who had been privy to deep, dark wickedness. They could act all innocent, but their previous, unatoned sins were creeping like shadows out of the past, ready to embrace those responsible for them. The bargemen sat, Mistress Alice included, mouths slightly open, staring fixedly at the coroner who, like a herald, was summoning up their past.

'I assure you,' Moleskin spluttered, 'we had nothing to do with the Goat. A midnight soul, close to the Oriflamme. When his master disappeared, so did he. But Sir John, why are we here? Why are we discussing these matters now?'

'Well, we have these poor dead whores,' Cranston replied. 'Logic dictates that their murder might well be the work of the Oriflamme, who must have returned to London and be hiding here. Just as importantly, there's the business of *The Knave of Hearts*, a royal cog and its crew utterly destroyed except, of course, for its master.'

'Dorset,' Moleskin broke in, 'Reginald Dorset. He was also a member of our company. A good tiller-man. He, and his henchman Bramley, who served alongside him, once the war was over they returned to London, very skilled and experienced; they soon gained preferment at court.'

'Patronized by no lesser a person,' Cranston declared, 'than Thibault, my Lord of Gaunt's Master of Secrets, who entrusted Dorset and his cog with a special task.'

'Which was?' Father Ambrose asked.

'That's secret business,' Cranston retorted. 'Anyway, Dorset was the only survivor found floating, grasping a piece of charred timber. He died soon after the Fisher of Men's retinue plucked him out of the water. However,' Cranston eased himself in the chair, 'before he died, Dorset gabbled about some hellish apparition wearing a white mask and a fiery, red wig which appeared on board *The Knave of Hearts*.'

Cranston poured some drink. Athelstan stared round; he was completely caught up in the twisting lines of the mystery the coroner was now describing whilst, at the same time, more than aware of the deepening fears of this group. They were desperate to discover the true reason for the Lord High Coroner's questioning, and the possibility that they might have to confront the sins of their youth.

'So,' Cranston continued, 'to go back down the passage of the years. The free company, your free company, retreats from Normandy. *Le Sans Dieu* was probably burnt and abandoned. You gather your plunder and flee. The Oriflamme and his two henchmen, one of whom was Jacques Mornay, vanish. Well, not exactly,' the coroner added grimly. 'I have received fresh intelligence about that felon's activities during the great English retreat towards Calais. The Oriflamme and his henchmen perpetrated more outrages. For all I know, these may have included some of you. The Oriflamme apparently attacked a remote château, one of those great houses out in the woods of Normandy, hidden from view and only approached by twisting lanes. Now its châtelaine was a young, beautiful countess, Madeline de Clisson. The Oriflamme and his henchmen cruelly violated both her and her maid after they had slaughtered the few old retainers who resisted.' Cranston drew a deep breath. 'Madeline survived long enough to tell everything to her father, the Vicomte Pierre de Clisson, who is now a high-ranking member of the French King's Secret Chancery.'

'Oh sweet heaven,' Father Ambrose breathed.

'I was not there,' Moleskin protested. 'None of us were, were we?'

A chorus of agreement rang out.

'Whatever,' Cranston continued drily, 'the Vicomte now directs the Luciferi, the servants of the French King's Secret Chancery, led by a mutual friend of mine, or he is now, Hugh Levigne, the Candlelight-Master. Now my friends,' Cranston continued sarcastically, 'Levigne is in London. Let me make this very clear. He is not interested in you or others, but he has petitioned my Lord of Gaunt, and Master Thibault in particular, that if the Oriflamme and his henchmen, especially the taverner Jacques Mornay, be hiding here in England, that all such criminals be arrested and handed over to the French Crown. Once in Paris, these criminals would be tried and punished for their dreadful crimes, in particular the rape and murder of Madeline de Clisson. Now the depredations of the free companies in France are notoriously well known. The Luciferi have no mandate to pursue you, but they are determined that the Oriflamme should hang on the great gallows at Montfaucon.'

'But is the Oriflamme in London?' Moleskin demanded. 'Is he here with his henchmen? Sir John, you do not know, neither do we.'

'Ah yes, but once he was your leader, Master Moleskin. Perhaps he will drift back to you. But, there again, as I have said, the Luciferi do not pursue you, though they might show a deep interest in who you are and what you do. They are mailed clerks, skilled in the matters of the chancery, but also in the use of arms, be it on the tournament field or dagger play along the alleyways. Monseigneur Levigne is not threatening. Indeed, he has said that he will reward any help you may wish to give.' Cranston paused. 'You are in no danger. You are followers rather than leaders, yet walk carefully. The secret chancery at the Louvre is hot in its desire to capture the Oriflamme and his henchmen. They have offered gold as well as the release of English prisoners if the criminals they hunt are handed over. Master Thibault, as he says, is aware of the grander picture. Neither he nor his master wants war with France and, if Englishmen have to be hanged in Paris, so be it. Gentlemen,' Cranston scraped back his chair, 'be careful, be prudent, for you live in very dangerous times.'

PART THREE

In media vitae sumus in morte: *In the midst of life we are in death*

A thelstan sat in his stone-flagged kitchen, which also served as his solar, chancery, meeting room, whatever he wished to call it. Athelstan glanced to his left. He glimpsed the tidy bedloft, the sheets and counterpanes freshly washed, thanks to Pike the Ditcher's wife. The stone-flagged floor had been scrubbed, as had the table top, as well as every other empty surface. The small priest's house still reeked of the pine juice his parishioners had so liberally used. Nevertheless, the house was clean, warmed by capped braziers, their smoke fragranced with herbs, whilst the fire roared in the mantled hearth, its flames greedily licking the dry wood and scattered charcoal. Bonaventure loved the fire. The great one-eyed tomcat now lay sprawled as imperiously as any emperor of Rome. Athelstan picked up a sharpened quill pen and stared into the fire. He was not really tired, just agitated by the events of the day. Athelstan constantly reminded his good friend the coroner that every individual man or woman is first and foremost a spiritual being. The friar passionately believed this, as he did that today his soul had confronted true wickedness. This evil now shadowed his spirit and threatened his peace of mind, like some savage animal hiding deep in the shadows but waiting, watching, ready to pounce. So what had caused all this? Athelstan dipped his pen into the night-black ink and began to write.

'Item: the parish treasure. Years ago Roughkin, owner of The Piebald tavern, keeper of the death house here at St Erconwald's and parish gravedigger, had mysteriously disappeared. The same could be said for Roughkin's son Senlac, who allegedly might have joined the King's array. Apparently Roughkin was an enigmatic, lonely man who had little time for his neighbour. Indeed, the taverner, along with his hostelry, enjoyed a rather sinister reputation, though it was difficult to establish why. Item: Roughkin had been described as a miser, a man who had amassed considerable wealth and, again, according to gossip, hid that wealth either in The Piebald, St Erconwald's church, or the great stretch of God's Acre around it. Rumour and parish gossip undoubtedly enhanced the stories about such hidden treasure. Item: all such stories had come to fruition when Roughkin's son Senlac recently reappeared, vainly searching for a chart or map which was eventually discovered in The Piebald.'

Athelstan opened his chancery satchel and took out the document he'd plucked from Joscelyn's fingers. He traced the words, 'Angels stare down at earth's treasure.' Athelstan then studied the oval drawings containing those small rectangles in a square ten by ten. Some of these contained triangles. And that was it. A roughly etched chart with doggerel Latin and mysterious symbols. Was it genuine, Athelstan wondered, or just a mischievous jest by the enigmatic Roughkin? 'Item: Master Senlac. A former soldier who now returned to the parish he'd been brought up in. A secretive, mysterious individual.'

Athelstan truly believed that Senlac had not told him the truth. 'You are a mummer so there's more to you,' Athelstan asserted, glancing up, 'than meets the eye.'

The friar shook his head. He had the deepest reservations about Senlac. Crim and Harold Hairlip had kept the new arrival under close scrutiny, as the friar had instructed them. However, when Athelstan returned from his meeting with Cranston, both boys could tell him little about the man they had watched for most of the day. Senlac had apparently moved back into Southwark recently. At first he'd stayed at a decaying tavern, The Owlpen, before journeying on to The Piebald.

'Item: the recent meeting at The Leviathan. The past had certainly caught up with those present. Years ago the bargemen served as a free company on a war barge named *Le Sans Dieu* – "The Godless". The company soon assumed a more terrifying reputation, their enemies calling them the "Flames of Hell". Like all mercenaries, Moleskin and his companions were greedy for plunder, the wealth rather than the lives of their enemy. The mysterious Oriflamme, who assumed leadership over the company, had changed all this. A true killer, deeply feared by his own men, the Oriflamme enjoyed inflicting horror upon horror upon some hapless, female captive; he'd been eager to bedeck them with same fiery red wig he sported himself.'

Athelstan paused in his writing and listened to the noises of the night. There was a roar in the wind which had persisted since darkness fell. Athelstan felt an abrupt jab of fear, as if some malevolent spirit had passed by, brushing his soul. He imagined the Oriflamme with his white mask and macabre wig. Such an apparition seemed to haunt him. The friar found it difficult to ignore this visitor from Hell. Why?

Athelstan abruptly glanced up at the crucifix nailed above the hearth. He'd seen such an apparition in his past, something similar. What was it? Athelstan racked his memory, then sighed, smiling to himself. That was it! Athelstan recalled meeting a Coptic priest who had made pilgrimage through Egypt into Ethiopia, a much-travelled man who loved to collect whatever took his fancy. Athelstan had met similar wanderers. Indeed, it was becoming fashionable for people to travel here and there, bringing back wonders; be it objects they'd collected or descriptions of what they'd seen. This particular traveller owned an ancient manuscript, which he'd brought to England and presented as a gift to Father Prior at the Dominican motherhouse of Blackfriars across the Thames. The librarian there had allowed a curious Athelstan to pore over the manuscript, explaining how the parchment was rare, some form of papyrus, strong and lasting so it could resist the corruption of the years. The librarian also explained, as far as he could, some of the mysterious drawings, winged bulls and other exotic creatures. One drawing had immediately caught Athelstan's attention, and he became fascinated by the librarian's explanation of it. The picture in question depicted a black-skinned man with silver-sandaled feet, his body adorned with the most gorgeous necklaces, rings and pendants. This creature had staring, bulbous eyes and, though his skin was black, his face was snow-white, his hair thick and red as any whore's wig in London. The librarian explained in hushed tones how this was Seth, the ancient Egyptian God of the Underworld, the left-handed destroyer, hence the blood-red hair and white face. The forerunner, or so the librarian explained, of Holy Mother Church's teaching on the Lord Satan and the powers of Hell.

Athelstan now recalled this, and wondered if the same knowledge, or something like it, had inspired the Oriflamme, whoever
he might be. Or was it something else? A scar on the soul inflicted
during childhood? The great Augustine argued how every human
soul housed a collection of emotions, experiences and memories,
be they good or bad. More importantly, these hidden feelings
would eventually manifest themselves. Did this explain that
hideously bizarre figure that had appeared in that French tavern,
The Dancing Goat, so many years ago? A truly evil soul who
drew others, such as the owner of that hostelry, into his web of
wickedness? But that was the past. Had the Oriflamme survived
to crawl like the monster he was out of the darkness again? But
why? And why now? Was the grotesque's reappearance connected
to the presence in London of the Luciferi and their desire to seize
the Oriflamme so he could be punished for his horrid crimes?
Indeed, the slaughter of young whores and the degradation of
their corpses almost seemed a challenge both to the power of
France and that of the English Crown. Surely, it was more than
a coincidence that the Oriflamme had re-emerged at the very
time the French began their hunt for him? It almost seemed as
if this killer was mocking them; that he revelled in what he was
doing and what he had done.

Athelstan recalled the corpse he and Cranston had inspected
and repressed a shiver. Yes, there was something deeply frightening about what he'd seen and heard today. A cloying fear now
clung to him. He had experienced the same as a young boy in
his father's cellar. He'd go down and crawl amongst the shiny,
wax-sealed pots as he searched for a particular one. He was
always mindful of the silvery gleam of the bats which nested
close by, hanging from the beams, watchful and waiting, ready
to take flight.

'You are frightening yourself,' Athelstan whispered. 'I must
calm my soul, soothe my mind.' He pushed away the memorandum he'd been drawing up and pulled across the ledger of
the parish council. He opened the leather tome and sifted through
its parchment leaves. Mugwort the parish bell clerk had a good
hand, and he'd already listed the items for the following day.
Athelstan mentally groaned as he reached an entry about Judith
the Mummer wanting to stage an Advent mystery play around

the life of Herod the Great! Such mummery always brought out the worst in his parishioners, as they fought each other over the different roles and tasks. Watkin and Pike would certainly vie for the part of Herod.

'Oh Lord save us,' Athelstan murmured. 'Why on earth did Judith choose Herod?' He returned to the ledger, noting with wry amusement how Mugwort had commented on Watkin, Pike and others. These parish worthies had drifted away from their various daily tasks to survey God's Acre and carefully inspect different headstones and funeral crosses. 'Treasure hunters,' Athelstan whispered. Mugwort had also described how Watkin and company had become embroiled in a rather strident confrontation with Godbless. Apparently, the beggar man had wailed long and loud about the past breaking through. How ghosts had come to confront him and that he and his pet goat should be left alone. In the end, Godbless was reduced to screaming and shouting in a gibberish no one could understand, before retreating back into the old death house, slamming the door shut in the face of other parishioners.

Athelstan rose, stretched, and went to crouch by Bonaventure, still toasting himself by the roaring fire. Athelstan listened to the wind rattling in the chimney stack. He recited an ave, stroked Bonaventure and went back to the parish ledger. Mugwort's entry about Godbless was echoed by Benedicta's concern at the beggar man's behaviour. She had been waiting for Athelstan to return and informed him immediately. Apparently, Godbless had wandered into the nave of the church and prostrated himself before the rood screen, shouting words which Benedicta couldn't understand. Eventually she had managed to calm the poor soul, bringing him a jug of ale and a platter of bread from The Piebald. Athelstan decided that tomorrow he would meet Godbless and question him closely. He pushed the ledger aside and grasped his psalter. He would finish his divine office and then take a well-earned sleep.

'The devils are coming,' Godbless confided to his sole bosom friend, Thaddeus the Younger. The goat simply kept on eating, crouching close next to its master. Godbless ran his dirty fingers across the coarse skin of the young goat. 'Doors are bursting

open,' Godbless continued. 'All sorts of doors, Thaddeus: gate-
ways to the past. Tunnels along which demons can slink. Holes
where monsters fall through.' Godbless ran his tongue around his
dry, cracked lips as he stared up at the eerie, much faded paintings on the ceiling of the death house. Godbless often studied
those, but he could not make out what they meant. Nevertheless,
he was certain that demons nestled there, like a horde of bats
waiting to take flight. Godbless wondered if that would happen
tonight. After all, everything else was breaking down. The beggar
man was deeply worried. He was trying to recall where he had
come from, where had he been born? What had happened to
his life? Why the memories, and why did strange words echo
through his poor, tangled brain? Why did he think, as he always
did, that some of the people he met in St Erconwald's, he had
seen before in a previous life? Sometimes he could hear voices
speaking a language he could not understand, and yet he should.
Deeply frightened, Godbless clutched Thaddeus so tightly that
the little goat whimpered.

'I hold on to you, Thaddeus, and I stay here in my cottage, I
will be safe.'

Godbless nodded to himself. He must guard this old death
house; his great friend and protector Brother Athelstan had told
him to do that. The friar had instructed him to be most vigilant
so that witches and warlocks did not flock here like carrion crow,
to dig up old graves and use the bones of the dead for their
midnight rites. Godbless extended his hands towards the fire
crackling in the small hearth. He now felt warm. The cemetery
outside provided enough kindling and bracken, both for the
fire and for the two rusty old braziers glowing either side of
the chimney stack. Godbless patted his stomach and stared at the
empty platter and tankard on the floor beside him. Benedicta had
brought them earlier in the day, both tankard and ale jug were
now empty. Godbless was grateful. He closed his eyes. What had
he done today? He recalled Benedicta staring anxiously at him,
but he couldn't tell her why he was so agitated, with so many
voices and faces appearing from the past. Nevertheless, Godbless
was grateful for her concern. He felt calmer even though he kept
remembering disturbing visions, about sailing on choppy waters
or walking through woodland flanked either side by flitting

shadows. Who were they? Where was that place? Why did he keep seeing that ghost, or one of them, wandering around St Erconwald's?

Godbless recognized the world he now lived in; he was aware that it was different from others. All kinds of dire apparitions appeared to him. Cruel, bold and big-headed maggots prowled around him, slimy creatures hunted by yellow, great-jawed monsters. Sometimes at night he glimpsed bent, bony wasps swarming in hordes over sharp-snouted flies and inky-black scorpions. Faces came and went. Voices called in tongues Godbless did not understand. Sometimes he did, as he stumbled across the blighted landscape of his soul, with its fiery streams pouring across a bare, burning plain under a black-red sky. Yet he was safe here. Brother Athelstan had told him that. The death house stood on consecrated ground. Was that true? The beggar man stared down at the ancient paving stones which covered the floor of his cottage. Godbless knew each of them. He could tell the differences between some and others which bore strange etchings on the corner. He wondered what these symbols meant. Godbless scratched his head. Now it was night. The cemetery outside lay quiet. No sound could be heard, except for the usual screeching and rustling of the night birds and the small, slithering creatures which crawled out once darkness fell. No warlock or witch had lit their hellish fires. Godbless could hear no chanting or murmured invitations to the sinister Lords of the Air. Abruptly frightened, as if caught by an icy breeze, Godbless stretched down and rubbed one of the paving stones. He wondered if the strange carvings were warnings against demons and other evil spirits, especially those blue-faced, red-eyed hags who sometimes winged their way through here and floated out across the cemetery.

Godbless recalled his promise to Brother Athelstan that he would guard the cemetery. He tweaked the nape of Thaddeus's neck and walked to the thick wedge of oak which served as a door. He took the key from its wall cleft and undid the two locks. He opened the door and immediately pushed away the visions which swept in with their dark, wicked faces. Godbless flinched at the bitter, wintery wind. He stepped outside. He was aware how baleful spirits floated like owls over the cemetery.

He wondered if those ceiling paintings in the death house and
the etchings on the paving stones kept him safe. Godbless blinked
and shook his head. Why did he think of a tavern? The memory
had afflicted him all day. It wasn't The Piebald but somewhere
else, a true house of demons. Godbless closed his eyes and
began to sing a song in a language he really didn't understand,
a voice within him which he didn't recognize. Godbless opened
his eyes. But why now? Why did ghosts from the past come
swarming in here?

Godbless retreated back into the death house, slamming the
door shut. He feverishly checked the window shutters, everything
was in place. Perhaps it was time he slept. He went back to squat
before the hearth. All was quiet, yet those voices were calling
him, a name he recognized in a tongue he knew but it was all
so confusing. Thaddeus was also agitated. The young goat stumbled to stand and bleated at a gust of billowing coldness, as if
the door to the death house had quietly opened and shut. Godbless
sprang to his feet. He turned and gaped at the ghastly apparition
which stood leaning against the door.

'You have returned,' the beggar man whispered, yet he did
not understand why he said that. 'You have come back to claim
me, haven't you?' Godbless retreated, knocking into Thaddeus,
who bleated and scampered away as the apparition closed
in on his master, one hand raised, the dagger it held winking in
the light . . .

Athelstan was wakened early the next morning by a furious
pounding on the door. He clambered out of the bedloft and
hastened down, asking who it was.

'Watkin, Father, Watkin and Pike.'

Athelstan paused as the bells of St Erconwald's began to toll
the tocsin, a warning that something terrible had happened, as
well as a summons to the people of the parish.

'What on earth . . .?' Athelstan unlocked the door and drew
back the bolts at top and bottom. As soon as he opened the
heavy door, a mist swirled in, as if eager to draw the priest into
its cold embrace. Watkin and Pike, wrapped in thick cloaks
reeking of the sewer, shouldered by him to warm their hands
over the weak fire.

'Build it up,' Athelstan declared. 'But what is the cause of all this? Never mind. Let me first change.'

The friar went into the enclave beneath the bedloft, shivering with cold; he drew off his nightshirt and swiftly dressed in fresh linen underwear over which he drew his thick woollen black and white robes. He walked back to the fire, rubbing his unshaven face, and stared at his two parishioners who rose to meet him.

'Well?'

'Godbless.'

'Oh no.'

'No Father, don't groan. We are concerned. We entered God's Acre. Pike and I wanted to discover if there is a pattern of gravestones and funeral crosses . . .'

'Which reflects what you have seen in that so-called treasure chart?' Athelstan tightened the white cord around his waist so it displayed the three knots, symbols of the vows he'd taken to observe poverty, chastity and obedience. 'So why the alarm now?'

'Godbless never wakes early, Father. The old death house is firmly shuttered, its great door with its two locks hangs fast. Yet we could see the glow of lantern light through the chinks of a shutter. If Godbless did rise early, he would be clattering about, but we heard nothing. We banged on the door, there was no reply.'

'Very well.'

Athelstan swung his cloak around him. 'Get a message to Mauger, no more bell tolling! Come!'

The friar, followed by his two parishioners, hastened into the shifting mist, making their way towards the heavy lychgate and so into God's Acre. The toscin had certainly aroused the parish; shadowy shapes carrying lanterns, capped candles and fiery flambeaux were already making their way through the murk. Athelstan shouted that they should go home and that there was no real danger. Eventually they reached the death house. The windows either side of the fortified entrance were firmly shuttered. Athelstan pushed against the door and both shutters, but they all held fast. He noticed the gleams of light and reckoned that at least two of the ancient lanternhorns within were burning fiercely. Athelstan asked Watkin and Pike to shoo away the other parishioners, except for Benedicta, Crispin and Mauger. Once he was satisfied his parishioners were returning to their beds, the friar walked slowly around the death house, trying to curb the fear twisting inside him. Something was very wrong. The harmony of God's Acre had been disturbed. Some evil had swept in, taken up residence like some ferocious lurcher lurking in the dark. Athelstan had visited such scenes before and he sensed the desolation caused by lives brutally snatched away.

Athelstan completed his walk around the mortuary. He knew there were no other entrances except for its door and windows. He pointed to the shutter on the left and asked his companions to break it down. Watkin and Pike, assisted by Crispin, began to smash at the thick oaken slats. Benedicta, shrouded in a woollen blue robe, came to stand beside Athelstan, sliding her hand into his. At last the shutters were wrenched free.

Watkin pulled himself up and went in through the gap. He immediately began to scream and yell in horror. Athelstan shouted at him to remain calm and open the door. Pike swiftly clambered through. Again, cries of alarm, but the lean ditcher was of sterner stuff. Athelstan heard him curse as he turned the two locks in the door and pulled it open to allow Athelstan full view of the abomination awaiting him. The old death house was a long, barn-like hall with low rafters, its walls painted white though most of the plaster was flaking. At either end of the chamber hung a stark black crucifix, in the centre of the wall facing the door was a huge hearth, the fire long spent, and above this another crucifix. However, as if in mockery of such religion, the long mortuary table now served as a gruesome altar. On this, like some offering to an angry war god, sprawled Godbless's naked body, his white, scabby, vein-streaked corpse drenched in the blood which had poured from his cut throat. On his head a fiery red wig. The beggar man lay embracing his pet goat, Thaddeus the Younger. The creature's throat had also been slit before its blood-soaked cadaver had been thrust into Godbless's dead hands.

'An offering to Moloch!' Athelstan whispered. 'That's what it is like. The table is the altar, Godbless and Thaddeus the sacrificial victims. Some demon has been here.' Athelstan paused. Benedicta had knelt down, hands clasped, ave beads around her long, lovely fingers. The widow-woman crossed herself and intoned the 'De Profundis'. Watkin and Pike also knelt. Athelstan blessed himself and, once Benedicta had finished, hastily performed the rites for the dead. He recited the 'Confiteor' – the 'I Confess' – and bestowed absolution, adding that he would anoint the body later.

Benedicta and the others grouped around the table. The widow-woman had found dirty sheets and tattered blankets from the simple trestle bed to cover the gruesome sight. Crispin offered to fashion a coffin. Athelstan nodded, staring down at the mangled remains, helping Benedicta to pull up the sheets.

'Who?' he whispered. 'And why? What harm, if any, did God-bless or his little goat offer to anyone?' He heard a sound and turned. Senlac stood in the doorway.

'Good morning, Father. I heard about poor Godbless and his pet goat, their throats cruelly slashed. Why?'

'Why indeed?' Athelstan replied.

'Why indeed,' Senlac echoed, crossing himself and staring around. 'This is as I remember it, a long, dank, dark, hellish hall.' He gestured at the shelves fixed to the wall and the pots of pine juice ranged along them. 'Nothing,' Senlac declared, 'nothing can ever disguise the smell of death. I just wonder . . .'

'What?'

'Well, my father often talked about God's Acre being plagued by warlocks and witches. Could they be—'

'No, no. Not now.' Watkin came round the table. 'We keep a close and sharp eye on our cemetery. Isn't it strange?' The dung-collector pointed at the door. 'That's nothing more than a thick, oaken slab. There's no bolts to rust and it's held fast by two locks. The work of a craftsman, in fact, one of the best picklocks I have ever met, till he was caught and hanged over Tyburn Stream.'

'Does the same key fit both locks?'

'Yes, Father,' Watkin replied. 'You must remember before the new death house was built? How you insisted that both locks be turned? You wanted to keep wanderers out.'

'Of course, of course. And the key was in one of the locks?'

'Yes, yes it was,' Pike declared. 'And those shutters Father, they are both very sturdy and closely barred, whilst there's no secret entrance.' Pike beat the battered heel of his boot against the ground. 'Only hard paving stone, with narrow gulleys to take away the slops from the corpses when they were lodged here.'

Athelstan was now being watched by a growing number of parishioners, who clustered in the doorway murmuring their shock. Watkin and Pike hoarsely informed them about the dreadful slaughter carried out in that place of death. Athelstan half listened as he scrupulously scrutinized the doorway, the window shutters, and even the narrow fire stack, as well as the rusty braziers, moving with the toe of his sandal, the ale jug, platter and pewter goblet.

'It's all a mystery,' the friar declared.

'It certainly is,' Watkin agreed. 'We all know Godbless would never allow anyone in after dark. Only you, Father. If Godbless told us that once, he did so a dozen times, isn't that true?'

Athelstan nodded his agreement. Godbless was always fearful of warlocks, wizards, and those other denizens of the night who liked nothing better than to set up a makeshift altar and sacrifice to their own hell-born demons. Men and women who furrowed the earth for human remains to use in their macabre midnight celebrations.

'Ah well,' Athelstan beckoned Watkin and Pike closer. 'See to the dead. Clear this place up. God knows,' Athelstan sighed, 'what truly happened here. I will now wash, change and celebrate my Jesus Mass. Afterwards, I want to meet the parish council outside the rood screen.'

Once the Mass was over, Athelstan swiftly divested himself of his purple and gold vestments. He left the sacristy and sat down in the celebrant's chair, placed close to the doorway through the rood screen. Mauger perched at the small scribe's desk to the friar's immediate right. The rest of the parish council ranged on benches on either side of their priest. Athelstan intoned the 'Veni Creator Spiritus', blessed his parishioners and stood up.

'We all know what happened to Brother Godbless,' he began, 'and his poor little goat. A true abomination. I, we, have a duty before God to discover the truth and bring to justice those responsible. So, what happened yesterday?'

At first Athelstan's question created chaos, as the friar had expected, but he immediately recognized by the vociferous replies from his parishioners that Godbless had been truly disturbed. All the witnesses confirmed, once Athelstan had imposed order, that Godbless had been deeply agitated, wandering the parish and God's Acre, as well as striding up and down the church. Apparently he kept muttering gibberish no one could understand. The only sense they could get from him was that he babbled about ghosts from the past, evil spirits haunting him, and how he and Thaddeus the Younger needed God's protection. On one matter Godbless had been very insistent and clear: Thaddeus was to stay close to him. Athelstan heard his parishioners out. He let them chatter, then raised his hands for silence. Once he had this, the friar loudly listed a number of questions. First, was any stranger glimpsed closeted with Godbless? Secondly, did anyone see anything untoward in God's Acre, around the old death house or, indeed, anywhere in the parish? Silence greeted both his questions.

'Very well,' Athelstan folded back the cuffs of his gown and glanced up as the copse door opened. A figure slipped through the shadowy transept and into the nave. Athelstan peered through the murk and raised a hand in greeting at Tiptoft, Cranston's green-garbed courier, calling out that they would soon speak. Tiptoft nodded and squatted down close to the base of one of the drum-like pillars.

'One further question,' Athelstan continued, 'was anyone, and I mean anyone, seen entering God's Acre last night?'

Again silence.

'Next, who would Godbless, especially when he was so agitated, admit into the old death house once darkness fell?'

'We've answered that,' Watkin called out. 'Only you, Father.' A murmur of agreement echoed his words.

'In which case we reach the heart of this mystery,' Athelstan declared. 'How did someone gain entrance, murder poor Godbless and Thaddeus, mock their corpses and leave as silently as any ghost? The death house being locked and barred from within?'

'It must be the work of demons,' Watkin bellowed, drawing a chorus of approval from the rest.

'Oh, I am sure it was a demon,' Athelstan replied, 'but one in human flesh, and that is a matter for me and Sir John to discover

so let us leave this for the moment.' Athelstan gave the council
a final blessing, collected his cloak and chancery satchel and
hurried down to where Tiptoft rose to greet him.

'You know why I am here?' the courier lisped, his voice hardly
above a whisper. The pallid-faced courier, his red, spiked hair
generously greased with nard, plucked at Athelstan's sleeve. 'My
Lord Coroner awaits you, Brother Athelstan. Some bloody affray
in Queenhithe . . .'

On their journey across the Thames, being rowed by a morose
Moleskin and his equally glum archangels, Tiptoft informed
the friar in hushed tones how Sir John had received a message,
anonymously, with the same to the French, that the Oriflamme and
his henchmen had hidden themselves, along with other malefactors, in a derelict mansion. They had resisted any proclamation
to surrender so Sir John had sent for Tower archers. In addition,
another whore, Meg Tumblekin, had been found naked, her
throat cut, a red wig pulled over her head, the corpse set adrift
in a narrow cockle boat until it was found by local fishermen
and brought to Queenhithe. Cranston had set up house in The
Leviathan; as Lord High Coroner he could use any room or
chamber in the city as his court. Cranston had the power to
organize an inquest and the formal viewing of any corpse found
in mysterious circumstances.

According to Tiptoft's description, Athelstan realized this must
be another hideous murder, a further outrage by the Oriflamme.
Moleskin, who'd sat deliberately close so he could eavesdrop,
raised a hand and said he'd already heard whispers about the
whore's murder as well as news of a bloody affray somewhere
between St Olave's and The Leviathan. Athelstan simply smiled
thinly. Moleskin was one of his parishioners but the past was
opening up and the bargeman, along with others, had a great
deal to be ashamed of. Indeed, he must regard Moleskin and his
comrades as possible suspects.

At last they reached Queenhithe. Tiptoft led Athelstan up along
the tangle of filthy, reeking alleyways. The narrow streets were
strangely silent. The usual hustle and bustle of the runnels leading
down to the quayside had faded away. The overhanging houses
were shuttered, doorways empty; even the tribe of beggars and
counterfeit men had fled from the growing storm. The appearance

of the Tower archers dressed in their war garb had imposed a watchful silence. People decided to stay indoors until the tempest had passed. Both messenger and friar reached the enclosure before St Olave's. Athelstan noticed the church was closed as he followed Tiptoft into The Leviathan only a brief walk away.

Cranston had turned the tavern's taproom into his coroner's court. The dimly lit, heavy-beamed chamber seemed well suited to the grim proceedings about to take place. A fire burnt fiercely in the hearth, the leaping flames caught the shadows of those gathered around the table and sent them dancing. Athelstan peered through the murk, raising his hand in greeting to the sept of bargemen – Cromer, Desant, Falaise and Hornsby. They were now joined by Moleskin. Mistress Alice was also there, organizing the servants, who flitted in and out with platters of food and jugs of strong ale.

'We will be with you soon enough,' Cranston bellowed as he swept into the taproom. Cranston pulled down the fold of his tawny-coloured military cloak and exchanged the kiss of peace with Athelstan. The coroner hugged the little friar close. 'Come,' he whispered, 'you might as well view the horror.'

Both coroner and friar left the tavern. They crossed the smelly stable yard into one of the outhouses. Meg Tumblekin's corpse, with lanterns placed at head and feet, lay stretched out on a trestle table, a fiery red wig pulled drunkenly over the back of her skull. In life, Meg may have been comely, even pretty, but her nasty death had transformed her into a heart-rending horror. The dead woman's corpse was puffed and slimed by dirty river water. The slit in her throat was like a gaping mouth, whilst her eyes, nose and lips had been sharply nibbled. The outhouse reeked of death and Athelstan gratefully accepted the scented pomander Cranston thrust into his hand.

'Found like this close to a cockle boat,' the coroner declared, 'no other sign or indication of who was responsible; why, when or where.' Cranston paused as Tiptoft came into the outhouse. The courier took one glance at the corpse, gagged and hastily retreated back into the yard. Cranston and Athelstan followed. Tiptoft, busy cleaning his mouth, gestured at a figure, cloaked and cowled, standing outside the taproom door. The man came over, pulling back the deep capuchon to reveal a merry, olive-skinned face with pleasing features under bristling black hair. Athelstan immediately recognized Hugh Levigne the Candlelight-Master, leader of the Luciferi and the special envoy of Monseigneur Derais, the French ambassador residing at the Maison Parisienne just off Cheapside. He had the smooth face and courtly ways of a high-ranking chancery clerk, but Athelstan knew Levigne was more than this. The Candlelight-Master was a born street fighter, a true dagger man, whose choirboy looks masked all the virtues and strengths of a mailed clerk. Levigne pulled off his leather-studded gauntlets to clasp hands and exchange the kiss of peace with both Cranston and Athelstan. Levigne then stood back and pointed at the outhouse.

'Another one, Sir John?' The Frenchman's voice was low, cultured with only the slight trace of an accent.

'Another what?' Athelstan queried.

'*Fille de Joie*. Didn't you know, Brother?' Levigne's hand fell to his sword hilt. 'Every single girl killed, her corpse desecrated and mocked with those wigs, was patronized by our ambassador,' Levigne gave a crooked smile, 'and the ambassador's people, including both myself and my companions.'

'In God's name,' Athelstan breathed, 'could that be the reason for their murder?'

'Perhaps,' Levigne shrugged, 'but, just as importantly, their assassin could be the same evil soul who manifested himself on that war-barge, *Le Sans Dieu*, so many years ago.'

'And why are you here now? I mean, at The Leviathan?'

'Like you, Brother Athelstan, to view the abomination and to follow up certain information. Early this morning, both myself and Sir John received a message, a simple strip of parchment, informing Monseigneur Derais and Sir John that the criminal known as the Oriflamme, along with his principal henchmen, including Mornay, former tavern master of La Chèvre Dansante, were hiding in a derelict house overlooking the Court of Thieves here in Queenhithe. We received this memorandum at the Maison Parisienne; I understand Sir John's was delivered at the Guildhall. Now Brother Athelstan,' Levigne beat his gauntlets against his thigh, 'as Sir John must have told you, our masters at the Louvre want these criminals delivered into our hands for just punishment on the gallows at Montfaucon.'

'I ordered Flaxwith,' Cranston declared, 'my chief bailiff, to break into the house, but he and his men were beaten back. So,' Cranston stamped his feet, 'Monseigneur Levigne has brought some of his bullyboys whilst I sent for a cohort of Tower archers. These lovely lads must now be waiting for my orders, so come.'

All three made their way out of The Leviathan. Moleskin, Mistress Alice and the others had gathered near the main door with a litany of questions, but Cranston ordered them to hold their peace. The coroner was met outside by his chief bailiff, Flaxwith, accompanied as always by his mastiff Samson, whom Athelstan secretly considered to be the ugliest dog he had ever seen. Flaxwith had a hushed conversation with the coroner, even as Sir John gently kicked Samson aside, as the dog, as he always did, tried to embrace the coroner's booted leg. After he finished whispering to Sir John, Flaxwith led them along a maze of twisting runnels and filthy alleyways into the Court of Thieves, an ancient square bounded by buildings with a cracked statue of St Dismas, the Good Thief, on a plinth in the centre. The court was cobbled, its stones glistening with dust, empty except for two corpses sprawled in ever-widening puddles of blood. Along all sides of the square rose tall, lofty mansions, much dilapidated and decayed, their doorways, porches and windows now crowded with Tower archers, bows at the ready. Cranston swiftly explained how the corpses were two of Flaxwith's comitatus, slain as they tried to force an entrance to the soaring townhouse which dominated the far side of the square, a three-storey building of timber and plaster on a red stone base. Its paintwork, as with the other dwellings, was flaking heavily, the plaster sagging. Nevertheless, its shuttered windows and fortified doorway made it look impregnable enough.

'We have demanded their surrender,' Flaxwith hissed, 'but all we received in reply was a hail of arrows, yard-long shafts. Whoever hides there has skilled bowmen in their company.'

As if in answer to this, a shutter on the top floor of the mansion was abruptly flung back and three arrows hissed swiftly through the air, forcing the Tower archers back into the protection of their own hiding places. The arrows, undoubtedly loosed by long bows, smashed into the plaster and wood around those laying siege. A voice screamed something and the shutters were hastily pulled

back before Cranston's bowmen could even aim and loose. A
Tower archer hurried at a half-crouch out to a narrow alleyway
further along; he almost threw himself into the doorway where
Cranston and his party were sheltering.

'Captain Armitage is ready, Sir John.'

'Then tell our noble captain of archers to begin our attack, but
slowly, the shield men first.'

The soldier nodded, gaspingly repeating Cranston's instruction
before he hurried back, narrowly missing another volley of shafts
loosed from the windows of the mansion opposite.

'Let's wait and see,' Cranston whispered. 'It's a question of
slowly, slowly.'

Athelstan, the sweat cooling on his skin, peered down towards
the mouth of the alleyway where the archer had returned. A
trumpet brayed shrilly and a cohort of hobelars carrying huge
kite shields debouched out of the alleyway. They held their shields
up and slowly began to form an interlocking wall at least twelve
men long. Again the trumpets shrilled. The line advanced slowly
across the square, Tower archers fanned out behind them. More
trumpet sounded. The phalanx was now a moving shield wall of
armed men. They shuffled forwards; behind them trailed a group
of men-at-arms, pushing and pulling a small trebuchet, its sling
already pulled back, taut and tight, its cup primed with rags
and shards of wood coated in oil and tar. The phalanx crept
closer to the mansion opposite; its shutters were abruptly thrown
back. A rain of arrows fell but they either missed their mark
or thundered into the shield wall; this parted to allow Tower
bowmen to race forward and loose, in some cases, with deadly
effect. Athelstan saw one of the enemy tumble from an open
window, arrow shafts in his chest and belly. The phalanx edged
closer. An archer, following the trebuchet, now lit the oil-soaked
mass in its cup. Flames flared high. A horn sounded. The phalanx
stopped. The trebuchet was positioned more carefully to the
screech of rope, wood and iron. A shouted order and the cup
was released, a heavy, heart-jarring sound followed by a
resounding thud as the throwing arm met its cushioned barrier.
The fiery bundle that the trebuchet loosed streaked across the
square and crashed through an open window of the mansion
opposite.

The Tower archers now had the upper hand, confidently moving forward whilst the trebuchet's constant hail of fire set the entire building alight. Indeed, the flames flared so fiercely, the heat grew so intense, that Cranston ordered a recall and the shield men carefully fell back. The derelict mansion was now completely torched. Cranston noted how every entrance to the sides or rear of the building was closely guarded: those who sheltered within would either have to surrender or be burnt to death.

The smoke and flame grew more intense. Suddenly a window opened and a white cloth fluttered to the ground. Athelstan watched as the door to the mansion swung open. Smoke billowed around, almost shrouding the figures who staggered out, led by a man carrying a crucifix, the symbol of total surrender. Athelstan calculated there were about eight men still walking and these helped others who appeared to be sorely wounded. They were weaponless and their leader, whom Athelstan thought he recognized, shouted for water and help for the wounded. Tower archers hurried forward, forcing the surrendered men to kneel with their hands behind their backs. Cranston ordered a bucket of water to be passed along the line. The prisoners were also helped by others. Father Ambrose appeared, accompanied by Mistress Alice, Moleskin and Falaise. The bargemen explained how this square was part of St Olave's parish, so they had a duty to assist any hue and cry. Cranston agreed and told them to give whatever assistance was necessary. Ambrose and Mistress Alice immediately knelt before the wounded, offering whatever help they could, both physical and spiritual. Athelstan, too, made to assist, but the priest, eyes brimming with tears, just smiled.

'These poor souls,' he murmured, 'are in great distress.' He placed a hand on a wounded man sprawled on the cobbles, a bubbling wound to his throat. An arrow had pierced the back of the man's neck and, in his agony, he must have broken half of it off, but the barbed arrow point had dug deep. Mistress Alice knelt on the other side of the man. She looked pleadingly at Athelstan and pointed at two other wounded further along the line, one of whom was thrashing about in pain. Athelstan, assisted by a Tower archer, did what he could, aware of Cranston striding about trying to impose order. The fire was allowed to burn. The square was sealed off and a cart arrived to collect the dead.

The rest of the prisoners were given water and a small loaf of bread. Athelstan distributed these, studying the prisoners closely; all of them looked harassed, tired and desperate, their clothing nothing more than a motley collection of rags, though their boots, swordbelts and other harness of war, piled beneath the statue of St Dismas, looked sturdy enough. The prisoners were difficult to distinguish; their hair was thick, long and matted, their faces almost hidden by bushy moustache and beard.

'Follow me,' Cranston whispered, plucking at Athelstan by the sleeve. He pushed the friar to a man in the centre of the line of prisoners, a tall, bulky individual who raised his head and grinned at Athelstan.

'Do you recognize me, Brother?'

'Of course I do. As soon as I clapped eyes on you. Simon Grindcobbe!' Athelstan exclaimed. The friar stared in shocked disbelief at a man who, only months earlier, had wielded as much power as John of Gaunt. Grindcobbe had been a founder member and leader of the Great Community of the Realm. A true prince amongst the Upright Men, with tens of thousands of peasants waiting to do his will, not to mention the Earthworms – the Upright Men's fierce street warriors – here in London.

'Don't be shocked,' Grindcobbe peered up at Athelstan. 'Such is life, friar. Our world has changed. The wheel has turned. Mistress Fortune has shaken her cup for another throw and it looks as if the meek will not inherit the Earth.'

'You weren't so meek months ago.' Cranston pushed back his beaver-skin hat and scratched the sweat beads, pausing to roar orders at the archers still clearing away all the detritus of the recent battle. Cranston took off his hat and beat it against his leg as he looked up and down the line of prisoners.

'They are all here,' he declared, 'the dukes and earls of the great peasant army. Look around, Brother, as you do too, Master Grindcobbe: this is what it has come to.'

The friar muttered his agreement. Cranston was correct. All the dreams, all the high-sounding phrases of the Upright Men were now nothing but dust in the wind, finally crushed in a squalid, sordid street fight. The Court of Thieves now looked desolate. The dead had been carted away. A local physician had been summoned and, assisted by Father Ambrose, Mistress Alice and the rest, was tending to the wounded prisoners, forcing wine laced with a coarse opiate into the mouths of the injured. The fire in the blazing mansion was burning down, the timber and plaster crackling and crashing in the heat. The dark pall of smoke slowly thinning.

'They are all here,' the coroner continued, 'at least those who survived the Great Revolt and the hangings which took place afterwards.' He gestured along the line. 'Robin of the Greenwood, Little John, Friar Tuck, Will Scarlett, and all the other fairy names they assumed to disguise their true identity. Oh yes, little monk.'

'Friar, Sir John.'

'Whatever, my friend. Anyway, I doubt if any of these know anything about the Oriflamme, La Chèvre Dansante or that ill-named war-barge, *Le Sans Dieu*, as Monseigneur Hugh Levigne is about to discover.'

The Candelight-Master, escorted by a group of Luciferi, swaggered across the square. Levigne nodded at Cranston, then squatted down to question a prisoner, speaking softly in English and French, but all he received in reply was a shake of the head and whispered abuse. Levigne rose and strode over to Sir John, languidly throwing back his cloak to reveal the hilt of a thin, rapier-like war sword. He stopped before Cranston and Athelstan and gave a mocking bow.

'Sir John,' he smiled, 'it seems we were both misled. These men are your concern, not mine. They have nothing to do with the Oriflamme or any crime in France. We were tricked.'

'It's called buying a horse without riding it,' Cranston retorted. 'We were sold dross for gold and I wonder why. Let us see if the Oracle will speak.' Cranston went and crouched before Grindcobbe, who lifted his bound hands in greeting.

'Well, Sir John? How did you know?'

'We didn't. We were searching for the Oriflamme.'

'Never heard of him but, if the French are interested, then I suspect it's something to do with the ravages carried out by our great lords in France. Our allies there, the Jacquerie, claim that the savagery of our Masters of the Soil in France was even more devastating than here. It must be. We've heard rumours about the French hunting down certain individuals, but that's just babble in the taverns.' Grindcobbe sat back on his heels, licking dry, cracked lips. 'Ah well, Sir John, the day is done and we are for the dark.'

'You were preparing to flee?'

'What do you think?'

'You have money, treasure hidden away?'

'Of course.' The former rebel leader nodded towards the smouldering ruins of the mansion. 'Our monies are probably molten metal by now.'

'You were going to flee by ship?'

'No, Sir John, the Angel Gabriel was to take us across the Narrow Seas in the shadow of his wings.'

'Which ship were you leaving on?'

Grindcobbe just grinned.

'Which ship?' Cranston insisted. 'Who was going to help you?'

Again the grin.

'Very well.' Cranston rose to his feet and stared around. 'Brother Athelstan, this is finished but my suspicions are aroused. All these mysteries seem to revolve around the Queenhithe sept of the Guild of the Bargemen and their meeting place at The Leviathan. So,' he shouted at Flaxwith to summon Tiptoft, 'let us hold court in that taproom.'

John Falaise, former member of the free company which served on the war-barge *Le Sans Dieu*, now a worthy bargeman, knelt in front of the statue in the narrow lady altar to the left of the main sanctuary in St Olave's. The ancient church, as always, was dark and shadow-filled. A few torches danced in the icy breeze which pierced beneath doors and through window shutters. Apart from their flickering flames and the light of tapers burning on their spigots in the chantry chapel, there was very little light. Nothing to fend off the encroaching darkness. Falaise, however, welcomed the sombre silence. He needed to reflect and so plan a way forward. He could not believe what had happened. Grindcobbe and his henchmen seized and taken up, their planned escape on board a Flemish cog completely frustrated. Who had betrayed them? Falaise had visited the Court of Thieves. He had learnt the rumours that both the French and Cranston believed the Oriflamme and his henchmen had been hiding in a derelict mansion. Who had caused all this confusion? Who had sent misleading information to both the coroner and the French ambassador? Who was behind this chaos? Falaise rubbed his face. He had always regretted his past. He and his comrades had perpetrated sins of deep scarlet. They had shed innocent blood. True, he and other members of the free company had not joined the Oriflamme in his disgusting treatment of women prisoners but, there again, they had done nothing to prevent it.

'We did nothing wrong,' Falaise whispered to the darkness as he got to his feet. 'But we did nothing right.'

Falaise paused to light a taper before the wooden statue carved in the likeness of Our Lady of Walsingham. He was still deeply distracted. Why had the Oriflamme reappeared now? More importantly, who had betrayed the Upright Men? Most of the guild members in the parish of St Olave's, including their priest, had been secret members of the Great Community of the Realm and had counted themselves as Upright Men. The sept had certainly known how truly desperate Grindcobbe and the others were to escape. Nevertheless, only Falaise had been privy to the actual details of how and when the Upright Men would leave. He had bought supplies from Mistress Alice for Grindcobbe and the rest, but that was all.

So who had been behind their betrayal, and why? It must have been the Oriflamme, but who was that monster? He and his henchmen always hid from the light, their identity and appearance cunningly concealed. Indeed, was the hideous abomination who now prowled along the Thames the same malefactor who had carried out similar outrages in Normandy? What proof did they have that it was? Falaise went back to his prayers, pleading for a remedy for the fear curdling in his stomach. He desperately tried to list all those who might have known about Grindcobbe. Falaise broke from his prayers to sip at the deep-bowled goblet of Bordeaux from the wineskin kept there in the nave. So caught up was he in his drunken anxiety, Falaise was totally unaware of the sinister figure who stood in the deep shadows of the nave. A dreadful apparition dressed in a woman's gown, face hidden by a white mask, with a fiery red wig pulled down tight over its head.

*   *   *

Cranston and Athelstan sat in the sacristy at St Olave's. The friar gazed round at those assembled by Master Tiptoft: Hornsby, Desant and Cromer, together with their priest Father Ambrose and Mistress Alice. Moleskin had also been summoned, along with a disgruntled and sullen Senlac. He vociferously objected to being there until the coroner shouted at him to be quiet or he would personally ensure Senlac was flung into Newgate's filthiest dungeon for being grossly contemptible towards a royal justice. Senlac now sat, silent and morose. Cranston, enthroned at the top of the sacristy table, clapped his hands, shouting for silence.

'First,' the coroner declared, pointing at Senlac, 'does anyone here, including you Moleskin, recognize this man as a soldier who served on *Le Sans Dieu*? Is he a former member of your free company?'

A chorus of immediate denial greeted the coroner's question, Moleskin adding that few people, if any in St Erconwald's parish, remembered either Senlac or his father.

'Why are we here?' Hornsby spluttered, wiping his mouth on the back of his sleeve. 'Oh, by the way,' he gazed around, 'where is Falaise? Why isn't he here?'

Hornsby's weather-beaten face was deeply petulant, a mood shared by his comrades. Any further conversation was stilled by the booming of the church bell.

'In God's name,' Father Ambrose rose, 'Mistress Alice come, let us see what is happening.' He bowed towards the coroner. 'Some alley urchin must have forced their way into the bell tower. Sir John, Brother Athelstan, please excuse us. We will soon be back.'

Both priest and taverner hurried out of the sacristy.

'We shall continue,' Cranston declared. 'Let us cut to the quick. We were given information, wrong as it now proves, that the Oriflamme and his henchmen, whoever they might be, were hiding in a derelict mansion overlooking the Court of Thieves. In fact, that house was the refuge of former Upright Men desperate to flee across the Narrow Seas. They were betrayed, I suspect by the Oriflamme, who is now baiting us as well as slaying whores and,' Cranston patted Athelstan's arm, 'according to my learned colleague here, the criminal is also responsible for the murder of a poor beggar out at St Erconwald's. Now . . .'

Cranston broke off at a piercing scream which echoed down the nave, followed by the patter of footsteps. The sacristy door was thrown open and Alice flung herself into the room. She stood half bent, hands on knees, gasping for breath.

'In heaven's name, woman!' Cranston exclaimed.

'Falaise,' she gasped, 'Falaise has hanged himself, or so it seems.'

Cranston and Athelstan, followed by the rest, hurried out of the sacristy and down the nave into the dusty, ancient bell tower. There was a spiral staircase, its narrow steps twisting up behind the bell rope; Falaise had used this to hang himself. Apparently he had tied the end of the bell cord around his throat and slipped off the high, narrow ledge step, the rope swiftly tightening around his throat. He might have tried to regain his footing, but the knot he'd tied was twisted and hard as stone and could not be loosened. The bell rope, hanging straight down, was so tight and taut that the hapless victim could not move to a very steep higher step, its stonework crumbling, without worsening his situation. Father Ambrose was already murmuring the words of absolution in the dead man's ear.

Athelstan waited until the priest had finished, whispering to Cranston to impose order. The coroner told the others to withdraw and tell any parishioners alarmed by the bell to return to their homes. Athelstan pushed by the hanged man, quietly apologizing to Ambrose as he went up the steep steps towards the bell chamber. He rounded a corner and his gaze was immediately caught by a gargoyle, a monkey, carved in stone with a human body, perched on a plinth beside the door to the belfry. An identical one stood on the other side. Both small statues had been adorned with fiery red curls, which rendered them even more ghastly. Athelstan stared at the macabre scene before hurrying back down the steps.

'This is no suicide,' he whispered when he reached the bottom. 'Let us cut the body down.'

He and Cranston, assisted by Father Ambrose, severed the oily, twisted bell rope. Athelstan tried not to stare at the murdered man's stricken features, the purple tinge to the face transformed by all the horrors of sudden death; eyes dead and glassy, the much-bitten tongue greatly swollen. Cranston cursed as he fought to sever the hard, oil-soaked rope. But at last he did, and Athelstan had to turn away at the dead man's last gasp and the stink of his stomach being emptied. Athelstan composed himself, asking both coroner and priest to stand aside as he crouched down and studied the dead man's wrists. There was no sign or trace of binding or any ligature, though the tips of the dead man's fingers and nails were chapped and broken, the skin rubbed raw.

'Falaise tried to free himself,' Athelstan declared, blessing the corpse. 'But the rope is strong as the flail on a steel whip, whilst the knot forming the noose is cleverly fastened, hard as any link in an iron chain.' Athelstan prised open the dead man's mouth, trying to move the swollen, wounded tongue so he could sniff. He caught a rottenness but also the sweet tang of Bordeaux. 'He drank wine just before he died,' Athelstan asserted and glanced up. 'Father Ambrose, what was Falaise like? I mean, what was he doing here?'

'He was bell clerk to the parish,' the priest took a deep breath. 'Falaise did like his wine and often came here with a wineskin or a goblet but,' the priest shrugged, 'look around, there is no sign of either.' He pulled a face. 'Falaise was a bargeman, a good guild member, a parishioner who kept to himself. I can add little more.'

'In which case, thank you,' Athelstan smiled. 'Father, please join your parishioners, ask them to wait for a while. Oh Father,' Ambrose turned at the door, 'when you and Mistress Alice first came here, you glimpsed nothing amiss?'

'No, Brother. The door to the bell tower was closed, we opened it,' the priest flailed a hand, 'and what you see, so did we.'

Athelstan smiled his thanks and asked Ambrose to organize the removal of the corpse to the parish death house.

'Oh, by the way,' Athelstan winked quickly at the coroner, 'I have changed my mind. Sir John and I will be leaving. At this moment in time, we have no questions. But, rest assured, we shall return.'

'And tell your parishioners,' Cranston pointed at the priest, 'including Senlac, that no one summoned here today can leave London or they will be put to the horn as an outlaw, a wolfshead. Do you understand?'

The priest nodded in agreement. He opened the door and stepped aside as Cranston swept through followed by Athelstan.

Both coroner and friar ignored those they had questioned in the sacristy and left the church, hurrying along the lanes. Once clear of the parish, Cranston stopped and grasped Athelstan by the shoulder.

'Little friar, what was all that about, the sudden, dramatic departure? I need to question those suspects as well as issue orders to Flaxwith and the Tower archers.'

Athelstan gently poked the coroner in his generously endowed stomach. 'Sir John, your questions will wait and so will the bargemen. Let them stew in their own juices. As for Flaxwith and the rest, they know where to find you and such matters will wait. We must talk. So come, let us adjourn to your favourite chapel.'

Cranston grinned, took a generous slurp from his miraculous wineskin and offered it to the friar who drank a good mouthful.

'You see, Sir John,' Athelstan declared, handing back the wineskin, 'we must keep up a pretence. Let us at least act as if we are wise and knowing even though, in truth, I am deeply confused.'

'I would certainly drink to that,' Cranston agreed. 'So, let us go where we don't have to pretend.'

The coroner surged through the busy streets, Athelstan keeping close beside him. The coroner was soon recognized; greetings were shouted, as well as the usual catcalls from the hordes of counterfeit and cunning men who flooded the different market places hungry for prey. Sir John seemed to know them all, shouting warnings at 'No Nose', 'Rawskin', 'Shadow-Dancer', 'Moonlight-Man' and all their tribe garbed in garish rags, though well-armed with knife and stabbing dirk.

By now the day's trade was in full swing. The air reeked with a score of smells: smoke from the ovens where rancid meat was cooked, grills decorated with all kinds of offal as well as the welcoming sweetness of the pastry shops and tavern kitchens. They passed one such tavern and Athelstan glimpsed whores in their fiery red wigs and his mind turned back to the evil which had thrust its way into his life, like some ravished rat bursting out of its sewer. So immersed was he in his tumble of thoughts, Athelstan startled as Cranston gripped his arm. The friar glanced around. They were now in Cheapside, passing the Standard and

Tun. All along the broad thoroughfare ranged hundreds of stalls
selling everything, be it Moroccan leather goods to silk from
kingdoms far to the East. The crowd swirled backwards and
forwards, their voices carrying like a low peal of distant thunder.
Bagpipes and trumpets made themselves heard, whilst different
groups – be they mourners or the schoolboys of St Paul's – tried
to shove their way through. Athelstan heard a scream and turned.
A group of whores found touting beyond Cock Lane were being
stripped and caned before being locked in the pillory. On the
ground beside them, those hideous wigs. Athelstan tensed as he
experienced the onset of that deep anxiety which sometimes
assailed him whenever he felt trapped in a crowded or narrow
space. Cranston gripped his arm more tightly but Athelstan found
it difficult to move. He whispered his apologies until the coroner
embraced him gently, coaxing him forward.

'Only a few more paces.'

Athelstan glanced up, took a deep breath, and walked quickly
into the welcoming warmth of The Lamb of God. They were
immediately greeted by Minehostess, a bright-eyed, cheery-faced
lady who ushered them into Cranston's favourite chamber, a
comfortably furnished solar overlooking the hostelry's richly
stocked garden. Athelstan allowed the coroner to settle in the window
seat and greatly welcomed the goblet of wine which thawed the
chill of both body and soul. Food was served. For a while, they
ate and drank in silence, a period of calm only interrupted by
Cranston's constant shadows whenever he entered the tavern. Leif
the one-legged beggar and, behind him, Rawbum, Leif's comrade-
in-crime, a cook who had scalded his backside whilst drunk.

Both worthies crept into the solar all a-flutter, Leif loudly
declaring there was trouble brewing along Cheapside. Cranston
tossed each a penny and bellowed at them to leave, slamming
the door shut behind them. The coroner had barely regained his
seat when there was a roar from outside followed by the shrieks
of Minehostess. Cranston and Athelstan sprang to their feet,
hurrying out across the taproom to join the hostess standing in
the richly decorated tavern porch. She daintily stepped down
from the chest her servants had brought, inviting both coroner
and friar to take her place.

Athelstan climbed up and looked out over the crowd; this now parted to reveal a furious street fight between a fire-eater, a travelling minstrel, and three dwarves who earned their living by juggling. Apparently all three parties had clashed over a space which they claimed as their own. The fire-eater was now acting like some dragon, drawing in the fire from his torch and billowing it out at the dwarves, who retaliated by throwing anything they could whilst the troubadour swung a heavily knotted rope to protect himself. The fight drew closer and closer to the tavern.

'Satan's tits,' Cranston breathed, asking the hostess to fetch his sword, but Athelstan plucked the coroner's sleeve and pointed to a column of city guards battling through the crowd to seize these disturbers of the peace. The minstrel was now close to the porch, his rope trailing around him. Cranston roared at the fellow to drop the rope, which he did. The affray began to subside and the coroner made to return to the solar. Athelstan, however, stood staring down at the rope lying coiled and knotted on the ground.

'That reminds me of something,' he murmured, 'something I glimpsed in St Olave's but, for the life of me, I cannot recall it.'

'Brother?'

Athelstan smiled at the coroner and stepped down from the chest. 'Sir John, my apologies, I was distracted. Braised beef, sweet capon and spicy veal demand our attention. Let us do justice to our feast.'

Once they had returned to the solar and finished their meal, Athelstan opened his chancery satchel. He laid out his writing implements beside a square sheet of scrubbed vellum, the best the Guildhall could provide.

'Right, my learned coroner, I shall speak as I scrawl. Interrupt me whenever you wish, so . . .' Athelstan dipped his quill pen into the ink and began to write in cipher known only to him and the coroner. 'Item: during the war in France the free company of the battle-barge now known as *Le Sans Dieu* were joined by the mysterious Oriflamme, who liked to dress in women's garb, his head festooned by a thick red wig, his face always masked. He was joined in his cruel forays by the tavern master Mornay, as well as an anonymous henchman who eventually disappeared. Item: the Oriflamme apparently knew a great deal about the river Seine and the countryside stretching along either bank. He suborned the free company with information which provided them with great plunder, as well as the means for the Oriflamme to indulge in his vicious, cruel pleasure, the abuse and torture of female captives. It would seem, though we only have their word for it, that the rest of the free company were totally in thrall to this monster. They certainly did not participate in his cruelties, but they definitely profited from the plunder they seized. Father Ambrose was one of their company, but he refused to follow the Oriflamme, whilst the rest kept a still tongue in their head as any complaint or grumble was ruthlessly dealt with. Item: the war eventually ended. The Oriflamme and his ilk disappeared whilst the free company returned home and, like Moleskin, settled down as respectable members of this city's community. In truth, they probably used the plunder to finance their life of civic responsibility. Item: as I have said, one person who did not join the Oriflamme was Father Ambrose. I am sure that others like him could not stomach the malefactor's wickedness. Nevertheless, it's apparent that what happened along the Seine weighs heavily on all their consciences. We must remember that the human soul's hunger to be absolved of unresolved guilt must never be underestimated. I pray Sir John that one or some of those bargemen will provide us with more information. Item: the past is the past, the bargemen hoped it would remain so.

'The years roll by but then matters take a violent turn. A war cog, *The Knave of Hearts*, is commissioned to take treasure to the English garrison in Calais. In fact, this is only a ploy by Master Thibault to distract attention from the gold and silver being secretly transported by sumpter pony to other ships waiting at Dover. Item: *The Knave of Hearts* is under the command of Master Dorset and his henchman Bramley.' Athelstan paused and turned to Cranston. 'Did you search their houses, their muniments and manuscripts for any information?'

Cranston, sitting, his eyes half closed, nodded. 'Of course, Brother, but you know how it is. Such men rarely keep records and, in particular, a catalogue of their previous sins.'

'Very well my friend,' Athelstan continued writing. 'It's a pity because both Dorset and Bramley were former members of *Le Sans Dieu*. They certainly would have known about the Oriflamme but, of course, we can never probe that. Item: *The Knave of Hearts* suffered a disaster. Its hold contained barrels of black cannon powder. These caught fire and the cog simply ceased to exist. The crew were slaughtered; none survived except for Master Dorset, who must have been flung into the water after he sustained a deadly head wound. Now, before he died, Dorset babbled about a nightmare figure. According to him, the Oriflamme mysteriously emerged on board his ship. Did he really, or was that a phantasm of Dorset's muddled soul, a bitter memory of previous sins? I suspect the Oriflamme was on board *The Knave of Hearts* and that he was responsible for its destruction, but somehow escaped, probably by using the bum-barge which was later found floating on the Thames.

'Item: the Oriflamme, or someone who certainly knows the workings of that creature's hellish soul, has recently reappeared in London, intent on inflicting his depravities on poor whores. He slits their throats. He pulls a red wig over their heads and their naked corpses are sent floating in some cockle boat as open testimony to the Oriflamme's wicked, dead soul. Item: the murdered women have two things in common: they were all members of the household of The Way of all Flesh, the Lady Alianora Devereux. Yes?' Cranston, half asleep, nodded. 'Secondly,' Athelstan continued, 'the slain whores were all favoured by the retinue of the French ambassador, Monseigneur Derais, and, in particular, by the Candlelight-Master, leader of the Luciferi. And so, my friend, we come to the next item. About two months ago Monseigneur Hugh Levigne made it very clear to the English Crown that they were highly desirous of seizing the Oriflamme and his immediate henchmen. They wanted these outlaws arrested and brought to trial in Paris for their crimes; in particular the violation and murder of a French noblewoman whose father is now a leading member of the Secret Chancery at the Louvre. So, I ask myself. Did this news have anything to do with the resurgence and reappearance of the Oriflamme? If so, how did he know?'

'Gossip,' Cranston shook himself awake. 'Let's face it, Brother, nothing remains a secret in London for long. Already it is being whispered how *The Knave of Hearts* was not carrying that gold, which was sent by another route. Don't forget, little friar, the slaughtered whores were favoured by the French? Perhaps those ladies of the night, comforting and cosseting members of the Luciferi, discovered that they were hunting the Oriflamme.'

'Oh, my dear coroner,' Athelstan gripped Cranston's arm, '*in vino veritas* – in wine the truth . . . The Oriflamme must have learnt about Levigne's intentions through those whores, yet why kill them? To silence them about other customers they may have favoured? To punish the French for their actions? More importantly, how did the Oriflamme, and I am sure it's he, learn about Grindcobbe and his comrades hiding out in that derelict mansion? He used that information to bait us! That's what this killer is doing, Sir John. He's playing a deadly game and enjoying every second of it. He taunts us. He thoroughly revels in this murderous mayhem. He sees himself as master of the masque. Sir John, we have confronted killers before, many of them men and women who've slain to protect themselves or for greed, lust, revenge, and all the other demons which prowl the human soul. But this Oriflamme is an archangel demon, a lord of Hell who loves to sup blood. So,' Athelstan picked up his quill pen, 'further deaths. First Godbless slaughtered in the old death house which was locked and sealed from the inside. How was that done? By whom? And why? What threat did that old beggar man pose? Why was he so barbarously executed? And, the day before he died, why was Godbless so frenetic, shouting and crying, prostrating himself before the rood screen in St Erconwald's? Above all, why did he allow the killer into his lonely, desolate cottage at the dead of night? Did the assassin force himself in? And, to return to a question I have listed, who could the killer be? Senlac? He's a new arrival in our parish, could he be behind all this mischief? Yet I've established on the night *The Knave of Hearts* was destroyed, Senlac was gambling in The Owlpen, as he was during those hours of darkness when Godbless was murdered.'

Athelstan shook his head. 'And so we move on,' he continued. 'The next death is equally mysterious and macabre: Falaise, guild member and former companion on the war-barge *Le Sans Dieu*. Falaise was murdered in that church tower, a rope tied around his throat. The rope was cleverly fastened. Falaise could only fumble at the knot, wary of missing his step. Eventually he did and the rest we know. Again, our devilish master of revels, who crowned those gargoyles with little wigs in mocking testimony, knew exactly what he was doing. Falaise would struggle, try to save himself, but then make a slip. He was hanged as good and true as any felon on a gibbet at Smithfield.'

Athelstan paused at a knock on the door. Minehostess came bustling in, leading a woman wrapped in a tawny cloak. She pulled back the hood to reveal a lined, grey face redeemed by sad, dark eyes, framed by iron-grey hair under a thin gauze veil. She was clearly agitated, weaving her fingers together, lips slightly parted, eyes watchful.

'Mistress?' Cranston demanded.

'Mistress Margret Bramley. Widow, relict of Master Bramley, henchman on the war cog *The Knave of Hearts*. I,' she gazed beseechingly at Brother Athelstan, 'Brother, I journeyed to St Erconwald's. They informed me that you were with Sir John Cranston and that I would probably find you here at The Lamb of God.' She smiled thinly, 'The widow-woman Benedicta was most helpful.'

'Yes, Mistress, so you have found us?' Athelstan gestured at a cushioned chair close to the table. 'Do you want something to eat and drink?'

'A little watered ale.'

Athelstan nodded at Minehostess, who hurried out and promptly brought back a pewter tankard. Athelstan waited until the door was closed again and watched this highly nervous woman settle herself.

'I am sorry,' she began, 'but I need to speak to you.' She cradled the tankard and then put it on the table, her hands were shaking so much. 'I am terrified,' she blurted out, 'truly terrified.'

'Hush, Mistress,' Athelstan soothed. 'Tell us in your own time. You must be here about your husband and his tragic death aboard that war cog?' The woman nodded, lips moving soundlessly. 'Mistress?'

'A good man,' she told him. 'We had two children.' She took a deep breath. 'But my husband was like a castle with long, dark passageways and sombre rooms. Sometimes he would hint at the horrors he'd seen, but then falter at describing his own involvement in them. He suffered nightmares, which roused him, screaming and shouting, from his sleep. He did tell me about the Oriflamme, a red-wigged monster and some of the outrages he committed.

'The years passed. The nightmares receded. We lived a good

life, my husband, me and our two children.' She blew her cheeks out. 'Then, one night, it must have been about a week before he set sail on *The Knave of Hearts*, we had a visitor, I don't know who. Hooded and visored he was. He arrived at our house on Firkin alleyway in Queenhithe. I never really had an opportunity to see him clearly, he was just a moving shadow. Anyway, he and my husband were closeted in our buttery for about an hour. When the stranger left, my husband was deeply agitated. No, no,' she shook her head, 'I don't know the cause, except that he kept muttering about how the past had sprung on him like a demon in the dark. I did not know what he meant. However, the next morning we were woken by a rapping at the door. We hurried down. It was still dark, a thick river mist curled along the alleyway. The person who had roused us had disappeared but he left, what I knew, was a stark warning to my husband.'

Deeply agitated, she supped at the ale. 'A sow and its piglets used to roam our alleyway. Sir John, Brother Athelstan: all three had been slaughtered, their heads severed and poled with a cresset torch on the ground between them. On each of the severed heads, a red wig. Truly grotesque! I shall – can – never forget those ghastly heads, the blood glistening in the torchlight and those horrid wigs.' She broke off, hands outstretched towards Athelstan. 'A visitor from Hell, Brother, to my husband. Clear enough. The sow and her two piglets were a warning to me and my two children. My husband became a ghost to himself. He told me to stay within. I was not to go out until he left on *The Knave of Hearts*. And that's all I know.' The woman sighed noisily and made to rise, but Athelstan gently pressed her back into the chair.

'You can tell us no more?' he asked.

'What I know, you now do, Brother Athelstan. My husband lived a troubled life and died a most troubled death. I heard about the murdered whores, the red wigs left on their heads. I thought I should come and tell you what had happened to me. I have done, so now I will be gone.' She rose.

Cranston took a sip from the miraculous wineskin, got to his feet and embraced her. 'Rest assured,' he murmured, 'you will have justice.'

PART FOUR

Timor mortis conturbat me: *The fear of death disturbs me*

Matthew Hornsby, member of the Worshipful Guild of Barge- and Watermen, was truly afraid. He felt guilty about the past but, as the years rolled by, the memories of the bloodshed in France had faded. Now they had returned, full, foulsome and fearsome. The guild had ceased to be a band of brothers; each member nursed their own secrets. Indeed, so deep had the fear grown that Father Ambrose had decided it would be best to leave the parish for a while, seek sanctuary elsewhere before going on their parish pilgrimage to Notre-Dame in Boulogne. Till then, however, there were still tasks to be done, especially by himself as clerk of stores in the parish of St Olave's.

Hornsby had come to the arca house, which stood deep in the ancient graveyard of St Olave's. He'd entered the dark, squat building and quickly lit the lanternhorns, then he drew the bolts on the door, pushing them firmly into their clasps before turning the battered key in the even rustier lock. Hornsby leaned against the heavy, iron-studded door and stared around. The arca was dark and gloomy: nothing more than a square of hard sandstone blocks, similar to those used in castles where Hornsby had served as a hobelar along the Welsh March. The windows of the arca were mere arrow-slits to allow in meagre light and air. The roof was strongly beamed, its outside covered by hard tiles cemented fast together. The floor was of pure rock, probably the foundations of some ancient building which had long disappeared. In all, the arca was a small fortress chamber, where people could shelter or treasures be stored.

Hornsby felt weak with a clammy fear: he gave a great sigh, sliding down the door to sit on the ground with his back against it. He stared around at the heaped parish possessions: the small tuns of altar wine, pots of holy water, bundles of vestments and linen, small coffers crammed with altar cloths. Once this chamber had been a refuge for the priest and others during times of bloody turbulence such as the recent Great Revolt, when Father Ambrose and others had sheltered here after nightfall. Hornsby slowly got up. Such days had returned! Or at least for him.

Hornsby clasped the key to the arca, now safely deposited in his belt wallet. He had come to this fortified chamber to do the odd task and, above all, to reflect. Father Ambrose might have plans to move away from the parish for a while, but what was the use of that? If the Oriflamme truly was a member of their community, they would simply be taking that killer with them. Other members of the guild thought the same. Memories were being stirred. People were beginning to recall what happened on that war-barge.

Hornsby closed his eyes. Falaise had been murdered, that's what the gossip said. Was that the work of the Oriflamme? Had that sinister assassin, finished with murdering whores, decided to turn on members of the guild? Hornsby picked up a lanternhorn and moved to where sacks of incense were stacked. He needed to fill the small boat in the sacristy. He paused as he heard a sound. At first he dismissed it as vermin scurrying about, but then he recalled how the arca was free of such a nuisance. Again the sound. Hornsby slowly turned and stared in horror at the dreadful apparition which seemed to glide out of the murk. He stood, mouth going dry, so terrified he couldn't speak as he gazed at this hellish vision: a figure garbed in a grey gown, a warbelt strapped around its waist, a white mask covering the face and a fiery red wig pulled tight over the head, its strands curling out like a host of serpents.

'Matthew Hornsby,' the apparition rasped, 'fearful, are you? Thinking, are you? I bring you peace.' The Oriflamme lifted the crossbow he had primed and, before Hornsby could even move, the bolt smashed into his forehead, shattering flesh, bone and brain.

Cranston and Athelstan made themselves comfortable in the parlour of The House of Delight, one of the city's most ornate and lavish brothels. Athelstan gazed around at the walls, decorated with the finest tapestries from Bruges, a truly gorgeous array of coloured, precious threads celebrating the theme of love, be it Diana of the Ephesians, Lancelot and Guinevere, or the love themes of romantic poetry. The floor of the parlour was cleverly tiled, the high ceiling exquisitely painted, whilst the furnishings were of the finest polished oak, which caught and reflected the delicately beautiful silver and gold ornaments arranged on shelves around the room. Nevertheless, the two women who sat before him and Cranston were a stark contrast to their surroundings. They were garbed in simple brown gowns, white wimples on their heads, with sandals on their bare feet. Both women looked like devout nuns, members of some strict religious order. Nevertheless, the elder woman, despite her hard face and prim ways, was Alianora Devereux, The Way of all Flesh, the greatest whore-mistress in London, whilst the younger, pretty-faced woman was, according to the introductions, one of her favourite novices. The Way of all Flesh was studying Athelstan carefully, though now and again she would glance sharply at Cranston who, as he had proclaimed when they first entered the house, had known The Way of all Flesh for many a year. Athelstan had certainly heard all the rumours about this remarkable woman, whilst this was not the first time he had visited her in pursuit of some malefactor.

'Well, Sir John?' The Way of all Flesh lifted her hands. 'Once again you and Brother Athelstan grace my presence. What brought you here? What business?'

'Murder! Treason! Grievous threat. A whole basket of felonies, Mistress, which could send those involved to a hempen necklace or the butcher's block at Smithfield.'

'Now, now Sir John, you are not intimating—'

'Of course not. I am sure,' Cranston added wryly, 'no crime is ever committed within these love-soaked walls. Other things, but not crime. To cut to the quick, Mistress, to move to the arrow point, you must surely know about the murdered whores—?'

'*Filles de Joie!*' the woman sharply interrupted.

'Same thing. Young prostitutes, their throats cut, their bodies stripped naked and their heads festooned with red wigs before being despatched to float down the Thames in some skiff or herring boat.'

'Yes, yes I have.'

'They were all members of your household?'

'I take in many a poor girl from wandering the streets and show her great compassion.'

'Quite, quite, but listen my Lady,' Cranston pointed a finger, his face all severe, 'do not joust with me, Mistress. All those girls were from this house?'

'They were.'

'And they were all favoured by the French, members of Monseigneur Derais' household? In particular, Monseigneur Levigne and his Luciferi?'

'Yes, yes that is so.'

'Don't you think it's strange that all the slain girls had this in common?'

'It's a thought. But, there again,' the woman shrugged, 'they were led and organized by Mathilde Makepeace.'

'One of your ladies?'

'Yes, and the first to be slain. She would receive an invitation from the French to organize certain revelries in some tavern or, more usually, in the Maison Parisienne, the French ambassador's residence.'

'Mistress, I can guess the details but,' the coroner's voice turned hard, 'you are not being as helpful as I wish. We can talk here or I can summon you to the Guildhall.'

'Sir John, Sir John,' the woman dropped all pretence, the prim, cold smile disappeared and her voice turned businesslike, 'of course we mourn these deaths. The dreadful murder of young women, their corpses desecrated and mocked. Naturally we realize there must be a connection between their murders and the French envoys here in London. So I ask myself, as you must have, were these slayings punishment, some sort of revenge against Monseigneur Levigne?'

'And why should that be?'

'Again, Sir John, you must hazard a guess. You may well know the answer to your own question. The Luciferi are in London to hunt down and capture a criminal called the Oriflamme and his immediate henchmen. One of the Luciferi told the same to Mathilde Makepeace. As I have said, she informed me a short while before she was murdered.'

'What you say is very logical and makes sense,' Cranston bowed mockingly. 'Mistress Alianora, we walk the same path.'

'Hand in hand?' she teased.

'If you wish, and then I could lead you onto a different path,'

Cranston retorted. 'I would love, Mistress, to learn what you know about certain doings in London?'

'Sir John, let us keep to the business in hand.'

'Tell me, Mistress,' Athelstan demanded, 'was Mathilde Makepeace, or any of her companions, particularly friendly to someone else?'

'Such as?'

'Members of the Worshipful Guild of Barge- and Watermen, the sept which gathers at The Leviathan in Queenhithe?'

'Not that I know of.'

'You are sure that neither Mathilde, or any of the other murdered girls, consorted with members of that guild?'

The Way of all Flesh shook her head and glanced sharply at the novice, who nodded in agreement.

'So,' Athelstan pressed on, 'Mathilde must be the key. She may well have unwittingly informed the Oriflamme, whoever he may be, about Levigne's intentions in London, as well as supplying him with a list of girls the French have enjoyed dalliance with in this city.'

'I would agree with that, Brother.'

'And is there anything else you can tell us?' Athelstan insisted.

'The red wigs?' The young novice spoke up.

'Oh yes there is! Well done, Sister Monica!' The Way of all Flesh patted her companion on the hand. 'One thing we did learn was that Mathilde bought sacks of garish red wigs fashioned out of coarse horsehair.'

'From whom?'

'From one of the greatest suppliers in our city. Two brothers, Hengist and Horsa. They ply their trade from an old slaughter-house in Offal alley. It's not far.'

'I know it,' Cranston grinned. 'Oh yes, I surely do. You can smell it long before you reach it.'

'Is there anything else?' The Way of all Flesh demanded.

'You have told us everything?' Athelstan retorted.

'I have and, in which case, gentlemen . . .' The Way of all Flesh rose to her feet, so Cranston and Athelstan did likewise.

'Don't forget me.' The coroner seized the woman's proffered hand and raised it to his lips.

'Sir John, how could I ever?'

*   *   *

Cranston and Athelstan left The House of Delights. The day was
already dying, the crowds dispersing. Stallholders were packing
away their wares: the fleshers, cooks and taverners laying out their
tubs of food, the sweepings of their particular business. Already
the legions of poor were gathering to feast. Beggars whined
incessantly whilst the shadow-people, the night-walkers, pimps,
wolfmen and all the inhabitants from the squalid dens of the city,
the catacomb of dark cellars and filthy pits, were crawling out
of their lairs, ripe for mischief and hungry for profit.

The coroner and friar reached Offal alley. Athelstan swiftly
realized why Cranston bought pomanders from the stall of a
one-eyed chapman just before they turned into the alleyway. The
reeking smell was deeply offensive, the stench of corruption
became all-pervasive, and it certainly grew worse when Cranston
ushered him towards the gates. Here, they paused to take deep
sniffs from the pomanders. The coroner led Athelstan forward
into a yard where the cobbles glistened with the blood and gore
from a stack of slaughtered horses, their bloody carcasses piled
high in oaken stalls, the severed heads stuck on a range of poles.
Torches, fixed into every available crevice, illuminated the gruesome scene. The severed heads were particularly monstrous, with
their popping, glassy eyes and half-opened mouths, lips curled
back to reveal long, yellowing teeth.

Cranston strode towards two bulky figures in long leather
aprons who emerged from an outhouse, their arms and hands
coloured a brilliant red. Athelstan at first thought this was more
blood, then realized it was a coarse dye. The men introduced
themselves as Hengist and Horsa and openly acknowledged they
knew Sir John, whilst they had heard of Brother Athelstan. Both
men were bald as an egg, their long faces almost hidden by bushy
moustaches and beards. They raised their hands in greeting, the
elder Hengist explaining that they had best not clasp their visitors, as the dye was almost impossible to wash out.

Cranston heartily agreed, refusing any offer of refreshment.
He pointed around the great slaughter yard.

'You bring the corpses of horses here?'

'We buy horses past their use. We slaughter them, sever their
heads and tails, then we fashion, or rather our wives do, wigs
from the hair.'

'Who buys these?'

'Well, Sir John, every pimp, whore mistress and prostitute in the city. They all come here.' Hengist became expansive, 'We enjoy a fine reputation. We only sell the very best. No one—'

'Yes, quite.' The coroner steadied himself against the slopping swill seeping out over the cobbles.

'We use the mane and the tail,' Hengist continued, 'they provide the best. You see the coarser they are—'

'Again, I understand,' Cranston testily retorted, 'but have you recently made a large sale of your wigs to any particular individual?'

'Oh yes, a few weeks ago. Mathilde, a girl who works for The Way of all Flesh, arrived in our yard with good pounds sterling. Mathilde wanted to buy sacks of wigs and have them transported to a place she indicated . . .' Hengist paused.

'And?'

'I loaded them into an old dung cart and took them, with Mathilde leading the way, to a derelict warehouse along a deserted alley in Queenhithe. I unloaded the cart and left her to it. A few days later, I learnt about Mathilde's murder. I hurried back to the warehouse but all the sacks were gone.'

'You haven't told them about the conversation you had with her,' Horsa declared, nudging his brother.

Athelstan tried not to flinch at the gust of sweaty odours which seemed to cling to both these men.

'Come on lads,' Cranston stamped his feet, 'I am a coroner investigating hideous murder. Mathilde was cruelly slaughtered. Consequently, what she may have said in the days before her death is important.'

'When I led the cart down, Mathilde trotted beside me. She chattered like a sparrow on the branch about one of her customers, who liked to tumble her in an alleyway, pressing her up against the wall. She said she was used to all kinds of revelry when it came to playing the two-backed beast. She didn't mind as long as they paid her good coin and gave her something to eat and drink. This one paid well. Anyway,' Hengist hurried on, 'this customer who wanted the wigs, liked to wear a white mask with a hood over his head. Mathilde never knew what he looked like.'

'Are you sure?' Cranston demanded. 'Didn't she ever ask to see the man's face?'

'Sir John, Mathilde was a whore. She was there to please.'

'Surely she would wonder why he wanted to buy so many wigs?'

'Ah, Mathilde did ask! He'd replied how he hoped to open his own house of delights and, if he did, Mathilde would be his whore mistress.'

'Ah, I see,' Athelstan declared. 'This character seduced and traduced poor Mathilde, weaving dreams about her becoming a lady in her own right equal to The Way of all Flesh.'

'Mathilde said the same,' Horsa declared. 'She was full of plans about managing her own domain with its retinue of whores.'

'Anything else?'

'No, Sir John, I promise you. Nothing at all. All I can guess is that Mathilde handed over those wigs and, a few days later, she was murdered. I suspect that customer must be her killer.'

'Very true, very true,' Athelstan half whispered. 'My friend, I believe you are correct.'

Cranston and Athelstan left the slaughter yard and made their way back along the alleyway. The coroner paused halfway up, took a generous swig from the miraculous wineskin before walking on, one hand on Athelstan's shoulder.

'Do you know my little friar, I do wonder . . .'

'What, Sir John?'

'Well, the Luciferi may be the envoys of the French King, but they are also assassins. I keep thinking about Falaise. Was he murdered by the Oriflamme?'

'Remember those red wigs, Sir John? They are almost the personal seal of this killer.'

'True, Brother. But what if the Luciferi have decided to carry out their own execution of anyone associated with that war-barge, *Le Sans Dieu*, and the depredations of the Oriflamme? Why not seize a man like Falaise and arrange matters so he hanged himself and leave those red wigs as a taunting insult?' Cranston scratched the side of his face and took away his hand. 'It's just a thought, little friar. I do wonder if we are dealing with one or two killers. But, only time and the truth will tell.'

Benedicta squatted before the fire in Athelstan's house. She leaned down and stirred the fiery mass of wood. Beside her, Bonaventure stretched and purred in pure contentment. The widow-woman had come out in the dark to make sure all was well. She had left most of the other parishioners seated before a roaring fire in The Piebald. The night was cold. The frost already settling. Nevertheless, accompanied by Crim, Benedicta had visited the freezing, empty church, then looked in to watch Philomel feasting on his feed before coming here. Bonaventure, of course, had been waiting, a silent shadow beside the door. Benedicta stroked the great tomcat and wondered how late Athelstan would be. She had matters to report about what had happened in the parish. In particular, she had kept a sharp eye on their visitor Senlac, yet he seemed harmless enough. True, he had protested vociferously at being summoned to the meeting at St Olave's, yet he had returned with tales of more murder. The newcomer had quickly taken the place of honour in the inglenook at The Piebald, regaling all the customers about what he'd learnt across the river.

Benedicta felt her mouth go dry with fear. The stories about the red-wigged slayer were spreading, and she feared for the little friar whom she loved so dearly. Benedicta had also listened very attentively to Cecily and Clarissa. Both these ladies of the night had learnt all the gory details from their sisters in the trade. This killer seemed to revel in his murderous forays. Moleskin had confessed the same. In fact, the boatman seemed completely terrified, and kept muttering about the past, about old sins pursuing him like dogs from Hell. Benedicta had encountered this sort of guilt before. The war in France had been sharp and bitter. Many men in the parish, including Watkin and Pike, had fought the length and breadth of Normandy. They had been in the free companies, cohorts of mercenaries who feared neither God nor man. They had plundered and pillaged to their hearts' content: châteaux, churches, palaces, and even the occasional abbey or monastery. True, they were not killers, but they had wreaked hideous devastation and destruction. More significantly, they had brought their ill-gotten wealth home to finance a new trade, be it Crispin the carpenter, Simon the skinner, Beadle Bladdersmith or Merrylegs and his cook shop. Benedicta had also noticed how these men were markedly reluctant to discuss the past. They realized in their heart of hearts that, whatever their excuses, they had pillaged the property of others whose lives they had deeply blighted. Such men were reluctant to reminisce and, as Athelstan had once remarked, even more reluctant to confess such sins because, if they did, reparation would have to be made.

The news about the Frenchman Hugh Levigne and his Luciferi had disturbed many of the parish. A new peace treaty had been reached between England and France. According to Mauger, who was an authority on everything because of his skill at reading and listening at doors, the masters at the Louvre Paris were keen on hunting down the captains of certain free companies so they could face inquisition and trial in Paris. Giles of Sempringham, the Hangman of Rochester, had also heard how the seizure of former mercenaries had taken place in his native city Canterbury, as well as other towns in the shire. So keen were the French, that they were offering bribes and concessions to Regent Gaunt and his Master of Secrets to surrender certain named individuals. Benedicta wondered what would happen.

She stared into the fire, her eyes growing heavy. She heard a sound and started, abruptly remembering she had not locked the door behind her. Now fully awake, the sweat starting on her body, Benedicta rose and slowly turned to confront the macabre figure who stood leaning against the door. The nightmare was dressed in a woman's long, grey gown, a thick garish wig, the colour of blood decorating its head, face covered by a ghostly white mask with gaps for eyes, nose and mouth. In one hand the dreadful visitor held a serrated dagger, in the other a coiled rope.

'In God's name,' Benedicta gasped.

'Aye, widow-woman, and in Satan's name, I greet you.'

The voice was that of a man, but heavily disguised, as if he had something in his mouth.

'What business, sir, do you have with me?' Benedicta fought to remain calm as she glanced to the right and left looking for a weapon; there was nothing.

'Come, Benedicta.' The dreadful apparition beckoned her close with the rope; he brought the knife up to point at her. 'Come quietly or I will do what I have to do here. Come.' The hideous figure moved forward. Benedicta made to lunge towards the table; her assailant stepped to one side. Benedicta swiftly turned, seizing the fire prongs, even as the door was flung open, crashing into the intruder as Crim burst into the house. The altar boy who had come to escort Benedicta, staggered and stood still, eyes startled, mouth gaping. He glanced at the widow-woman, then at the intruder, who had been knocked sideways. Crim sprang forward but the assassin shoved him away and fled out into the darkness.

Athelstan sat in his beloved chantry chapel, deep in the northern transept of St Erconwald's. The friar loved this little shrine to his patron saint, a place of serenity, hallowed and beautiful. The small window high in the outside wall to his left was filled with exquisitely stained glass, a gift from Sir John. The floor of the chapel was carpeted in the richest turkey rugs, deep blue and so thick, they deadened all sound. The furnishings were of the finest polished oak and elmwood, whilst the altar cross was edged in silver to match the candlesticks on the snow-white cloth. Two small braziers kept the chantry warm and sweet smelling. Indeed, it was a place, as Athelstan had confided in Cranston, which combined all the comforts, both physical and spiritual.

Athelstan took a deep breath and stared at the carved statue of St Erconwald standing on its corner plinth to the left of the altar. He closed his eyes and prayed for strength. This most hallowed place had been grossly violated! Athelstan had returned the previous evening to find his parish in uproar over the attack on Benedicta. The friar had spent some heart-lurching moments when Watkin first informed him, but he was soon comforted that his beloved friend had escaped unscathed. Watkin had summoned a local leech, who had fed Benedicta The Piebald's richest Bordeaux laced with an opiate. The widow-woman was now sleeping in a chamber at The Piebald, guarded by other parishioners. Athelstan had visited her as soon as he rose that morning, but Benedicta had still been sleeping, so Athelstan had continued with his parish activities.

The friar had celebrated Godbless's funeral mass then buried both the beggar man and the remains of his pet goat in a grave deep in God's Acre. During the ceremony, Athelstan's parishioners could see that their little priest was totally distracted. They did their best to assist at Godbless's requiem; they also brought fresh news about the sleeping Benedicta but, apart from that, they had left the friar alone. Athelstan was pleased at this. He had certainly not informed his flock about the other abomination which had been perpetrated. On his return the previous evening, the friar had come into his church to douse any candles and ensure all was well. Of course he had visited the chantry chapel, and been horrified to see a grotesque red wig pulled drunkenly over the head of St Erconwald's statue. Not only was this a sacrilege but a clear threat, a stark warning along with the assault on Benedicta that neither Athelstan – nor any of those he held dearest – were safe. Fighting the red mist which sometimes descended, Athelstan had torn the wig off and thrust it down a sewer behind the church.

Athelstan lifted his head and smiled tearfully at the statue. 'I am sorry,' he whispered. 'I truly apologize for the grievous insult offered.' Athelstan had eventually calmed himself. He had sprinkled the statue with holy water yet the heinous insult still rankled. The friar blessed himself and closed his eyes. 'You truly are a child of Hell,' he whispered. 'A treacherous demon who revels in the pain and hurt you inflict, yet you are arrogant. You have all the overweening pride of your father in Hell. You resent my interference. You believe that both me and mine should be punished for even trying to hunt you.'

Athelstan leaned back in the celebrant's chair. 'So much slaughter and destruction,' he reflected. He mentally listed the litany of bloody chaos the Oriflamme had recently caused. *The Knave of Hearts* and all its crew obliterated from God's earth. Those poor whores sent floating mockingly down the Thames. Godbless slaughtered, as if he was some offering to a pagan god. Falaise tortured until he made a mistake, slipped and strangled himself to death; those poor Upright Men, desperate to escape, now seized and destined for a hanging outside Newgate. Benedicta and Crim threatened and terrified out of their wits.

'Oh, I will settle with you,' Athelstan whispered. 'This is *usque ad mortem* – to the very death.' But whose death?

Athelstan felt deeply threatened. He had locked himself here in this church; only the corpse door remained open. He had satisfied himself that the parish was settled, even visiting the old death house. He had found Senlac busy with the paving stones yet, as Athelstan could see, there was nothing beneath except packed earth, certainly no indication of how Godbless had been so brutally murdered. Nor did the paving stones, some of which had been lifted, conceal any secret place. Athelstan heard a sound. He rose, opened the door in the lattice screen and glimpsed a figure emerge through the darkness of the transept. At first he felt a spasm of clammy fear, but relaxed as Father Ambrose, swathed in a thick cloak, came forward, hands extended. Relieved, Athelstan clasped them in welcome, pulling the priest close to exchange the kiss of peace before ushering him into the chantry chapel. Ambrose made himself comfortable on the cushioned wall bench, pulling down the edge of his cloak and murmuring how lovely the shrine looked.

'It's so bitterly cold outside,' the priest smiled at Athelstan, his dark, lined face becoming softer. 'I first visited The Piebald; Moleskin informed me about what had happened.' The priest leaned forward. 'Athelstan, I confess to you as a fellow worker in God's vineyard, I am truly scared. What we face—'

'Is evil incarnate,' Athelstan, still feeling waspish, finished the sentence.

'I agree.' The priest glanced away. Athelstan, regretting his sharpness, made himself more comfortable as he studied Ambrose: the black thinning hair, the healed scar to the right of his neck, the broad brow, firm chin and clever eyes. A self-composed soul, Athelstan thought, a man comfortable in his own skin.

'Brother, why do you stare at me?'

'Because I am curious,' Athelstan smiled. 'Why on earth are you here? Why cross the river in such freezing weather?'

'To put it bluntly, Brother Athelstan, I am terrified. My parishioners are terrified. The Guild of Bargemen are terrified. This red-wigged killer stalks us like a weasel in a rabbit warren. Now he pursues you and yours,' the priest pointed down the church, 'or so they told me at The Piebald.'

'And you have no suspicion about who this killer is?'

'Brother, it could have been one of our former company, a member of our parish, or just a demon who's prowled the deadlands and has now swept in to wreak vengeance on the sins of men.'

'Quite poetic!' Athelstan rejoined, trying to lighten the mood. 'Where are you from, Father?'

'Bardby in Lincolnshire. I am a son of a freeholder taken into the de Lacy array and shipped off to Normandy. Once there, I slipped away. I have some knowledge of barges and so I drifted along the Seine until I reached La Chèvre Dansante and the Flames of Hell. Though,' he shrugged, 'they weren't given such a title: that came later. Anyway, I enjoyed their company and they accepted me. We camped at that sprawling tavern, our war-barge pulled up on the bank. We roistered, we revelled, then we would go on our forays.'

'And the Oriflamme appeared?'

'Yes, yes he did, some time before I joined the company.' Father Ambrose sighed. 'He apparently swaggered in, as he always did, garbed in that woman's gown, a red wig on his head, a white mask concealing his features. He offered our company fresh fields for more plunder. He was knowledgeable and skilled about the countryside, able to converse in Norman French. He was also a deadly dagger man, sharp as any fox. He could sniff out mutiny and rebellion. As we told you, Brother, he weaved his web and held us all in fearful dread.'

'But not you?'

'Oh yes he did, Brother! I just wanted to have nothing to do with him, and I didn't. I avoided any expedition led by him. I did not bother the Oriflamme. I kept a careful, still tongue in my head and so he did not bother me. A true monster, Brother, a soul full of hate who despised both priests and women; though why he did,' Ambrose shook his head sorrowfully, 'I just don't know.'

'And you have no physical description of him, nothing distinguishing?'

'God be my witness, Brother, if I did, I would tell you.'

'And so why are you here?'

'As I have told you, Brother, we are terrified. I am here to seek sanctuary, both for myself and my parishioners, or at least those who belong to the sept of Barge- and Watermen. Brother, we do not feel safe. St Erconwald's is a sanctuary church.' Ambrose paused, drawing in his breath. He held up his right hand as if taking an oath. 'On behalf of us all, I invoke the rights of Holy Mother Church. I claim sanctuary in these sacred precincts.'

Athelstan was about to reply when he heard a sound from outside, as if footfalls echoed along the nave. A sharp, slithering noise followed by silence. He gestured at Ambrose to sit still and rose, carefully opening the chantry door. Athelstan hid his disquiet as he walked past the rood screen to the centre of the nave. He knew the church was locked except for the corpse door. Athelstan warily walked down to this. He was surprised to find the bolts at top and bottom drawn full across, and realized Ambrose must have locked the door behind him. Athelstan stared around but he could not see or hear anything untoward. Satisfied, he returned to the chantry chapel. Ambrose was still sitting on the bench staring down at the floor.

'Father?'

Ambrose took his hands away and lifted his head, his cheeks all tear-soaked.

'I am sorry, Brother,' he whispered, 'but I am truly terrified. We need to bring the guild and their families here. I know St Erconwald's has the right of sanctuary for those fleeing from the law, but it also extends the same privilege to any Christian who believes their lives are in utmost peril. Believe me, that is certainly true of myself and my parishioners. They will all come here. Mistress Alice will stay to look after the church and priest's house. I shall also write to Master Tuddenham at the archdeacon's chancery. I promise you, Brother . . .'

He faltered and Athelstan jumped as the door to the chantry chapel was flung open and that macabre figure, so closely described by Crim, slipped like the most sinister shadow into the hallowed shrine. Athelstan made to step forward, but the night-mare visitor lifted a small arbalest, its bolt already primed, the cord winched back; the intruder also had a similar one hanging on a belt hook. Athelstan tried to remain calm as he stared at this phantasm from the realms of midnight. The dire apparition was garbed like a woman in a long grey gown, a warbelt fastened around its waist, face covered by a white mask, its head hidden under a grotesque red wig.

'You are the Oriflamme?' Athelstan whispered hoarsely, pointing at the intruder. 'You have swept up from Hell, for that's where you dwell.'

The Oriflamme did not reply but advanced threateningly, raising the arbalest as he indicated that both priests should kneel. Ambrose did not move swiftly enough to join Athelstan, so the

Oriflamme lashed out with a booted foot, its toe catching the priest's knee. Ambrose groaned and hastened to obey.

'Why?' The voice grated as if he had small sponges in his mouth, the type tooth-pullers use to soak up blood when they drew a tooth. 'Why will you not let sleeping dogs lie? Why do you interfere and try and roll back the past?'

Athelstan heard the crossbow cord screech, followed by a thud as the bolt smashed into the plastered wall behind him.

'Take that as a warning,' the voice gasped. 'I know you, Ambrose Rockwood, you lily-hearted bastard. You always were so, now you are a mewling priest. You can beg for sanctuary, but that won't protect you. As for you, Athelstan, the interfering, meddlesome friar, all busy with fat Cranston. Stay out of my business. Tell the coroner to dismiss the French and I shall disappear as I do so now. So, both of you, lie down.'

Athelstan glanced up. The assailant held a second arbalest, primed and ready. 'On your faces,' the voice ordered. Athelstan glanced at Ambrose and nodded. The two priests prostrated themselves on the floor. The chapel door opened and closed, then silence. Satisfied that they were safe, Athelstan rose, helped Ambrose to his feet and hastened into the nave. The corpse door hung open, but when he went out and looked across the cemetery, he could see nothing but the houses of the dead, the gorse and brambles bending under a bitterly cold breeze. Athelstan returned to the chantry chapel, where Ambrose sat all trembling on the bench. Athelstan gently walked the priest down the nave. He unlocked the narrow postern door and took the priest out onto the steps. Tab the tinker was standing in the lychgate. Athelstan called the tinker over. He asked him to take Ambrose to The Piebald, promising the priest that he, and all those who wanted to, could seek sanctuary at St Erconwald's. Once both tinker and priest had left, Athelstan strode back into the church. He assured himself that all was well, then returned to the priest's house, locking and bolting the door behind him. He filled a deep-bowled cup with the richest Bordeaux Cranston had given him, took a generous gulp then, sitting at the table, put his face in his hands and wept.

Sir John Cranston followed the bulky, shadowy outline of the keeper of Newgate. They went deeper and deeper into that antechamber of Hell, the House of Iron, a place of utter desolation and misery. The coroner had visited the prison more often than he could care to remember, yet Cranston could never lose the chilling fear – even terror – this place of stygian darkness provoked in him. A true warren of the underworld, Newgate's galleries and passageways reeked of every foul odour. Its ceilings, walls and floor, fashioned out of the hardest stone, glistened with filth. Rats, dark and supple, scurried backwards and forwards, oblivious to anything else. Cockroaches and other insects carpeted the ground so thickly they crunched beneath Cranston's boots. Little light pierced the murk. The only source of warmth and visibility was provided by rows of thick-tarred cresset torches pushed into wall sconces. Cranston quietly acknowledged to himself the accuracy of the prison's reputation as a House of Iron with its padlocked doors, grilles, pits, cages, cells and dungeons. A constant raucous noise set his teeth on edge, the clanging and clashing of doors, the screams and shouts of prisoners and the strident obscenities of the jailors. Cranston pressed the pomander closer to his face as they passed an open chamber where the sickly remains of those crushed in the press yard lay bloated and rotting, ready for burial in Newgate's lime pits. The chamber next to it housed the severed, torn limbs of traitors executed for treason; these were being soaked in brine before being tarred for display above the city gates.

'In God's name!' Cranston murmured.

'Never mind, Sir John,' the keeper replied merrily over his shoulder. 'Here we are at what we call our long room.'

The keeper took the huge ring of keys from a hook on his belt and opened an iron-plated door. The room within was low-beamed. Torches, high in the wall, flared and spluttered in the draught of cold air. Beneath these sat a row of prisoners, chained to each other as well as to the wall behind them.

'The Upright Men,' the keeper joked with a dramatic flourish. 'Upright no longer, aye Sir John?'

'Wait outside Hubert,' Cranston retorted.

The coroner waited until the keeper slammed the door shut behind him, then he went and squatted before Grindcobbe, sitting in the centre of the group, his comrades manacled either side.

'Well Jack,' Grindcobbe cleaned the filth from his dirty, sweaty face, 'have you come to wish us well, to give us your best regards before we dance in the air at Smithfield?'

'Simon, my friend, you know that's not Merry Jack's way. I heard you want to talk to me.'

'For a price.'

'There always is. And?'

'Our sentences commuted.' Grindcobbe stirred in a rattle of chains and a gust of sweaty odours. 'We'll take exile, Jack. Permanent exile beyond the Narrow Seas. On pain of death, if we dare return.' Grindcobbe paused as his comrades murmured their agreement, moving backwards and forwards, chains and manacles jangling.

Cranston kept his face impassive. He did not want these men to die. The Revolt was over and Master Thibault had given him the power of life and death in all these cases.

'Well, well, well,' the coroner pulled a face. 'If you are gone from these shores, that might make my work a little easier. I won't speak for myself, but Brother Athelstan always had great compassion for you and your cause, even though he decried the means you used to achieve it.'

'Hurling times, Jack. We put all our fortunes on the table. We played the deadly game of hazard, shook the cup and let the dice roll.'

'True, true,' Cranston nodded. 'Anyway, what do you offer?'

'Information.'

'Let me hear it.'

'Now, Jack, you may first wonder how we, all locked and bolted in this hellish pit, would know anything.'

'The thought has occurred to me.'

'Come, come Jack. You know the way of the world. News in London is like the air we breathe. It seeps in and through everything, even to a place like this. We've heard the news about Falaise found hanging on a bell rope in his church.'

'And?'

'Jack, Falaise was one of our company. We gave him gold and silver to arrange our journey across the Narrow Seas to Flanders, Hainault or Brabant. He was the one who knew about our hiding place and what we intended.'

'So Falaise betrayed you?'

'No, no,' Grindcobbe's reply was echoed by those chained with him. 'Falaise was an Upright Man, good and true to the marrow of his being. He was one of us, body and soul, but he kept that well-hidden. What I believe is that somehow, that creature from the fiery chambers of Hell, the Oriflamme, must have also discovered our whereabouts as well as our intentions.'

'And so he informed both the French and myself to draw attention from himself?'

'Or herself!'

'Simon?'

Grindcobbe shrugged. 'Jack, it wouldn't be the first time some gentle lady is in fact a dyed-in-the-wool killer. But . . .' Grindcobbe paused and licked his dry lips, trying to wet them with his tongue. Cranston took the miraculous wineskin from beneath his cloak and allowed it to be passed so each prisoner could take a sip. Once he received it back, Cranston cleaned the mouthpiece and took a deep gulp, rolling the full-bodied wine around his mouth to cleanse it from the filthy humours of this horrible place.

'Continue,' Cranston pointed at Grindcobbe.

'Well, Sir John, it's obvious. The Oriflamme was very successful, and he certainly made a fool of those Frenchmen.'

'Never mind them. Do you know of any reason for Falaise's murder?'

'The same as you, Sir John. Falaise may have begun to suspect who truly betrayed us. He must have then concluded that the traitor and the Oriflamme were one and the same person.'

'You have won yourself a stay of execution,' Cranston edged closer. 'But I can tell from your eyes, Simon, you have not yet finished your hymn. What fresh news?'

'Fresh news indeed,' Grindcobbe nudged the man next to him, his long, blond hair, moustache and beard smeared with filth, though the light-blue eyes were clear enough. 'Tell him,' Grindcobbe urged. 'Tell him what you told us.'

'My name is Robin of the Green Wood.' The man's voice was thickened by a strong burr. 'I am Robin of the Green Wood,' he repeated.

'I am sure you are,' Cranston peered closer. 'But in the warrants issued for your arrest, you are also named as Robin Goodfellow, Little John,' Cranston waved a hand, 'and so on, and so on. Never mind who you are, what's your story?'

'I was a captain of the Earthworms when our leader Wat Tyler invaded London. We plundered and pillaged certain houses and other places, the property of our enemies, the rich dwelling places of the Lords of the Soil—'

'Such as Regent Gaunt's Palace of the Savoy?' Cranston interrupted. 'And, thanks to you, a palace no longer. Nothing but blackened ruins, though I understand Master Thibault dances on these because they cover a huge cellar where many of your comrades were burnt alive.'

'Such is war, Sir John.'

'I call it criminal but continue.'

'I was commissioned to search the streets and alleyways of Queenhithe ward. We were looking for foreigners as well as those indicted by the Commons and the Upright Men. Now there was an old house on the corner of Slops Alley, one of those crumbling tenements, a mixture of plaster and wood. Nothing remarkable yet, unlike other tenements along that runnel, it had not been ransacked, pillaged or plundered. Instead we found the corpses of two old ladies hanging by their necks from a roof beam, frail, fairly emaciated. Nevertheless, someone had hated those two so much, they had invaded the house and cruelly hanged them. Now,' the prisoner lifted a manacled hand, 'this will certainly interest you, Sir John. The corpses were dangling, hands and ankles tied, but the thickest coarse red wigs had been pulled over their heads.' The prisoner paused. 'I have been a soldier. I've journeyed the length and breadth of this kingdom, but I have never seen anything like that, nor had any of my comrades. My curiosity was pricked. You see, Sir John, there was nothing in the house to plunder. Dirty, desolate and derelict. The furnishings were shabby. The floor was covered with a mess; even the dead women's garb was frayed and moth-eaten.' He took a deep breath. 'I cast about to discover who was responsible for inflicting such deaths on two harmless old women. I knew it wasn't one of our own company. In the end I discovered that perhaps both women were not so harmless.'

'What do you mean?'

'Both old crones used that house to care for foundlings—'

'Ah yes,' Cranston intervened. 'The council pay well, or at least used to. And these two?'

'Well, they managed that house of foundlings. They also had a fearsome reputation for ill-treating the poor unfortunates committed to their care: beatings, lack of food, cruel punishment. Eventually the house was closed down. The women, two sisters, disappeared but re-emerged shortly before the Great Revolt; I reckon that must have been about nine months ago. They had apparently moved away to escape their sins but then returned due to a lack of sustenance elsewhere.' The Upright Man paused. 'Someone, a former foundling, now a man, decided to use the chaos to settle scores and, apart from that, Sir John, Robin of the Green Wood can say no more.'

'Oh, I think you can,' the coroner declared. 'But I will take your word and that of Master Grindcobbe. One further matter . . .?'

'What?' the rebel leader demanded.

'You must have lurked around London before moving to that derelict mansion in the parish of St Olave's. Who knew you were there? I mean, amongst the guildsmen, those parishioners.'

'I think we've answered that, Sir John, but let me repeat it. Falaise was the only person. He swore to keep confidence. My Lord Coroner, what we did was common to the Upright Men. The more people who know our plans, the greater the danger of betrayal. Oh, I admit, the likes of Moleskin and others might have suspected, but the actual details were known only to Falaise. If he had been captured, he could betray none of his companions. Yet, in the end, it would appear that he did inform somebody.'

'Yes, yes I agree,' the coroner said. 'And can you tell me more?'

'Nothing, Sir John.'

'And that goes for all of you.'

A chorus of agreement echoed through the cavernous chamber.

'Well, Sir John,' Grindcobbe rattled his chains, 'what now?'

'For you, my friend, and your comrades, a shave, a bath, some strong boots and a thick cloak. You will be given two pence, a fresh loaf, a pannikin of water and licence to board any cog crossing the Narrow Seas.' Cranston got to his feet. 'You will be released tomorrow. Bugger off and don't come back!' The coroner readjusted his warbelt. 'If you do, I will hang you myself.'

'God bless you, Sir John.'

'God bless you too,' Cranston replied and, with the cheers of the Upright Men ringing behind him, Cranston left the hellhole of Newgate for necessary refreshment in The Lamb of God.

Cranston's pleasure at leaving the Newgate was short-lived. He swept through the huge iron gates onto the great cobbled area which stretched in front of the prison. The daily execution procession was assembling. The hangmen busily preparing their carts to carry the condemned either to Smithfield or Tyburn Stream. The prisoners, chained and manacled, were pushed into the carts around which friends and relatives piteously jostled, desperate to make their farewells to those who, as one executioner shouted, would not be making the return journey. The Guild of the Hanged Men were busy offering jugs of ale both to the condemned and those milling around the carts. A Friar of the Sack stood on a barrel, intoning songs of mourning as well as a psalm for the dead. The great dray horses which pulled the carts, scraped iron hooves on the cobbles, impatient to be gone. A few of the prisoners recognized Cranston and shouted abuse, promising they would wait for him on the other side.

'I doubt it,' the coroner murmured to himself as he shouldered through the throng, nudging aside a gaggle of witches and warlocks garbed in black, dusty robes, who gathered in the hope of collecting some items from those about to die. Cranston hated these dark shadows from the underworld who lived around the gibbets and gallows of London. These malignants were desperate to cut the corpses of the hanged in the firm belief that such gruesome relics contained the most magical properties. Cranston wondered whether, in his great treatise on the governance of the city, he should recommend that these children of the night be put to the horn and regarded as outlaws.

A swift movement to his side caught the coroner's eye; glancing quickly to his left, Cranston recognized the Sanctus man, London's notorious relic seller, who sold the most astonishing array of objects: be it a comb used by Samson, the foreskin of Goliath or the robe worn by Naaman Syrian when he was cleansed of his leprosy in the Jordan. The Sanctus man, who had the innocent, cherubic face of an angel, raised a hand in greeting and promptly disappeared into the crowd.

'Not today,' the coroner whispered to himself, 'not today, but you, sir, are another one on my list.'

At last Cranston broke free from the throng and entered the great fleshers' yard where the butchers of London slaughtered the stock they had bought at Smithfield. They gutted and cleaned them before hanging the bleeding chunks on great makeshift scaffolds whilst their apprentices shouted for custom. The place reeked of blood and offal. The ground underfoot was slippery with grease and gore and the sight of row upon row of slaughtered geese, chicken, rabbits, pigs and ducks turned Cranston's stomach. The coroner pinched his nose and closed his mouth firmly against the rank, fetid stench. He glimpsed the beautifully gilded tavern sign of The Lamb of God and heaved a sigh of relief. He was about to push himself through a gap in the stalls when he heard his name being called. Cranston groaned and turned to meet Oswald and Simon, his clerk and scrivener from the Guildhall; between them stood two individuals Cranston immediately recognized. He pointed a finger at them.

'My cup overfloweth,' he rasped. 'What on earth does the Sicarius and his constant companion Wrigglewort want with me?'

'They came looking for you, Sir John,' Oswald declared mournfully. 'They have been hanging around the Guildhall, refusing to go until they see you.'

'Well now they have seen me.' Cranston glared at the two hooded figures, dressed so simply they looked like Cistercian friars.

'Sir John, they claim to have information.'

Cranston sighed, dug into his belt wallet and flicked a coin at Oswald, who caught it neatly. Cranston snapped his fingers.

'Simon, Oswald, back to the Guildhall.' The coroner stamped his feet. 'Buy a pie and a pot of ale to warm yourselves. You two,' he gestured at his visitors, 'follow me.'

Simon and Oswald hastened off, crowing with delight. Cranston pushed his way through the few remaining stalls and into the welcoming warmth of The Lamb of God. Minehostess welcomed him and swept Sir John into his solar. The coroner doffed his cloak and promptly sat down in the great throne-like chair before the fire, indicating that his two guests, as he called them, should sit on stools facing him. Only when Minehostess had served blackjacks of strong ale and a platter of diced, spiced chicken sprinkled with herbs and vegetables, did Cranston's visitors pull back the hoods which concealed head and face.

Cranston, his eyes on both, lifted his tankard and silently toasted them. He knew these two of old. The Sicarius, with his lean, bony face and narrow, watchful eyes, was a henchman of Master Thibault's household: his assistant and constant companion, the perpetual shadow Wrigglewort, looked exactly the same, though was of smaller stature. The Sicarius enjoyed a most unsavoury reputation as an eavesdropper, a spy and, at times, a subtle assassin: one of those malignants of Master Thibault's household who lived in the twilight world of both court and city. The Sicarius shared his name with others of his ilk – the Sicarii – dagger men who could be hired for all types of murderous mischief. His companion and comrade, Wrigglewort, slender as a wand with ever-blinking eyes and pointed features, looked like the ferret he truly was. A young man who enjoyed a chilling reputation as a searcher-out of other people's secrets. Wrigglewort took his name from his considerable skill at being able to sidle into any situation or, indeed, room or chamber, to gather intelligence for his master, who now sat clutching the young man's hand as they both sipped at their drink, eyes all watchful. Cranston took one last mouthful and put his tankard down.

'Well, well my beauties. And what have you come to tell me?'

'My friend and constant helpmate,' the Sicarius raised Wrigglewort's hand, 'has heard about the slaughtered whores. We established that they all came from The House of Delight in Queenhithe. We also know,' he added in a soft, sibilant whisper, 'that Master Thibault is now deeply interested in such murders.'

'So far you have told me nothing that I don't know already.'

'Well, well Sir John, listen to this. My good friend here was out a few days ago, busy down near Queenhithe quayside, when he glimpsed Meg Tumblekin being accosted by a stranger.'

'Who?'

'Sir John, if we knew, we wouldn't call him a stranger, would we?'

'Less of your sauce and more of the meat,' Cranston snapped.

'Well, the light of my life here followed both stranger and whore across to some steps which led down to the very edge of the river. A murky, gloomy day, Sir John. Wrigglewort could move and hide without being detected.'

'I am sure he did.'

'Sir John, the bosom of my heart watched the stranger slit the whore's throat. There was nothing he could do to prevent it. The assassin then stripped the corpse, fastened the red wig on her head and sent her adrift in a narrow cockle boat.'

'I know all this.'

'Ah, Sir John, but as he did, he softly sang, as if he was enjoying himself.'

'And what song was this?'

'Sir John, the "Song of the Sea". You know what that is, the official hymn of the Worshipful Guild of Barge- and Watermen. And, as he pushed the cockle boat out, he paused in his soft singing to wish *Le Sans Dieu* happy sailing.'

'So the assassin could well be a member of that guild. I already suspect that.'

'Very good, Sir John, I am sure you do. But now we come to our second tasty morsel. The French are in London, yes? They seek the Oriflamme and would love to take his head adorned with that red wig. Did you know they have offered rewards for any information leading to that killer's arrest, but they have also promised that anyone who kills the Oriflamme and brings his head to them will be rewarded?'

'Do they now?'

'And, did you know, Sir John, there are members of Levigne's household who believe that anyone who followed the Oriflamme should suffer swift but secret execution here in London? I mean, Sir John, we have heard about the death of Falaise. Perhaps that could be the work of our French guests.'

'Do you know anything else?'

'No, Sir John, we do not. But I am sure you will agree, such information is worth some coin?'

Cranston raised his tankard in salutation. 'My friends,' he smiled, 'on that, I do agree, so I bid you adieu!' Cranston got to his feet. 'But, my beloveds, I do have a task for you. Listen now . . .'

* * *

Cranston was fastening on his cloak and warbelt when Tiptoft, looking all solemn, slipped silent as a ghost into the solar. The grim-faced courier gave a small bow.

'Sir John, my apologies, the hour is late, but we have received messages at the Guildhall from Mistress Alice Brun. Something about the arca house in the parish cemetery at St Olave's being locked and bolted from within. Matthew Hornsby, a member of the guild and clerk of the stores, is allegedly inside, but he will not answer to any knocking or calls. Sir John, I have taken the liberty of asking Flaxwith to join you in the cemetery. My Lord Coroner, I think you'd best come.'

The day was greying when Cranston arrived in the cemetery of St Olave's. He immediately judged it to be an eerie place at an eerie time, the hour of the bat and the time of the fox. St Olave's cemetery was fairly small. The graves, memorials and coffin crosses were all well tended, as were the hummocks of soil which stretched across the graveyard. Ancient yew trees, gnarled and twisted, clustered close, their branches stretching out, moving slightly in the breeze, as if they were the arms of a monster ready to emerge from the murk. A few people stood there holding torches, the flames leaping up, as if to capture the tendrils of tar-reeking smoke. They all clustered close to the arca house, a squat square of the hardest sandstone, darkened and weathered by the years. It had arrow-slits for windows whilst the iron-studded door was a thick slab of oak.

Cranston studied it carefully as Mistress Alice Brun came hurrying through the poor light, grasping another woman by the hand, whom she introduced as Katherine, Matthew Hornsby's wife, a small, wiry woman with the jerky movements of a sparrow. Katherine Hornsby tearfully described how her husband was clerk of the parish stores. He had left their house to do work in the arca but had failed to return. She and others had hastened here. They had rapped on the door and shouted through the arrow-slits but there was no reply. Now she was alarmed, fearful at what might have happened.

'And where is your priest?' Cranston demanded. 'Father Ambrose and the others?'

'Sir John,' Mistress Alice replied, 'I believe they have moved across river to St Erconwald's. Father Ambrose wishes to take sanctuary there. He and the others truly believe that Brother Athelstan and yourself are their best defence.'

Cranston nodded understandingly, as if he was aware of what was happening, though secretly, he was completely nonplussed.

'Sir John,' Alice's voice turned all pleading, 'what can be done?'

'Mistress, bear with me.'

Cranston heard his name called and turned as Flaxwith and his cohort of bailiffs arrived. The coroner issued his orders. The bailiffs kicked and pounded on the door, shouting through the arrow-slits.

'Sir John,' Flaxwith drew close, 'there's no reply and I do fear the worst.'

Cranston agreed. He had been to such places before. He stared at the arca house and felt a shiver of fear as he sometimes did when he approached any place where murder may have taken place.

'Very well, Flaxwith,' Cranston asserted himself. 'Tell the others to leave, they have no business here. Only Mistress Alice and Master Hornsby's widow . . .' Cranston hastily corrected himself, 'Master Hornsby's wife.'

Flaxwith and his cohort cleared the cemetery, then brought an old bench from the church: they used this to batter and pound the thick wooden door, concentrating on the side where the locks and bolts were. The bailiffs swung the heavy bench backwards and forwards until both lock and bolt ruptured in a screech of metal and wood. Cranston told everyone to stay out. He took a lanternhorn, mentally listing what Athelstan would do in such circumstances.

The coroner paused in the entrance to the arca and examined both bolt and lock on the lintel of the door; these had definitely been twisted and violently torn. Cranston was satisfied that no trickery had taken place, no sleight of hand to depict the door as firmly held fast. The coroner walked further in, lifted the lantern and stared around at the various chests, coffers and sacks. He breathed out noisily as he glimpsed the body sprawled on the floor, arms and legs extended. Cranston drew closer and stared down at Matthew Hornsby. The cause of his brutal death was obvious. A crossbow bolt embedded so deep in his forehead that flesh and bone had erupted on either side, whilst only the feathered flight protruded from the victim's forehead. Blood had seeped out of the wound and poured from both nose and mouth to form a gruesome mask over the dead man's face, covering everything except the popping, glassy dead eyes.

Cranston crouched by the corpse and recalled what Athelstan would do. He swiftly scrutinized the man's wrists and ankles for any sign of ligature or binding but there was none. Hiding his distaste, the coroner lifted the blood-soaked leather jerkin and the linen shirt beneath. Again, there was nothing. Finally he scrutinized the man's skull but could find no trace of recent bruising. Cranston crossed himself and stared around that gloomy chamber. He had seen similar buildings in other church cemeteries, especially those parishes which bordered the river, where the depredations of pirates and the river-robbers were a constant threat. Such fortified rooms were strongly built; this was no different. Cranston glanced up at the roof, noting the beams tightly lined together and, above them, tiles, cemented so hard and thick, not even a chink of light could pierce them. The floor seemed to be of hard rock and Cranston believed the arca was probably built on the foundations of some earlier building. The coroner sighed, got to his feet, and returned to stand in the doorway. He summoned Flaxwith and shouted at Mistress Alice that no one else was to enter the arca. The chief bailiff stomped in, glimpsed the corpse and whistled under his breath, tightening the leash around Samson as the mastiff lunged towards the blood-drenched cadaver.

'Sir John,' the chief bailiff whispered hoarsely, 'a man cruelly slain, but there is no one here! And how could the assassin leave? That door was locked and bolted from within.'

'Then let us search for an answer,' Cranston retorted. 'Flaxwith, tether Samson and help me.'

The chief bailiff did so and joined Sir John on a thorough search of the arca. Coffers, caskets and sacks were pulled away, but Cranston's original conclusion held fast. The arca was built on rock with no sign of entry through the floor, walls or roof.

'God will help us,' Cranston breathed when they had finished. 'Or, even better, send my little friar to assist.'

By the time Athelstan met Cranston at St Erconwald's, the friar had recovered from the hideous confrontation he'd experienced earlier in the day. He had visited both Benedicta and Father Ambrose and insisted that his parishioners help in settling all those who wished to seek sanctuary in St Erconwald's. The preparations for this were now very much in hand. Moleskin had already informed Benedicta, Watkin and Pike that Father Ambrose would be joined by the sept of barge and watermen, together with their wives and children. They would lodge in the church and be provided with every sustenance from The Piebald's kitchen and Merrylegs' pastry shop.

Athelstan had left them to it. He had visited Senlac, still busy in the old death house raising the paving stones. He admitted it was slow and arduous; only a few of the slabs had been lifted. So far, it was unrewarding, and he assured Athelstan that he had found nothing of note except for a few coins. Athelstan also received a visit from Master Tuddenham, the archdeacon's harsh-faced henchman. This church lawyer declared that Father Ambrose's petition to seek sanctuary in St Erconwald's was in strict accordance with canon law, adding that he had also granted permission for the priest to lead a pilgrimage across the Narrow Seas to visit the Cathedral of Notre-Dame in Boulogne.

Cranston's arrival was a welcome relief to that of Tuddenham. Seated in his locked and bolted priest's house, with Crim and Bonaventure on guard outside, Athelstan informed the coroner about what had happened: the desecration of St Erconwald's statue, the attacks on Benedicta, Ambrose and himself. The coroner kept whistling under his breath and, when Athelstan had finished, he banged the table top.

'I will send Tiptoft to the Tower. I will order Armitage to despatch a dozen archers; the idle buggers can camp out at the death house and keep guard over Ambrose and his flock. You take care, little friar. Now, I too have been busy.' Cranston took a generous gulp from the miraculous wineskin. 'There has been another murder.'

'What?'

'Yes, Brother, I will be succinct. Matthew Hornsby.' And Cranston, choosing his words carefully, described precisely his meeting with Grindcobbe, as well as what he had seen at St Olave's.

Athelstan listened intently, eyes half closed as he imagined the arca house, a square block of stone, no windows, no other entrance except that reinforced door, and the dreadful sin committed within. A man slain, murdered, his soul sent unprepared to God. The friar asked a few questions and carefully listened to Cranston's precise, detailed replies.

'There is no explanation for it,' Athelstan declared. 'None whatsoever. A man locks and bolts himself in a secure chamber and he is found murdered, a crossbow bolt loosed deep into his brain. There is not a shred of proof, any evidence of how the killer got in or left. As you say, Sir John, another murder, undoubtedly the work of the Oriflamme. Yet there is one item missing.'

'Brother?'

'No red wig left on the victim's head. Why?' Athelstan smiled drily. 'Has the Oriflamme's supply of such grotesque objects petered out? Or is he trying to create the impression that someone else is responsible for the murder?'

'Brother, I am sorry. What you are saying eludes me.'

'I refer to what Sicarius and Wrigglewort told you. How the French are offering rewards for the Oriflamme and his henchmen either dead or alive. Now, Sir John, in my heart of hearts, I believe Hornsby was killed by the Oriflamme. He may wish to lessen suspicions against himself, hinting that Hornsby's death could be the work of others. Someone paid by the French or, indeed, have members of the guild turned on each other? Anyway, believe me, Sir John, there must be a logical explanation of how the killer broke into that arca and left so easily. I certainly don't believe, my friend, that assassins enjoy the same gifts and virtues as the Risen Christ.' Athelstan smiled at Sir John's look of puzzlement. 'The ability, my good coroner, to pass through wood and stone without hindrance.' The friar paused. 'Let me think, let me reflect.' He said, 'What the Sicarius and Wrigglewort told you was interesting and what you asked them to do even more so. We must visit that benighted place. After all, this Robin of the Green Wood, what he said does point to that house of foundlings being the source of all this murderous mayhem.'

'Brother, you are correct.' Cranston cleared his throat. 'After meeting with the Sicarius, I went to the Guildhall to search amongst the records. I discovered petitions from former inmates of that foundling house. These bitterly complained about the cruelty shown them by those harridans supposedly in charge of their care: two sisters, Lucy and Magotta. According to the meagre evidence, this precious pair were as cruel and as barbarous as any Newgate jailor. As I've said, there wasn't much, just scraps of parchment, faded pieces of vellum.'

'Were there any names?'

'Oh yes.' Cranston smiled thinly. 'No less a person than Samuel Moleskin, an orphan foundling raised by the Minoresses till he was entrusted,' Cranston snorted with laughter, 'to those sisters of the night. Apparently an able scholar, Moleskin left the house but he never forgot. He was one of those who definitely petitioned the council about the cruelty he suffered.'

'So,' Athelstan replied, 'the two sisters were cruel and it now seems that a former inmate of that house used the recent bloody disturbances to settle grievances. This was probably the Oriflamme, who must have been raised in that infernal place where he was punished and abused from morning till night. Once this individual reached adulthood, the Oriflamme took on the guise of his tormentors during his forays through Normandy. The war in France ended and the Oriflamme promptly disappeared. However, he hasn't just emerged from the darkness, he did so during the Great Revolt last spring. Perhaps hanging those two old women whetted his appetite and made him keen for more.'

'I agree.' Cranston rose to his feet and stretched. 'But don't forget, little friar, the Oriflamme we are hunting in London may not be the one who prowled the Seine so many years ago.'

'But surely, Sir John?'

'Brother, what if it's someone who knew the Oriflamme? Someone else, a former inmate of that house of foundlings?' Cranston spread his hands. 'We still do not have definitive proof that the Oriflamme in London and the one in Normandy are the same person. Now,' the coroner sat down, 'what do you think of my meeting with the Sicarius?'

Athelstan scratched his head. 'Well, Sir John, the first part of his information confirms what we already suspect: the Oriflamme is a member of – or closely connected to – the Worshipful Guild of Barge- and Watermen. The second part of the information is more complicated. Undoubtedly Levigne is prepared to offer rewards; that's the obvious thing to do. He would pay dearly to seize the Oriflamme and his henchmen, bundle them aboard some cog and drag them back to Paris for trial and execution. However,' Athelstan tapped the table, 'I am not too sure whether Levigne is really interested in the likes of Falaise and Hornsby. Or, indeed, our own Samuel Moleskin.'

'Aye,' Cranston agreed, 'we must keep a sharp eye on your parish boatmen. Nor must we forget our visitor Senlac; he could be involved in this murderous mystery.'

'True, he is a possible suspect but, there again,' Athelstan pulled a face, 'when Benedicta was attacked last night and Ambrose and myself were threatened, Senlac was either drinking himself stupid in The Piebald or busy in the old death house. No, no, no,' Athelstan pronounced. 'We are making progress, Sir John, yet we still stumble and lose our way. Ah well, it's time I became busy. And you, Sir John?'

'Little friar, a walk around your parish. I will visit the church as well as those miscreants at The Piebald, then I shall return to the tender charms of the Lady Maude.'

PART FIVE

De profundis clamavi ad te: *Out of the depths,*
I cry to you . . .

The coroner departed all in a bustle. Athelstan heard him
go, reflecting on what he'd seen and heard. He recalled
what Cranston had told him about that arca house with
Hornsby's corpse sprawled within. 'But if the assassin didn't
come through the door, the floor, the walls or the ceiling,'
Athelstan wondered, 'then how? If it was through the ceiling, he
would have to climb onto the roof and remove hard-set tiles;
he might have been seen. The floor, according to our good coroner,
is hard rock. So that leaves the walls.' Athelstan recalled
Cranston's description of the sandstone blocks which formed the
arca wall. He stretched his hands towards the fire as he sifted
the possibilities. 'Lord have mercy,' he said, 'but staring into the
flames will not help me, not now.'

Athelstan left the priest's house and walked through the lychgate across the cemetery to the old mortuary. He went in and
stood for a while reciting both the 'Requiem' and the 'De
Profundis' for those whose corpses had been brought here, especially poor Godbless. Athelstan then walked around, noticing how
a few more of the paving stones had been loosened and lifted
but there was nothing beneath except gravel-packed earth. He
walked absent-mindedly, missed his footing and fell down,
sprawling backwards. Athelstan closed his eyes. 'Silly friar,' he
whispered. 'I could have done myself an injury.'

He lay for a while, arms outstretched. He opened his eyes,
stared up at the ceiling, and gasped in surprise as he studied the
faded paintings. Athelstan scrambled to his feet and pattered a
swift prayer in thanksgiving. He stared around and began to
carefully pick his way across the death house. Once again he
marked the paving stones which had been raised as well as those
which had not. All of the latter bore a faded inscription, a small

triangle within a rectangle very similar to what was on that old treasure chart. For a while Athelstan just stood, sifting the possibilities. He felt a surge of excitement. He now believed he had stumbled onto a path which might well lead him to the truth. Athelstan was determined, no matter what, to confront the terrors which had clenched him in their grasp. He would break free, seek the truth and, God willing, impose God's justice and that of the King to resolve this murderous mayhem.

Athelstan left the mortuary. Cranston had already gone so he searched out Watkin and Pike. Brushing aside their questions, the friar gave them the strictest instructions about the old death house being locked, sealed and closely guarded. No one was to enter without his express permission. Athelstan then returned to the priest's house and tried to recall all he had seen, heard and experienced. 'I glimpsed something,' he muttered to Bonaventure who was busy preening himself on Athelstan's table. 'I know I saw something else very important but it eludes me. God sharpen my wits for I cannot recall it.' Athelstan, still troubled by the murderous mysteries which clogged his mind and dulled his wits, left the house to welcome Father Ambrose and the sept of the Woshipful Guild of Barge- and Watermen into St Erconwald's.

For a while the friar walked up and down the two transepts, greeting the different families gathered anxiously around their priest. Ambrose was doing his best to comfort them but he was clearly distressed himself. Athelstan glimpsed Moleskin with his soft-faced, dreamy-eyed wife, her cheeks plump and red as an autumn apple. The boatman caught Athelstan's glance and looked away, a bitter expression on his face. According to Ambrose, Moleskin was all frightened, fearful that ghosts from the past were gathering to seize him. Athelstan sketched a blessing in the boatman's direction and moved down to the corpse door. Again, something troubled him, but he still failed to discern the reason for the anxiety gnawing at his soul. He recalled his training in the schools of Oxford. His masters used to lecture him constantly on his fiery temper. How, when the red mist did descend, his turbulent mood achieved nothing, but posed even greater obstacles to cold, logical thought.

'For heaven's sake,' Athelstan whispered, pinching his own arm, 'calm down. Watch, observe and recall; only then do you act. Keep your eyes sharp and your tongue quiet.'

Athelstan noticed the piled possessions of the new arrivals. He stooped down to move an ornate chancery coffer, admiring its metalwork coating, the way it was locked and bound. He stared hard and crouched down, staring at what might be another key to resolving these mysteries. The friar glanced quickly around. No one was watching him, so he returned to his scrutiny, whispering a prayer to the lords of light to stay and guide him. Athelstan then rose and inspected other chests and coffers. He was certain about their ownership and thanked God that his deadly opponent had made such a simple yet telling mistake.

Athelstan left the church and returned to the priest's house. He placed a primed hand-held arbalest on the kitchen table whilst ensuring the windows and doors were shuttered, locked and bolted. He pulled his chair out before the fire, poured himself a stoup of morning ale and sat down staring into the flames. 'This time,' he whispered, 'such reflections are essential.'

Athelstan tried to piece together this murderous tapestry, the various threads which he had to weave together. First, the total destruction of *The Knave of Hearts*. According to the dying words of its master, the Oriflamme had made his reappearance on that cog with devastating effect. Yet how did he get aboard and then escape? How could he overcome the guards, veteran archers as well as the crew? Why was he there? For revenge? True, Dorset and his henchman Bramley were former comrades on the warbarge *Le Sans Dieu*, but surely the Oriflamme had better reason than that? Was it the treasure allegedly slipped aboard, though, in fact, *The Knave of Hearts* only carried munitions. Secondly, what secrets did henchman Bramley hold? Why was he so terrified? Why was his family so brutally threatened? For what reason? Information? Or was Bramley forced to smuggle someone onto the cog? Yet, according to all the evidence, Master Dorset would keep strict watch on whoever came on deck. Again, according to reports, no one did except for Father Benedict from St Mary Le Bow. Cranston explained how this old parish priest had gone on board just before the cog sailed to give both ship and crew a formal blessing. So what did happen on that ship? Why? How, and who was responsible?

Athelstan's mind moved on. The Oriflamme. Was he a member of the guild who'd decided to resume his murderous career? Yet

Paul Doherty

years had passed since the end of the war and the Oriflamme
had remained hidden. So why had he re-emerged now? What
part, if any, did Levigne's arrival in London have in all of this?
Athelstan closed his eyes. Levigne had come to London under
strict instruction to use whatever means he could to seize the
Oriflamme and his principal henchmen. Had that provoked
matters? Was the Oriflamme so furious he decided to inflict
punishment on any whore favoured by the French delegation?
Moreover, Levigne hadn't helped matters by promising rewards
to anyone who gave him assistance in capturing the Oriflamme.
Did that killer take the Frenchman's mission as a personal insult,
as well as strengthening his determination to protect himself both
now and in the future?

Athelstan leaned down and placed another small log on the
fire, pushing it in with the long, blackened poker. And here in
St Erconwald's, further mystery with the reappearance of Senlac
and that so-called secret treasure map. Athelstan smiled to
himself. He raised the poker and stared at the handle carved in
the shape of a monkey.

'I think I know the truth here,' he whispered, 'though only
time will tell. Now, poor Godbless . . .'

Athelstan recalled the beggar's gruesome murder, his body
sprawled on that table like some blasphemous sacrifice with the
gory remains of his young goat beside him. Who was responsible
for such a disgusting act? And why did Godbless allow his murderer
in at the dead of night? Athelstan straightened up in the chair. He
recalled how on the morning that Godbless's corpse was discovered
he was certain he had seen or heard something untoward, something
out of sequence and illogical. And the other murders? Athelstan
sighed and got to his feet. Poor Falaise, tortured, forced to stand,
not daring to move as he struggled to loosen that intricate, iron-
hard knot. And Hornsby, slaughtered in that arca at St Olave's, a
building firmly locked and bolted from within? Hornsby definitely
went in there, though God knows for what reason. He met his
assassin, who killed him, then the murderer left, apparently moving
through thick stone wall. The door to the arca was found firmly
bolted top and bottom, its key turned; the windows were mere
arrow-slits whilst the floor was totally undisturbed.

Athelstan turned at a rattle at the door, his name being called.

He grasped the arbalest in one hand and unlocked and unbolted the door with the other. Benedicta, garbed in a deep red cloak and hood, slipped into the kitchen.

They exchanged the kiss of peace, Athelstan ushering the widow-woman to the chair whilst he fetched a stool to sit alongside her. Benedicta pulled back her hood, revealing a simple white wimple, beneath which only one lock of her night-black hair escaped the tight band around her forehead. She smiled as Athelstan grasped her hand.

'You look well,' he murmured.

'I feel better after a deep sleep,' her smile widened, 'and for seeing you.' She squeezed Athelstan's fingers. 'Brother, do not worry, what is done is done. I am here with news. Listen, I visited St Erconwald's. I sat with Moleskin and his company. They mentioned a tavern on the Seine where they would moor their war-barge. La Chèvre Dansante.' Benedicta stumbled over the French. 'Yes, that's it.'

'Are you sure?'

'Yes, Father, I am. That's what Godbless kept shouting on the day before he died. I am sure of it. He was ranting and raving, his speech was never clear at the best of times. Of course he was yelling in Norman French, slurring the words, mixing them up, but that's what he was shouting.'

'In sweet heaven's name,' Athelstan replied. 'Was Godbless French, and what did he have to do with that tavern and the free company it sheltered? Godbless acted the fool, but perhaps some of that was a mask, a means of sealing off memories. Was he a member of the free company? I have met men who cannot recall their past, either because they can't or because they don't want to.' Athelstan crossed himself. 'Do you know Benedicta, Godbless, like quite a few souls here, just wandered into this parish and was embraced by our community. We tried to help. We gave him good lodgings, food, clothing, and invited him to all our celebrations. But we never really learnt who he truly was, where he came from or why he acted as he did.' Athelstan paused. 'You've been across to St Erconwald's? Has Mistress Alice, a parishioner of St Olave's, arrived yet?'

Benedicta shook her head. 'No,' she replied, 'but the Tower archers have.'

'Good, good. Now listen, Benedicta. Get an urgent message to our captain of archers. He is to seal off and guard the old death house. Send Mauger to Sir John. I need to meet with my learned friend just after the Jesus Mass tomorrow morning. Mauger will take to our good coroner certain requests. So . . .'

Athelstan was preparing to leave the next morning. He'd celebrated his Mass, excused himself from his parishioners and hurried back to make the final preparations. He had put on his cloak when there was a knock on the door and the handle was tried. Athelstan picked up the small arbalest, winching back the cord over the hook so it was fully primed.

'Who is there?' he demanded. 'I will not open until you identify yourself.'

'Father, you would not believe my name. I am Robin of the Green Wood, a former Upright Man released from Newgate this morning and bound for foreign parts. I crossed the bridge to Southwark where a cog is waiting. I will be gone by the end of the day, never to return. I mean you no harm. I swear that on everything I hold sacred.'

Something in the strong, carrying voice convinced Athelstan that his visitor bore him no ill-will. He pulled back the bolts, turned the lock and opened the door. The thick river mist still swirled, so dense it looked like boiling steam. Athelstan made out the outline of a man, hooded and cloaked, his hands raised in the air.

'Father, for the love of God, I am cold and I am hungry. I have been released from Newgate through the mercy of Merry Jack Cranston. I am here to return a favour. I have information about the man you hunt, the Oriflamme.'

Athelstan recalled Cranston's description of his visit to Newgate, about the house of foundlings and what the Upright Men had discovered during the Great Revolt. Satisfied, he ordered his visitor to come in. The stranger entered and made straight for the fire. He crouched down, hands out to welcome the heat from the leaping flames. Athelstan waited until his visitor had warmed himself, then he invited him to sit down at the table where he served him a bowl of hot, steaming porridge laced with honey, a jug of morning ale and some bread that Benedicta had brought the previous day. He watched as the man wolfed both food and drink. Robin, as he styled himself, was a man just past his fortieth summer. He had a long, harsh face, but the eyes seemed kind, the mouth ever ready to smile. He had been freshly shaved and barbered, but not too gently, the skin on his cheeks and skull nicked raw by a sharp blade. He was dressed in threadbare jerkin, hose and cloak. Athelstan recalled how he had a fairly new robe, a gift from a pilgrim to St Erconwald's. He rose, took this from a chest beneath the bedloft, and insisted that his visitor take it, along with two pennies for his journey.

'I know of you,' Athelstan retook his seat opposite his visitor, 'you are well-known to Merry Jack, as you call him, but your hurling years are over.'

'True, true, Father, and they passed soon enough. So, I will be brief and to the point, for you have another visitor waiting for you. Moleskin.' The man answered Athelstan's questioning look. 'He said he'd wait in the church for a while, allow me to introduce myself. He wishes to talk to you alone.'

'Then you'd best tell me, though I am curious why you didn't speak first to Sir John.'

'Father, I am and I was an Upright Man. I gave the coroner information about what I discovered in that house on the corner of Slops Alley. What I didn't tell him, hence my visit to you, is that when we burst into that house, we found Moleskin there. He was sitting on a stool, cradling a wineskin, fairly drunk, and smiling up at those two corpses dangling by their necks from a roof beam. Now I knew Moleskin of old. I recognized him immediately. An Upright Man from Southwark who had taken many a comrade back and forth across the Thames. He recognized me. I asked him what he was doing there and he said that, like me, he was with a cohort of Earthworms; this was before matters got out of hand and Moleskin fled for his life.

'You may recall Father,' Robin added drily, 'how quite a few of your parishioners found they could not support the violence which broke out when Wat Tyler invaded the city. Anyway, Moleskin said he'd heard how these two harridans had returned to London and decided to pay them a visit. I asked if he was responsible for their deaths? He replied he was not, though he would give free passage back and forth across the Thames for life to the person who had hanged them. I asked him about the red wigs. Moleskin became surly – you know, sullen and with-drawn, a common mood with him. He said he had said enough, got to his feet and fled the house. I did not want to tell the coroner that Moleskin was a comrade, one of ours. It is best if such information is not handed directly to an officer of the law. Nor did I want Moleskin to be taken up as a suspect, even accused, of being this Oriflamme.' The man got to his feet, pushing back the chair. 'Father, I have made my confession. Let Moleskin tell you for himself.'

'In which case,' Athelstan got to his feet and clasped the man's hands, 'God speed you, Robin. May his angels keep you in his care. But do one thing for me, go back to my church and tell Moleskin I will see him now.'

The Upright Man left whilst Athelstan readied himself, walking up and down the kitchen, half smiling to himself as he realized how little he truly knew about his parishioners. Benedicta often referred to that. Men and women who drifted into St Erconwald's because they sought sanctuary, a way of sealing off the past and starting a new life.

A sharp knock on the door roused Athelstan from his reflec-tions. He drew back the bolts and a crestfallen Moleskin slipped through the door, cloak pulled tight, its large hood concealing the boatman's face and head.

'Moleskin, you look as if you are hiding. Sit down. Do you want some ale, some oatmeal?'

Moleskin pulled back the hood, loosened his cloak and shook his head, making himself comfortable on the proffered stool.

'Moleskin,' Athelstan sat down on the chair opposite his visitor and leaned forward so he could hold the bargeman's gaze, 'as I have said before, you are like a man who has lost a pound and found a penny. I also think you could have been more honest with your priest. True, you are a member of the guild and once served on that war-barge along the Seine. But there are other matters, aren't there?' Moleskin just tearfully looked back. 'Those two harridans found hanged in their dirty, shabby house during the Great Revolt: you were there, weren't you? Did you have a hand in their deaths?'

'Father,' Moleskin rubbed his face, 'I confess I could have been more truthful, but you don't know what it's like, the past.'

'Yes I do,' Athelstan snapped. 'I too, have a past, Moleskin. I would like to shut the door on it but I find it better to open that door, to confront the ghosts and so deal with any troubles they bring; either by prayer, alms-giving, or some other good work of charity. You were a soldier, you served in France. You have the blood of others on your hands?'

'But I didn't follow the Oriflamme,' the bargeman spluttered, 'I . . . I never did.' He glanced away. 'I did other things,' he mumbled, 'and I am sorry, Father.'

'Very well. Let us go back to that shabby house and the execution of those wicked sisters. Did you have a hand in their deaths?'

'No Father, you remember the Great Revolt. We were all swept up in it. Many of us here were Upright Men. We thought we'd build a New Jerusalem, a true community governed by law and justice but, of course, we were mistaken. Many of the rebels were no better than the great Lords of the Soil. As you know, Father, not many of your parishioners had the opportunity to join the rebels. Master Thibault swept us all up and kept us secure as a favour to you. Now, at the beginning of the revolt, I was as eager as anyone for mischief. More importantly,' the boatman now relaxed, eyes half-closed, as he recalled the events earlier that year, 'during my journey back and forth across the Thames, I learnt how those two sisters, who had supervised the house of foundlings, had returned to their lair on the corner of Slops Alley. Father, I hated them. I had petitioned the council but nothing was done. I decided to use the troubles to visit them.' Moleskin spread mittened hands. 'I confess, God knows what I would have done if I'd found them alive, but they were not.' He licked dry lips. 'Father, if I could have some ale?'

Athelstan poured him a tankard, Moleskin sipped gratefully from it.

'There was chaos everywhere,' he continued. 'Earthworms roamed the alleyway, they had been joined by all the felons of London. Nobody really bothered about a derelict house. I found the door open and slipped in.'

'Was there anyone else there?'

'No one, Father. Nothing but crawling insects and squeaking mice and rats scratching against the wood. The sisters had a small solar. I just found their corpses hanging by the neck from the ceiling beams. I pressed their flesh; it was cold, bodies and faces beginning to bloat. They must have been executed many hours earlier, if not the previous day. I searched the house but there was no one so I returned to the solar. I just wanted to stare at two bitches who had inflicted such cruelty on me and others. I admit I was lost in the past, so immersed in my own thoughts, I never even realized the Upright Men had arrived. I told them who I was, I showed them my medallion, the token that I was one of theirs, and I left.'

'Moleskin, I am your priest, is that the truth?'

'Father, it is, I swear.'

'So you were placed in that house of foundlings, for how long?'

'Between my eighth and eleventh summer, before I was taken in by kindly folk, a bargeman and his wife. He introduced me to his trade; he even sent me for schooling until, like so many others, I was picked up by the King's arrayers and journeyed to France, hungry for plunder and glory.'

'What was life like in that house?'

'Cruel, vicious. They had nasty souls and wicked hearts. They would eat and drink and make us watch, we poor children, hungry and thirsty. They loved to beat us. One punishment they prized above all others. If you were caught doing wrong, if you objected or protested, you would be stripped naked, a red wig put on your head, then beaten to make you dance. I hated them, Father, I still do.'

Athelstan refilled the boatman's tankard. 'Tell me, Moleskin, other members of your guild, those at St Olave's or, indeed, anyone who served with you in France?'

'Yes, Father?'

'Well, did any of them attend that house of foundlings?'

'Father, you must remember I was very young. People change, faces are forgotten, especially when you try to forget the past.'

'But you chatter and gossip with your companions. Surely you must have learnt if any of those also suffered in that house?'

'No, Father.' Moleskin glanced away. 'Perhaps Falaise did.'

'You are not telling me the truth, Moleskin, I can sense that.'

'Well, it's a suspicion, Father. You see, most of the foundlings were boys. Occasionally a young girl would join us. One of these became a favourite of the two witches, as we called them. A young girl of no more than five or six summers.'

Athelstan repressed a shiver and kept his face impassive. 'Who, Moleskin?'

'You may be able to guess her name, Father. Mistress Alice Brun, the widow, a member of our guild who owns The Leviathan.'

'Are you sure? Has she ever admitted to that?'

'Father, no. It's just a suspicion. Something about her face, her mannerisms. There is something chilling about her. I have never confronted her and she has made no reference whatsoever to her past. The only time she did mention it, was when she claimed to hail from a village in Essex.'

'You said there was something chilling about her? Your priest Father Ambrose seems attracted to her?'

'Oh no, Father, he is as suspicious as we are.'

'About what?'

'Just a suspicion, Father. Her husband did fall ill, but sometimes I wonder, and I think Father Ambrose does, if Mistress Alice helped her husband into the grave, gave him something to soothe the pain.'

'Permanently?'

'Yes, Father, permanently. Now her husband was a good comrade. I liked him and Father Ambrose certainly did, he told me as much. Sometimes I wonder if our priest is trying to discover the truth about what really happened.' Moleskin picked up the tankard and drained it.

Athelstan recalled something that Cranston had told him. 'My friend,' Athelstan tapped the table top, 'which of your company knew about the Upright Men hiding away in that house?'

'Oh, we heard rumours. We knew they were desperate for a ship. However, as far as I know, Brother, the only person privy to that secret was Falaise; that was the way of the Upright Men.'

'And can you tell me anything else?'

The bargeman shook his head. 'No, Father, I cannot.' He rose. 'I'd best be gone.'

Cranston looked the very picture of keenness when Athelstan walked into the solar of the coroner's second favourite resting place in London. The coroner had chosen to wear a red sarcenet cote-hardie and hose, with a matching beaver hat, a brilliant white cambric shirt and his favourite cordovan boots and warbelt. The latter, along with his military cloak, were slung over one of the tavern tables. Cranston clapped his hands and rose to exchange the kiss of peace with Athelstan. The coroner then held him at arm's length, looking the friar up and down from head to toe.

'You're tired, anxious, my friend? Come break your fast on the crispiest bacon and the softest manchet whilst the butter is as fresh as the dawn. Now, what news do you have?'

Athelstan made himself comfortable and told the coroner all about the visits from Robin of the Green Wood and Moleskin. Cranston heard him out then laughed sharply.

'Robin of the Green Wood should have informed me but, there again, I am an officer of the law and Robin would not wish to indict a former comrade. Nevertheless, I tell you this, Athelstan: that house of foundlings on the corner of Slops Alley was a truly wicked place. I just wonder if the girl Moleskin talked about is Mistress Alice. She's hard-faced, Brother: she may have helped her husband into the grave.' He glanced sharply at Athelstan. 'But you have been thinking, haven't you, my little secretarius?'

Athelstan made himself comfortable and began, haltingly at first, to describe his suspicions. By the time he had finished, Cranston had fully broken his fast. The coroner leaned back, whistling under his breath.

'The hour is fast approaching,' he announced, 'when we can settle this matter. I will send Flaxwith with his merry men to dig up all those flagstones. The Tower archers will mount a strict guard. So, how will you trap this demon?'

'I don't know, Sir John. I spent yesterday closeted, listing my suspicions, trying to plot a way forward.' Athelstan smiled at the coroner. 'With your permission I will stay here, safe and secure at The Lamb of God, and do the same again. A blessed rest for body, soul and mind. Now, before we part Sir John, let us go back to that arca house at St Olave's. No, not now. First, I want you to send an urgent message to the best master mason you know. He must visit the arca and study it carefully. Next, I need you to take me down to a war cog at Queenhithe. I have to question a veteran master on what might have happened on the *The Knave of Hearts* during its last fateful voyage.' He slipped a small scroll into Cranston's hand. 'And there's a list of questions for the Fisher of Men.'

Sir John looked surprised but promised he would do all this, adding that Athelstan must stay safe and secure in The Lamb of God until everything was ready.

Later that morning, the coroner collected his secretarius from the loving ministrations of Minehostess. The coroner informed him of the arrangements for the day before taking Athelstan down to the principal quayside at Queenhithe, where the war cog *The Glory of God*, lay moored ready for sail. Cranston introduced Athelstan to its master, an old comrade from the French wars, Adam Leyton, and his henchman Chingford, two burly seamen who, by their own admission, 'had seen the days.' Sitting in the small master's cabin beneath the stern, Leyton lifted his goblet and toasted both of his visitors. Athelstan had informed him what he needed to learn about *The Knave of Hearts*, and Leyton replied that he and Chingford would do their best to accommodate him.

'I knew Dorset,' Leyton declared, '*The Knave of Hearts* was a sound war cog in capable hands.' He cleared his throat as Cranston began to tap the table.

'His crew must have been about ten, yes, including himself?'

'I would say that's a fair reckoning.'

'And he also had two Tower archers,' Athelstan continued, 'guarding the arca in the hold, that's what you told me, Sir John?'

'Twelve souls in all,' Cranston agreed. 'A fairly light crew, yes Master Leyton? But Dorset was under strict instruction to sail fast and as secretly as possible to Calais.'

'So *The Knave of Hearts* leaves its mooring,' Athelstan mused, sipping at the goblet Leyton had poured for him. 'Darkness is falling. Where would Dorset be? How was his crew deployed?'

'Come, I will show you.'

Leyton led them out of the cabin and down a flight of steps in the centre of the main deck, deep into the ship's hold, black as night despite the glowing lanternhorns. The place reeked of tar, pitch, fish, salt, as well as a rich stench from the bales of freshly gathered wool heaped around the sides. Leyton explained how the forward and stern holds were screened off by thick wooden partitions with a narrow door in the centre: the former provided sleeping quarters for members of the crew whilst the stern hold contained the ship's arca or treasure chest. At Athelstan's bidding, Leyton unlocked the door to the arca and, carrying one of the lanternhorns, took them into the chamber, where caskets and coffers were stacked around an iron-bound chest suitably padlocked in the centre of the hold.

'Dorset's cog would have had the same,' Chingford explained. 'Like me, Henchman Bramley would have set up a watch. Two archers resting in here or outside.' He touched the heavy chain on his belt. 'Bramley would have probably held the keys to both the stern hold and its arca.'

Athelstan walked up and down the dark chamber, steadying himself against the slight rise and fall of the ship as the current grew more turbulent. He heard the patter of feet and the cries of sailors busy on the deck above. Other noises echoed hollowly: the clattering of ropes, the screech of levers and the constant shriek of the hunting gulls which swooped low over the cog. Athelstan paused in his pacing, leaned against the bulwark and closed his eyes. He tried to imagine what it was like below deck on board *The Knave of Hearts* during that last, fateful voyage.

'Brother?'

Athelstan opened his eyes and smiled at Leyton. 'Let us say my friend, that *The Glory of God* is making the same run down to the estuary as *The Knave of Hearts*. You must have done the same many a time? Darkness has fallen. The night is freezing cold. The river is fog-bound so the lanterns are lit and a strict watch set. Yes?'

'Very good, Brother,' Leyton laughed. 'You will become a sailor yet.'

'Let's go back to that night, a busy time. The river is full and fast-flowing. Eventually you approach the sandbanks, places like Sodom and Gomorrah; such stretches of the river are very dangerous for the unwary.'

'Very,' Chingford declared.

'So, Master Leyton, where would you be standing?'

'On the main deck below the central mast, a lantern glowing on a hook above me.'

'And Master Chingford?'

'I would be forward, keeping an eye on our watchmen in the

prow. I would be sensing the weather, ready to order the sail to be shifted if the wind moved or increased in strength. Most of the crew would have also gone forward. If matters are running smoothly, the watch is divided. Some take their rest whilst the others man the sail, ropes and lanterns.'

Athelstan murmured his thanks and stared at the arca. He could imagine Bramley, on board *The Knave of Hearts*, coming down into the hold assuring everyone that all was well. So, what else was there?

'Ah yes,' Athelstan clapped his hands gently, 'the bum-barge, you have one?'

'Of course.'

'And it's taken aboard when you sail?'

'Not necessarily,' Chingford retorted. 'And I know why you ask, Brother. River gossip says that *The Knave of Hearts* trailed its bum-barge. However, let me assure you, that's not too unusual. Many cogs, until they reach the estuary, keep their bum-boats riding alongside.'

'Why?'

'So the crew can deal with the vegetation which trails from the sandbanks. Not to mention the mounds of swirling mud and other rubbish which breaks free from such places.'

'Yes, yes,' Athelstan said, 'I can see why the ship's boat isn't taken aboard.' He gazed around. 'I must remember,' Athelstan continued, 'how dark it must be in the hold of a cog like this.' He pointed at the lanterns. 'They provide light, but they also create a world of shifting shadows.'

'True, true, Brother,' Leyton replied. 'It can be as black as pitch on board a ship at the dead of night.'

'If it's so dark,' Athelstan demanded, 'is it possible for someone stowed away to move around?'

Leyton laughed sharply and whispered at Chingford, who hurried back up the ladder onto the deck. 'Brother, when Sir John visited me earlier in the day, I wondered if you would ask that question, so I have sent for Walter and his weasels.'

'Pardon?'

'Brother Athelstan, you will meet them soon enough. However, do accept my assurances that *The Knave of Hearts*, like any cog preparing for sea, would be scrutinized and searched most carefully before it sets sail. Now, whilst we wait for our visitors, do you have any more questions?'

'I understand that Dorset allowed a priest aboard to bless his cog?'

Leyton pulled a face. 'Some masters do, it's not uncommon. We pay coin to Father Benedict, an old seafarer who now holds a benefice at St Mary le Bow. He's done the same for me and mine when we are about to sail into dangerous waters. Why do you ask?'

Athelstan just shook his head.

'And the bum-boat from *The Knave of Hearts*?' he asked.

'As far as I know, Brother,' Cranston responded, 'it's been impounded, kept in the water bailiff's yard further down the quayside.'

'We should visit that but . . .' Athelstan paused at the patter of bare feet on the deck above. Chingford called down the hatch. Leyton shouted back and a man, as lean as a beanpole, scurried down the ladder, followed by at least half a dozen urchins; the boys were dressed in rags, their hair spiked with dirty grease, faces blotched and stained. The beanpole introduced himself as Master Walter, leader of the weasels, a company of ship searchers. Athelstan nodded understandingly, clasping the man's hands. Once introductions were finished, Athelstan also met Walter's ragamuffin retinue, all of whom – he secretly thought – reminded him of Ranulf the rat-catcher's two ferrets, Audax and Ferox. At Leyton's bidding, Walter described how he was hired by the captains and masters of different ships and cogs to search their holds, cargo and other impedimenta before the ship slipped its moorings. He had done the same for *The Glory of God* as he had for *The Knave of Hearts*.

'And you found nothing amiss that day?'

'Nothing. I would swear to that.' Walter held up a calloused hand whilst his entourage danced around him, scrutinizing Cranston and Athelstan from head to toe. Silence abruptly descended when the coroner opened his purse and drew out two silver coins which winked in the poor light.

'I ask you,' the coroner's voice sounded like a trumpet through the hold, 'whether you glimpsed anything,' the coroner held the coins high, 'anything untoward on that cog, *The Knave of Hearts*, before it left on its fateful voyage?'

The weasels, like a chorus, eyes hungry for the silver, chanted in high-pitch voices that they had not seen anything untoward.

'Except . . .' the smallest of the weasels, a lad as thin as a willow-wand shouted.

Athelstan crouched down before the boy. 'What's your name?'

'Weasel Ten.'

'And what did you see, Weasel Ten?'

'Nothing, nothing.' The lad stepped closer and Athelstan felt a stab of pity at the boy's thin, bony face.

'What is it, Weasel Ten?'

'When I go on board a cog, the sailors are always kind. I have met him before, you see . . .'

'Who?'

'Bramley, Dorset's henchman on *The Knave of Hearts*. He was always kind. He told me he had children himself, but not on that day. He . . .' Weasel Ten's voice faltered.

'Yes.' Athelstan took a coin from his own wallet and pressed the penny into the boy's hand. 'Tell me now,' he coaxed.

'Bramley just seemed frightened, like a dog who fears a beating. He shouted at me. Told me to get out of his way. He never did that before.' Weasel Ten gripped his own chin. 'He looked stern, angry. I thought it strange that he should be like that, especially on a day when I wouldn't see him again.'

Athelstan thanked Weasel Ten and asked Cranston to take all those assembled back on deck.

'It's getting a little crowded down here,' the friar smiled, 'and I need to think.'

Cranston lifted the silver coins as if they were banners in a procession, and led the entire company back up onto the deck. Once they had left, Athelstan crouched down, willing himself into the darkness, not here but ensconced in the hold of *The Knave of Hearts* as it made its way down to the sea. Athelstan glanced to his left, the forward hold where a few of the crew would shelter, desperate for sleep. In the stern to his right the two Tower archers guarding the arca would probably sit with their backs to the door. They would have their bows at the ready and yet be half asleep. Perhaps they would be nervous at the strange shuddering of the cog as it battled the wind and strong current. All would be quiet. Bramley would come down but he wouldn't be alone. The killer, probably the Oriflamme, would be with him, though Athelstan, especially after his visit here, still could not understand how the killer got on board. Bramley would assure the guards that all was well; he would open the stern hold. He and the killer would enter. Bramley would be carrying the keys to the arca. Once inside that hold, Bramley was probably murdered. The assassin immediately seizes the keys. He removes the treasure chest then turns to the cannon powder. A fuse is lit and the killer flees. Outside there is no one except the two Tower archers, crouched half asleep. The Oriflamme kills them, probably with a crossbow bolt. He would act so swiftly the poor men would hardly realize what was happening. The Oriflamme then probably dons his disguise. He knows the long fuse is burning so it's time he left the ship. He goes up on deck and places the treasure chest next to the taffrail. He encounters Dorset and fells the master with a blow to the head. The assassin then prepares to leave with what he thinks is the treasure coffer.

Athelstan ran a finger around his lips. But what are the rest of the crew doing? Did they have time to react? The fuse is burning. The assassin leaves, going down into the bum-boat. Perhaps the crew were alerted, but the bum-boat is ready, it pulls away. A short while later the flame reaches the cannon powder and *The Knave of Hearts* ceases to exist.

'There are still gaps,' Athelstan reflected, 'gaps which must be filled, including just what really did happen on board that ship shortly before the Oriflamme fled. Ah well.' Athelstan climbed up the ladder to where Cranston, Leyton and Chingford stood talking.

'We've sent Walter and his weasels on their way,' Cranston declared. 'You are finished, Brother?'

'More questions, I am afraid Master Leyton. When you approach sandbanks such as Sodom and Gomorrah, where do you deploy your crew?'

'Oh that's obvious. In the main, they all move into the prow, vigilant for any obstacle.'

'And you?'

Leyton pointed at the mast. 'I will stay there and watch Chingford marshal the men,' Leyton pulled a face and Athelstan caught the master's impatience. 'You have other questions?'

'Yes, yes,' Athelstan glanced around. 'This is a strange one,

Master Leyton, but can you imagine you and your ship are on full flow down the river. The sail is unfurled, the crew are mustered, all eyes on the river. Is it possible for a killer to move about your cog, enter the arca hold, take what's there, murder the man who has let him in and kill the two guards outside. Once done, he then lights a long fuse and slips up on deck to inflict more mayhem before fleeing using your bum-boat?'

Leyton just stood staring at Athelstan. 'At first,' the master measured his words carefully, 'I would say no. But, there again, at the dead of night, the river flowing swift and my ship battling its way forward; well, everyone is distracted. The crew are busy with their different tasks. They are separated one from another. Matters are not helped by the ship being cloaked in darkness, whilst any strange sound can be dismissed as the work of the river. More importantly, the crew are not vigilant against any danger on board ship; their eyes are on the water so why should they be fearful? The killer would use all that to his advantage.'

'Of course he would,' Athelstan agreed. 'And your crew, they are handpicked?'

'Like cherries in a bowl,' Chingford nodded. 'Both the master and I do the hiring. We only take good seamen with wide experience and of sound character. We seal indentures with each and every one.'

'And the record?'

'Kept in the master's cabin with other manuscripts.'

'And on board *The Knave of Hearts*, Bramley would also be responsible for the hiring and the management of the crew?'

'Of course, he and Dorset would welcome each member on board as we do.'

'And if you had an escort of Tower archers?'

'Usually,' Chingford shrugged, 'there are two. Sir John, you know the type, they would arrive at the ship just before we sail in their chainmail coifs and hoods. They would wear the usual brown and green jerkins emblazoned with the White Hart. They'd also have warrants and licences sealed by the Constable of the Tower; that's all I can tell you, Brother.'

'Thank you, thank you.' Athelstan turned and walked over to the far taffrail, staring at the grey, swollen river with the mist slowly gathering. He narrowed his eyes and glimpsed the occasional barge, skiff, herring catcher and other fishing vessel, their lanterns glowing before a crude sketch of their patron saint, usually St Peter or, indeed, any man or woman blessed by the church who had spent their lives going out into the deep. Athelstan leaned against the rail and closed his eyes; the cold breeze wafted his face as he reflected on what might have happened on board *The Knave of Hearts*. He was now reaching specific conclusions, though certain pieces of this murderous mosaic still had to be inserted into their proper place.

'Brother Athelstan?'

The friar turned. Cranston was standing against the taffrail on the other side of the deck. The coroner beckoned him over as the Fisher of Men came up the gangplank and strode onto the deck as if he owned it. The Fisher was feared and respected by all river folk. Leyton and Chingford immediately welcomed him, but the Fisher, pulling back his cowl, shook his head at their offer of refreshment and pointed at Athelstan.

'Sir John passed your questions to me and,' the Fisher tapped the chancery satchel hanging from a hook on his warbelt, 'I have been through my records.'

'Yes, yes.' Athelstan came across, sketching a blessing towards the Fisher. 'And what have you found? There's no need to show me the record, just tell me in your own words.'

'Well,' the Fisher stepped back, bracing himself against the side of the ship, 'you asked if we had found a naked corpse, that of a man, his face damaged beyond recognition. Well, we found more than that.'

'After the *The Knave of Hearts* was destroyed?'

'Oh yes, about a week – not one corpse, Brother, but two.'

'And their faces?'

'That's it, Brother, they had no faces because they had no heads. Both had been decapitated and we found no trace of them. The corpses were taken back to our mortuary. No one ever claimed them, so they were buried in the poor man's lot at St Michael's.'

Athelstan stepped closer. 'And no mark of recognition?'

'Brother, I would say both men were soldiers, as two fingers on the right hand of each of them were calloused, so they were used to drawing a bow. Both corpses were found close together, caught in a reed bank about a mile downriver.'

'Of course,' Athelstan breathed, 'Master Leyton, if Tower archers came down to your cog, veteran soldiers not looking forward to days at sea, they would seek refreshment, a few blackjacks of ale and some hot food, yes?'

'Oh certainly.'

'And what tavern would they frequent?'

'Without a doubt, The Prospect of Whitby.'

'In which case,' Athelstan bowed at both the Fisher and the two sailors, 'Gentlemen, your help has been invaluable. Sir John, let us our wet our mouths in The Prospect of Whitby.'

The Prospect of Whitby was Queenhithe's grandest hostelry, dominating trade along that stretch of the waterfront. The tavern's taproom was a spaciously vaulted hall, its floor covered in coarse matting, and well furnished with proper chairs, stools and tables. The air was sweet with the flavours of cheeses, hams and flitches of bacon hanging from the rafters in white netting sacks, whilst the entire room was warmed by a blazing fire in a hearth that was shaped like the mouth of a wyvern. Minehost, a small, busy man, full of his own importance, presided over the frenetic serving and care of a host of customers. At first, he wasn't at all helpful, until Cranston banged the long serving table, roaring out who he was and that he needed certain questions answered as honestly as possible. Minehost visibly cringed and a pool of silence spread across the taproom. Some of the customers, realizing who Cranston was, immediately headed for the nearest door. Athelstan even glimpsed one, a mountebank, his tattered leather jerkin festooned with tinkling bells, pull back the nearest shutters and climb – as nimble as a monkey – through the open window.

'Right.' Cranston stood over the taverner. 'We will sit there.' The coroner pointed towards a window enclave furnished with a cushioned bench and a clean table and warmed by two small braziers. Once they were ensconced and ales had been served, the now abject Minehost spluttered how he was eager to assist the Lord High Coroner in his enquiries.

'Good,' Cranston murmured. 'Do you recall the evening that *The Knave of Hearts* set sail?'

'Oh yes, Sir John, its crew had visited our tavern the day

before for, as you know, cog masters will not allow any drinking on the actual day of departure.'

'True, true,' Cranston nodded.

'Let us cut to the quick.' Athelstan put down his blackjack of ale. He pointed at the taverner. 'I ask you to think carefully. On that day did two archers, Tower bowmen wearing the White Hart insignia, come into this tavern?'

'They certainly did; swaggered in, as is their custom. They ordered food and ale, and they were later joined by two others.'

'Tower archers?'

'No, Brother. Two ordinary bowmen. You know how they are. I would guess that they were mercenaries, garbed in Lincoln green, hoods pulled close over their heads. They came in here and joined the two Tower archers.' Minehost pulled a face. 'They were most welcome. They brought good custom, ordering ale by the jug. They drank deep and wolfed down platters of food. Then, early in the afternoon, all four left together, the Tower archers in particular much the worse for wear.'

'And these two other bowmen, did you see their faces?'

'Brother, these men like to act the warrior with bracers on their wrists, deep hoods, and those coifs which cover the forehead and come up over the chin. No, I cannot recall their faces so I cannot give you a description.'

Cranston and Athelstan left the tavern. The friar stopped, clutching the coroner's arm as he stared up at the sky.

'Come, Sir John, the day is drawing on. Let us visit the water bailiff.'

They walked along the busy quayside. Athelstan was very wary of the ground under foot, which was coated with the guts, heads and tails of the early morning fish catch. The cobbles were slime-covered and slippery, whilst the friar kept a sharp eye on the half-wild dogs that gathered to feast as well as fight the legion of beggars who scoured the quayside searching for anything edible. The air reeked richly of all the river smells, which mingled with odours from the makeshift ovens, grills and cooking stoves, around which the poor gathered to toast the morsels they'd found. Quayside officials, armed with sharpened willow-wands, moved along this horde of dispossessed, ever ready to lash out or lacerate.

They passed Queenhithe gallows, a six-branched gibbet decorated with iron cages containing the corpses of river pirates hanged earlier that day. They eventually reached the end of the quayside, which was barricaded off by a high wooden palisade guarded by two water bailiffs. One of these opened the wicker gate and led both coroner and friar into an enclosure littered with chests, coffers half-covered by tarred cloths as well as a row of small boats, coffer crafts, skiffs, herring rafts and battered bum-boats. The water bailiff now studied a greasy sheet of parchment, lips moving as he tried to make out what was written there.

'Ah yes, you are looking for *The Knave of Hearts* bum-barge? That's what you said, Sir John.'

'And that's what I want to see,' the coroner snapped.

'Ah yes, ah yes. Then you'd best follow me.'

The water bailiff picked his way around different craft and pointed to a squat, deep-bellied bum-boat with a scrap of oily parchment pinned to it.

'There it is,' the water bailiff declared. 'I'm afraid its oars were never found but it's still seaworthy and the small tiller still works.'

Athelstan thanked him and carefully clambered in. He could find nothing amiss, but then he noticed the rope attached to the tiller, which could be tied to a bench in the stern although it had been severed through. Athelstan crouched down and scrutinized the knot which had attached the cord to the tiller. Athelstan smiled in satisfaction.

'I have it,' he murmured.

'Brother?' The water bailiff came alongside.

'This knot,' Athelstan glanced up at the man, 'it's not a common one, is it?'

The burly official pushed by the friar, crouched down and studied the knot as if seeing it for the first time. 'No, no,' the fellow replied. 'That's a true sailor's knot.'

'Thank you.' Athelstan rose, rubbing his hands. 'Sir John, I want the remains of this rope severed and handed to me, but the knot must not be damaged.'

Once this had been done, Athelstan thanked the water bailiff, and both he and Cranston left his yard.

'Where to now, little friar?'

'You sent for the master mason?'

'The very best, my friend. Henry Tunstal. Master mason and the most high-ranking clerk in the office of the King's works. Henry loves stone and spends most of his life dreaming about what buildings he can fashion. He will be waiting for us in St Olave's cemetery. Henry is an old friend and will do anything I ask; even freeze with cold in that dank, dark place.'

Cranston and Athelstan found the graveyard entrance guarded by Tower archers. A serjeant, displaying the young King's personal emblem of the White Hart, informed Sir John that the master mason was still busy in the arca house and led them along the coffin paths to what Cranston dramatically described as 'the place of sudden death.' Athelstan gazed swiftly around. Both cemetery and church seemed eerily deserted and he experienced a sense of loneliness, a chill of the soul, as if the very spirit of this place had gone. So unlike St Erconwald's, where the bustle and business of everyday life spilled out of the church, across God's Acre and into the homes of his parishioners. St Olave's, however, was different, and this cemetery certainly so. It was house of desolation with its sprouting grass, ancient twisted yew trees, and row upon row of battered crosses and crumbling memorial stones. The only sound which broke the menacing stillness was the strident cawing of rooks and crows.

The arca house was as much as Athelstan expected: a squat, square building of darkening stone, with lancet windows and a formidable door recently rehung on its leather hinges by the carpenters working under the supervision of the master mason. Henry Tunstal was a genial-faced, small man with thinning hair, his clothing covered in a sheen of fine dust. He clasped hands with Cranston and Athelstan, gleeful in what he had learnt. Tunstal refused to tell them anything but asked them to wait outside, close to the door, whilst he entered the arca. Cranston shrugged and waved Tunstal towards the entrance. The mason skipped inside, slamming the door shut behind him, shouting at the coroner and friar to await a miracle.

'God bless him,' Cranston whispered. 'Henry was always excitable. Now he is like a boy who has been given a bowl of sweetmeats.'

'He's discovered the secret,' Athelstan replied. 'I can guess what it is, but let's wait here.'

Athelstan stood, staring at the fortified door and, even though he expected it, he jumped as he heard Tunstal calling their names from behind them. The friar turned and stared at the grinning mason.

'Satan's tits!' Cranston whispered. 'Are you fey, can you really walk through stone?'

'You found it, didn't you?' Athelstan asked.

'I did, Brother, come.'

Tunstal led them around to the rear of the arca and pointed to one of the square stones at the bottom of the wall now partially pulled out. The mason crouched down and slid the stone free, placing it within his grasp when he lay down. Tunstal edged into the gap created and pulled the stone towards him; crawling further back, he dragged the stone into place so it rested in its original position. Athelstan watched the mason go in then, crouching down, scrutinized the wall, noticing how the lichen, dried cement and sheer age of the arca created a covering crust so it looked as if the loose stone was as firmly cemented as the rest. Athelstan got up, wiping his hands and dusting down his robe. He gently kicked the weeds, gorse and wild strong grass which grew close to the base of the wall.

'No one,' Athelstan turned to Cranston, 'would notice anything amiss. The loose stone is at the bottom of the rear wall, disguised as if cemented in like the rest. This place is gloomy at the best of times whilst the weeds and bramble grow thick and fast. All of this helps to protect the arca's secret entrance.'

Athelstan squatted down again and ran his fingers across the stone until he reached a natural cleft in the rock which could serve as a hand grip. Athelstan placed his fingers in and glanced up at the coroner. 'It will be the same inside, Sir John. In fact, that's where the cleft really should be used.'

They went back around the arca. Tunstal opened the battered door and waved them inside, gesturing at the far corner, where he'd pulled away moth-eaten sacks and battered chests.

'Right, Master Henry.' Athelstan sat on an overturned barrel, whilst Cranston fortified himself from the miraculous wineskin and squatted down on a chest.

'Tell us,' Athelstan gestured at the far corner, 'why and how?'

The master mason beamed with delight.

'The short version,' Cranston growled. 'Henry, the day is dying and we have other business to attend to.'

'This is an arca house,' the mason declared, lifting his arms as if to embrace the entire gloomy chamber. 'It was built ages ago. The masons employed the hardest sandstone to create these dark blocks. A place of refuge in time of trouble.'

'Naturally,' Cranston interjected.

'Very good, Sir John,' the master mason blithely acknowledged. 'Now imagine you are someone who has fled here. It might be the priest or some other parish official. The attackers will naturally concentrate on the door at the front. The roof is too dangerous and too difficult to dismantle. It leaves the assailant exposed to spear, arrow or bolt. Naturally the attackers will believe the arca is a square of the thickest stone with only narrow arrow-slits for windows, so the door must be forced. Inside the prisoner, as his opponents would regard him, simply moves to that far corner. Now,' the master mason beamed again, 'Brother Athelstan, you must have found the cleft on the outside stone?'

'Yes we have.'

'Good, Brother. There's a similar one inside. The person preparing to escape simply pulls the stone in. He clambers through the gap and edges out, dragging the stone with him. You can imagine the attacker's surprise when they do break down the door?'

'And that would take some time.'

'Yes, Sir John, it would. Perhaps even hours. By then, the person who escaped would be over the hills and far away.'

'It's really to be used from within?'

'Yes, Brother, a means of easy escape. They could always use the arrow-slits to ensure nobody was at the back of the arca. Once they were satisfied, it would not take very long. As for entering the arca through that gap? Well, look around, it might be a little more cumbersome, but it can easily be done. At the end of the day, the cemetery is a gloomy place, whilst the moveable stone is extremely well concealed.'

Athelstan heard sounds from outside. He rose and walked to the far corner.

'Poor Hornsby,' he spoke over his shoulder, 'I believe his assassin entered secretly and stood here deep in the shadows. He killed Hornsby and left, pushing that stone free and creeping out . . .' Athelstan broke off and turned. Tiptoft stood in the doorway.

'I found out where you were,' Cranston's messenger mournfully intoned. 'And thank God for that. Sir John, Brother Athelstan, you are needed at St Erconwald's.'

'I am sure we are,' the friar replied. 'Nevertheless, Sir John, I understand we have one last place to visit.'

'We certainly have: that haunted house on Slops Alley.'

With Tiptoft hurrying behind them, Cranston and Athelstan made their way along a maze of dirty alleyways going deeper into Queenhithe ward. Cranston seemed to know each and every runnel, striding swiftly with Athelstan trotting behind him. They reached the corner of Slops Alley to find the Sicarius and Wrigglewort awaiting them with an escort of burly dung collectors, whom these two worthies had hired to force the door and, as the Sicarius whispered to Sir John, drag certain items out of the great sewer at the back of the house. Cranston made hasty introductions, both the Sicarius and Wrigglewort exclaiming they'd heard about the redoubtable Brother Athelstan. The friar smiled and bowed at their compliments, even as he wrinkled his nose at the foul smell which gusted out through the half-open door. The Sicarius gestured at the labourers to walk away; he then thrust a pomander into the hands of both Cranston and Athelstan.

'You are going to need these,' he lisped, 'follow me.'

The Sicarius went ahead, pushing the door to one side. Athelstan carefully followed, Cranston walking behind muttering curses at the rank stench and the sheer drab, squalidness of the house. The stink grew worse. Tiptoft, coughing and spluttering, said he could take no more, so Cranston told him to go back and stand in the alleyway outside. Athelstan peered to his left and right at the crumbling plaster; the splattered dirt on the paving stones beneath caught at his sandals whilst the squeak and scurry of vermin was constant. Athelstan recalled his visit to that chamber at The Piebald, of experiencing a deep, unnamed dread; this was no different.

'A place of great evil,' he whispered to Cranston. 'It should be razed to the ground.'

'Oh, don't you worry,' the coroner retorted, 'I have a list of things to do and the destruction of this house heads that list.'

They reached the solar where the Sicarius and Wrigglewort had left lanterns. They picked these up and led both coroner and friar through the filth-strewn kitchen and buttery out into an overgrown, derelict garden. The Sicarius, a pomander to his face,

gestured at a rickety table he'd found somewhere. On this
sprawled an old woman's corpse, a crossbow bolt still embedded
deep in her throat and, resting against her corpse, two severed
heads. The filth of the sewer where these remains had been thrust
had, in the main, been washed off, but they still looked ghastly.
Athelstan studied the old woman and recognized her as probably
one of the many such pathetic creatures who begged alms
across the city. She was a gruesome sight. Corruption had already
set in; one of her eyes was missing and the horrid wound to her
throat was clogged with mud. Keeping the pomander close to
his nose, Athelstan then scrutinized the two heads.

'Young men,' he murmured. 'Look, Sir John, possibly soldiers.
Their hair is cropped very close.'

Athelstan could take no more. He hurriedly blessed the
remains and, burying his face in the pomander, turned away,
gesturing at his companions to join him some distance from the
gruesome mess.

'In heaven's name,' the friar breathed, glancing up, desperate
to catch the chilly fresh air, 'what do you make of these?'

'As I told you when we met,' Cranston replied, 'I asked these
two worthies to visit this house and find what they could.'

'We discovered very little,' the Sicarius retorted, 'which made
us curious. Well, until we came out here. The sewer stank to
high heaven. I hired the labourers outside, dung-collectors with
their spades, mattocks and hooks. I asked them to search the
sewer and that's what they found.'

'And who do you think they are, little friar?'

'My Lord Coroner, I can only guess. I suspect the old lady
was in a place where she shouldn't have been. I also have a
suspicion, though I cannot prove it, that the Oriflamme was
accustomed to visiting this house fairly regularly, a place which
must haunt his soul. Well, at least he used to until we began
hunting him. Now it's too dangerous for him to visit.'

'And the two heads?'

'Sir John, remember what the Fisher told us about those decapitated corpses. I have my suspicions yet I, too, need to reflect.
But, enough for now. Pay these two worthies for what they have
done as well as to take care of those mangled remains. My parish
awaits . . .'

PART SIX

Absolve me Domine . . . *Absolve me Lord*

Cranston and Athelstan arrived back at St Erconwald's to find Flaxwith waiting for them at the lychgate leading into God's Acre. Other bailiffs patrolled the curtain wall whilst four Tower archers stood on guard outside the old death house. Flaxwith just shook his head at Cranston's questions.

'Sir John, Brother Athelstan, you'd best see for yourself.'

He led them up through the poor light to the old mortuary, unlocked the door and ushered them inside. The place was lit by lanterns and the dancing flames of cresset torches. Athelstan immediately noticed how all the paving stones had been lifted. Beneath some lay hard-packed earth, but others concealed hastily covered pits protected by stout wooden frames under layers of hard soil. Flaxwith escorted Cranston and Athelstan to one of these and pointed down at the jumble of skeletons – yellowing skulls, arms, legs and ribcages – which had survived the bitter-smelling lime poured over these pathetic human remains.

'There are—'

'Several of these,' Athelstan finished his sentence. 'You also found some treasure?'

'Yes.' Flaxwith pointed to a hempen sack just beneath a shuttered window. 'That contains coins, bracelets, rings and other valuables. I recognize one of these as belonging to a royal courier.'

'Shoreditch,' Cranston said. 'I remember him. A royal messenger, Matthew Shoreditch. According to reports, he disappeared once he'd crossed London Bridge. I was sent here to investigate but we could find nothing, whilst we were later informed that Shoreditch had used his warrants in Kent at different taverns on the pilgrim road to Canterbury.' Cranston shrugged. 'Roughkin must be responsible for Shoreditch's death and these others. Once he knew I was here, he decided to flee using the courier's warrants.' He glanced at Athelstan. 'You guessed that, little friar, didn't you?'

'No, the dead intervened.' Athelstan pointed to the ceiling. 'I stumbled, fell and looked up. You see, Sir John, the fresco painted there, it's now very faded. I remembered that phrase in doggerel Latin on the so-called treasure chart, 'Angels stare down at earth's treasure'. That's how Roughkin would remember where he had hidden both his murder victims and their treasure under certain paving stones.' Athelstan crouched beside one which had been pulled away to reveal a pit. He tapped the earth-encrusted right-hand corner. 'See this mark, a roughly etched triangle in a rectangle: it indicates a hiding place. Roughkin intended to come back one day to claim his ill-gotten plunder and lift such stones.'

'But he never did, only his son.'

'Is it really Senlac,' Athelstan mused, 'or his father Roughkin? It's possible. I was informed that Roughkin fathered Senlac when he was very young. Moreover, how would Senlac know about this?'

'He may have learnt his father's secrets and come searching; that's why he raised some of the flagstones, that's what you told me on our journey here.'

'Sir John, a sudden change of mind! I cannot prove this. However, I now believe it is Roughkin and he deliberately lifted some of these paving stones as if searching for some secret entrance which might explain Godbless's bloody murder. In truth, he was trying to divert my attention, as well as create the illusion that there was nothing beneath these paving stones.'

'So he only prised up those stones which he knew concealed nothing but packed earth?'

'Precisely, Sir John. He was trying to deceive me. He wanted to create the illusion that there was nothing hidden in this death house.' Athelstan paused at a knock on the door and one of the archers came in.

'Sir John,' the man declared, 'Flaxwith has something to show you.'

They left the death house. One of the bailiffs was whispering to Flaxwith, who nodded and gestured at the man to join them. They crossed God's Acre into its most forsaken part, near the far curtain wall, a desolate stretch of land peppered with rotting plinths, decaying wood and ancient yew trees, their branches stretching out to cover the ground.

'We decided to search here,' the bailiff declared. 'Earlier, I glimpsed a flash of colour, as if someone was hastening towards the wall. I thought nothing of it till later when the rumours spread about what had been found in the death house. I returned here and . . .' The bailiff crossed to one of the ancient yew trees and pulled back the branches. The man who called himself Senlac lay sprawled inside, his back to the tree trunk, blood coating his face and jerkin, his popping eyes looking up, as if transfixed by the crossbow bolt embedded deep in his forehead. Athelstan whispered a prayer and studied the corpse. He noted how the victim still had his belt with its dagger sheath next to a tattered purse which, on inspection, contained a few coins.

'I suspect,' Athelstan declared, moving deeper into the darkness, careful not to brush the sharp branches of the yew tree with his head, 'yes, I suspect that Senlac, or rather Roughkin, met his killer here, who despatched him very close – the crossbow bolt is deeply buried. As for the why and the wherefore well, let us see. Now Sir John,' Athelstan plucked Cranston by the sleeve and led him out of hearing by the bailiffs. Standing very close, the friar spoke swiftly and tersely, brushing aside the coroner's objections, adding that Sir John must follow his instructions if they were to unmask, confront and capture a most cunning and dangerous assassin. Athelstan then took leave of the coroner and went into St Erconwald's. Father Ambrose was talking quietly to the guildsmen and their families. The friar waited patiently until the priest was finished, then took him aside.

'Father,' he asked, 'where is Mistress Alice Brun?'

'Why, Brother,' Ambrose pulled a face, 'I left her busy in St Olave's. She will be hastening here and there. I asked her to look after the church and house, then join us here. I am surprised that she has not.'

'In which case, Father, it's best if we both go to see her.' Athelstan lowered his voice. 'The visitor to our parish, Senlac, has been found foully murdered. I need, we need, to question Mistress Alice.'

'Senlac! Yes, I saw him here . . .'

'Never mind for the moment.' Athelstan stared around and

glimpsed Moleskin sitting with his back to a pillar. 'Moleskin,' he called, 'I need you and your crew. It is important,' Athelstan turned back to the priest, 'that Moleskin is with us. Nothing Father,' Athelstan placed a hand on the priest's arm, 'nothing is what it appears to be, either in this parish or yours.'

Athelstan and Ambrose left St Erconwald's, threading their way through the warren of alleyways, a veritable maze of stinking, rubbish-filled runnels leading down to the quayside near St Mary Olave's. A dangerous place. The haunt and hunting ground for a legion of cunning men, pimps and felons, especially as darkness fell and a thickening river mist curled in. Despite this, Athelstan was soon recognized. Voices shouted who he was and that the friar and his companions should be allowed to pass unchallenged. Athelstan kept his head down, glancing to the right and left as the shadows which had emerged from the shabby doorways swiftly withdrew.

They reached Moleskin's barge. The archangels, who had kept very close to Athelstan as they hurried from the parish church, clambered in. Moleskin made sure that Athelstan and Ambrose were comfortably seated in the canopied stern and cast off. They were soon in midstream. The river was running fast, whipped up by a strengthening breeze as the darkness closed in and the night lanterns were lit. They reached Queenhithe. Athelstan told Moleskin to wait for a short while in a nearby alehouse then go home. Plucking at Ambrose's sleeve, Athelstan hurried the priest through the streets to The Leviathan. The tavern was cloaked in darkness, except for lantern light seeping through a shutter across one of the upper-storey windows.

Ambrose lifted the door rapper carved in a shape of a whale and banged hard so the clatter echoed through the house. Eventually Athelstan heard the sound of footsteps, Mistress Alice shouting about who it was? Ambrose answered tersely. The small hatch in the door slid back and the tavern mistress's face, bathed in the light of a lanternhorn, smiled at them through the grille. Bolts were drawn. The lock turned and Alice, garbed in a thick blue cloak, beckoned them in, along a narrow, dark passageway into the deserted taproom. At first, there were explanations and questions. Alice remarked how she'd heard that Athelstan and Cranston had visited the graveyard and why hadn't they called in to see her? The friar just smiled back as the tavern mistress lit candles and lanternhorns, asking Ambrose to wheel the braziers close to the hearth. Once this was done, Alice arranged a chair for herself and two more for her visitors, feeding the weak fire with bracken and logs until the flames leapt merrily. She offered them wine; both men refused. Ambrose rose and bowed to Athelstan.

'Brother, I have been away from my parish. I need to check on certain matters in both the church and my house. You will excuse me?'

Athelstan nodded. He sat quietly until the priest had left and, refusing Alice's further offer of food and drink, stretched out his hands towards the flames. For a while he and the tavern mistress exchanged desultory conversation about both St Erconwald's and St Olave's until Athelstan, who realized the woman knew nothing about the real purpose of his earlier visit with Cranston, straightened in the chair and stared fully at her.

'You are preparing to leave, Mistress, on pilgrimage to Notre-Dame in Boulogne?'

'Yes, Brother.'

'Is that the truth,' Athelstan pointed a finger at her, 'or are you really preparing to use the pilgrimage as a subterfuge so you and your lover Father Ambrose can disappear far beyond the Narrow Seas? He is your lover, yes?' Mistress Alice straightened up, her fixed smile disappeared, so in the poor light her face aged and grew more severe, her eyes watchful, staring hard at Athelstan as if noticing him for the first time.

'You are fleeing?' Athelstan asserted. 'And your poor late husband? Did he truly die of a wasting disease or did you help him on his way into eternity?' Alice, however, was no longer staring at the friar but gaped at some point behind him. Athelstan turned slowly in the chair and stared at the ghastly figure which had emerged from the darkness behind him. This phantasm of the night was clothed in grey, a white mask covering the face, a fiery red wig pulled down tight and bristling over his head.

'Ah,' Athelstan rose. The hideous apparition raised the small arbalest.

'Sit down, friar,' the grotesque ordered.

'Of course, Father Ambrose.' Athelstan replied. 'And so I meet the Oriflamme.'

The hideously garbed figure, still holding the arbalest, gestured at Athelstan to sit as he arranged a chair to face the friar squarely. The hideous mask and wig were removed and the priest slouched arrogantly, a half-smile on his face.

'Why?' Athelstan asked. 'Why do you confront me now, here in this place, at this time?'

'Because I want to, because you want to and it is only right. Darkness has fallen, Brother Athelstan. Now is the hour, this is the moment and I must seize it. But, of course if you must know, I watched you, little friar. I saw you scampering around your cemetery and church. I guessed a number of matters; in particular, you had visited the arca house in St Olave's cemetery and deduced whatever conclusion you did reach. Above all, I was not at all convinced by your story about Mistress Alice: that was a clever pretext to get me away from St Erconwald's and lure me here for a confrontation. Well, now you have it, but it will not go the way you planned.' Ambrose paused. 'In a word, we are done, friar. You, me and her. But soon, it will be only the two of us.' And, raising the arbalest, Ambrose loosed a bolt which shattered Alice's forehead. The woman jerked backwards and forwards, mouth gargling, eyes going up, she coughed as blood dribbled from her mouth and nose and then fell back. Athelstan could only grip the arms of the chair as the woman shivered and quivered in her death throes. She then gave a deep sigh and lay still. Athelstan, shocked at the sudden sheer brutality, half rose from his chair but sat down again. Ambrose had primed the arbalest with a fresh bolt whilst he rested a second hand-held crossbow on a stool beside him.

'In heaven's name!' Athelstan exclaimed.

'Whatever,' Ambrose smiled, running a hand down his grey gown. 'As I said, it's just the two of us, friar. She's gone and she's not coming back. Now, for the rest. I have sent a parishioner with an urgent message to that fat bastard Cranston.' Ambrose nodded as if he was trying to reassure the friar. 'The message says that you are hurrying back to Southwark and that he must wait for you at St Erconwald's as you have urgent and important business to discuss with him. So,' Ambrose raised the arbalest, pointing it at Athelstan, 'Fat Jack won't be coming whilst,' Ambrose nodded behind him, 'all doors and windows are shuttered and held fast. So, friar,' Ambrose's voice turned sweet and cloying, 'here we are, just the two of us.'

'You are going to kill me? That's what you do. You kill people for pleasure and to remove any obstacle from your path. What I wonder about is how you will explain my death?'

'Oh, quite simple. Look at Mistress Alice, now her cloak lies open. Yes, she wears a grey gown just like me and, when I am finished and I have killed you, as I surely will, I shall explain that you had a confrontation with her. I've already told the few parishioners I've met that you were meeting her in this taproom. So I will explain how I came back to join that meeting but I found the tavern locked and bolted so I went away.'

'But the message to Sir John?'

'Despatched by me in your name, friar. I shall say you told me to do so just after you arrived here, then I left. You came in here, had a confrontation with Mistress Alice, and that is the truth. You found an arbalest,' Ambrose gestured at the walls, 'you found an arbalest,' he repeated, 'hanging from a hook. You primed it, you loosed a killing bolt, but not before Alice had grievously wounded you with her own concealed crossbow. You collapsed bleeding to death, and so joined the choir invisible, or whatever heaven you friars peddle to your stupid faithful.'

'Is that what you believe?'

'I believe in nothing, friar, except my own good self. Anyway, to return to my story. You are left here with Mistress Alice and the confrontation takes place. More violence, more bloodshed. I grow anxious and I break in. I find both of you dead. Fat Cranston and his stupid bailiffs will eventually arrive and my mummer's play is complete. Oh, I will add a few little details. Alice will be wearing a red wig, a white mask pushed into the pocket of her gown; similar disguises will be found hidden away deep in the cellars of this mouldering tavern.'

'And so you will depict Mistress Alice as the Oriflamme?'

'No, don't be foolish. I will just depict her as someone who imitated the master. I will add a few details which are correct: that she killed whores because they may have infected her late husband and given him the wasting disease he later died from.

Anyway, I really won't be staying long in St Olave's to answer
Cranston's stupid questions. All I will arrange, and I am halfway
through it, is her death and yours. As for all the other mysteries
– well, they can remain mysteries, can't they? I will be far gone
and, I assure you, I shall never return.'

Athelstan nodded understandingly trying to control the fear
which chilled his heart. Ambrose was a true killer. He enjoyed
it, and the friar understood the subtle logic of what this Judas
priest was planning. There would be no solution, no resolution
to all the murders which had taken place. Nothing except the
finger of suspicion being pointed at Mistress Alice Brun who,
unfortunately, killed the man who trapped her. Athelstan determined to keep his nerve, to maintain his mask and just hope that
time would be his greatest ally. Athelstan smiled thinly, as if
marvelling at Ambrose's cunning.

'Only I know the truth and that will die with me,' Athelstan
conceded. 'You, of course, will be going on pilgrimage to
Boulogne in the next few days?'

'Of course,' Ambrose laughed, 'and I am never coming back.
I will take with me anything valuable,' he waggled the fingers
on one hand, 'that my greedy little paws can grab.'

'And her, why?' Athelstan sketched a blessing in the direction
of the dead woman. 'She was your leman, your lover. Did she
know the truth? Never mind the nonsense about whores infecting
her late husband. Did you help get rid of her spouse? The solicitous priest kneeling by the sick man's bedside, offering all sorts
of comforts, including poisoned wine.'

Ambrose moved his head from side to side, as if weighing up
what Athelstan had said.

'She fed him potions,' he replied. 'I know that. My silence
was bought by her splendid performance in both the bed and the
buttery. She may have suspected, she may have guessed, but who
cares? The stupid bitch is now dead.'

'You don't like women?'

'I hate them, I always have and I always will. I hate women
and I hate priests, even though I pretend to be one. As I have
said, I don't believe in anything except myself. So, tell me
Athelstan,' Ambrose smiled falsely, 'how did you reach your
conclusion? It's important, you know?' Ambrose's tone turned

patronizing, as if he were some magister in the schools waiting for a scholar's reply. 'It is important. I always learn from my mistakes.' He laughed sharply. 'And why not? I am the best of teachers.' Ambrose waved a hand. 'Now, before you begin, do you want something to drink, a cup of wine, a tankard of ale?'

'I want nothing from you.' Athelstan had now recovered from the brutal, sudden slaughter of Alice. He was tempted to tell this demon incarnate that, despite his arrogant certainty, he had already made a number of errors. Athelstan just quietly prayed that the traps this killer had set would spring back on him.

'I know you,' Athelstan cleared his throat. 'Do you realize that, Ambrose? I have reached that conclusion. You are clever but I know you.'

'Don't bait me, friar.'

'As a boy,' Athelstan blithely continued, 'you were abused. Your soul was twisted and tortured. An evil root was planted deep inside you to flower in even greater wickedness.' Athelstan peered at this smooth-faced demon priest. 'I wager you were the son of French parents. Your mother raised you probably till you were past your tenth year, then you were abandoned by choice or by circumstance. You were left as an orphan, a foundling sent to that dire house on the corner of Slops Alley. You fell into the power of two evil witches who, using the garb of grey gowns, white masks and red wigs, made your life a living hell.' Athelstan paused. Ambrose's face had changed, becoming softer, mouth slack, eyes tearful. Athelstan pointed at the dead woman. 'Was she there in that house? A young girl being trained in cruelty by those two harridans?'

'Yes, yes she was,' Ambrose answered dreamily. 'I remembered her but she didn't recall me. I revelled in that and made her pay between the sheets. She thought, silly bitch, that I was just another priest eager to get between her legs, like some spring sparrow, hot and lecherous.' He shook his head. 'She knew nothing about my upbringing.'

'A time of great sorrow,' Athelstan declared. 'At least for you. God knows where you went next. I wager you were schooled in the transepts of St Paul's, the halls of Oxford or Cambridge, perhaps even the Sorbonne in Paris. You are highly intelligent. No doubt you travelled to France, you are well-tongued in their

language. You are personable and charming. Holy Mother Church
is truly desperate for educated priests. Some French bishop
ordained you and found you a parish and benefice in Normandy,
not far from the river Seine.' Athelstan paused, as if listening to
the wind clattering at the shutters, rattling the loose wood, an
eerie sound which only enhanced the dire scene within: the fire
crackling, the flames leaping, as if to chase the shadows which
fluttered across the hearth. Ambrose slouched, a knowing smile
on his face. Beside him, Alice's crumpled corpse with her gaping,
bloody mouth, glassy dead stare and that horrid wound in her
forehead. Athelstan closed his eyes and quietly prayed. Surely
some passing lord of light would intervene?

'Friar,' Ambrose placed the arbalest in his lap and softly
clapped his hands in mockery, 'you are almost correct, though
some details are wrong. Never mind, do continue.'

'Rottenness gathers,' Athelstan resumed. 'It festers like pus in
a wound. So it was with your soul, scarred by those hideous
sisters. The seed is sown, the crop bursts forth, and soon it is
harvest time. I am sure that in whatever godforsaken plot of
Normandy you lurked, there were whores, town and village
prostitutes. They would be your first victims, butchered, stripped
and festooned with red wigs – or did that come later?' Athelstan
stared at Ambrose who just gazed stonily back.

'Ah well,' Athelstan shrugged, 'the war in France also
provided you with devilish opportunities for your evil cunning.
You allied yourself with an English reprobate, a murderer like
yourself, Roughkin, former owner of The Piebald tavern in
Southwark and keeper of the death house at St Erconwald's.
He became your henchman. You both learn about an English
free company sheltering at a riverside tavern, La Chèvre
Dansante. You join their company and, through sheer guile and
force, became their captain on expeditions up and down the
Seine where you could indulge all your evil ways. You always
appeared in that grotesque disguise, the wig, the mask and the
gown. You encouraged the war band to do the same. You would
be assisted by Roughkin, also disguised, though I suspect you
used him for other nefarious duties such as gathering information on places you had chosen to attack, ransack and plunder.
Of course, Roughkin could also act as the Oriflamme when

you wished to revert to your disguise as an ordinary mercenary, a member of that free company.'

Athelstan paused, straining his hearing for any untoward sound. He glanced swiftly at Ambrose who, like all his kind, was puffed up with his own cleverness. 'You boasted to me,' Athelstan continued, holding Ambrose's malevolent gaze, 'how, when the Oriflamme planned to visit the company, you were absent. Well, of course you were, as you or Roughkin donned the guise of that demon, to lead the company of *Le Sans Dieu* on one of their expeditions. Once finished, the Oriflamme would disappear and you could emerge as Goodman Ambrose Rookwood, or whatever name you call yourself.' Athelstan shook his head. 'A clever ploy. You pose as the Oriflamme's enemy yet, at the same time, you could also search out any dissension in the group. And so you did. You were the ideal lure. Members of the free company knew your support for the Oriflamme was lukewarm, even non-existent. On reflection, I did consider that to be deeply suspicious.'

'Why, friar?'

'Oh yes, you made a mistake,' Athelstan taunted. 'The Oriflamme was ruthless. According to what I learnt, he dealt harshly with any objectors, yet you remained untouched. Why?'

Ambrose's smile faded.

'God knows what Roughkin's part in all this truly was.' Athelstan crossed himself. 'I cannot question him as he now lies dead, murdered by you, but I shall come to that by and by . . .' Athelstan paused. 'Roughkin died unrepentant. A killer, he has the blood of Godbless on his hands. But, as I've said, I will come to that later.' Athelstan stared into the flames. He had to keep his killer close and under even sharper watch.

'Friar?'

Athelstan raised his head and gave what he hoped was a weary smile. This assassin must not realize, not yet, the mistakes he had made. Over the years, Athelstan had made a particular study of the sons and daughters of Cain. Men and women who killed not on a spurt of violent emotion, but coolly plotted the destruction of another human being. Athelstan had concluded that they shared a number of characteristics. They were arrogant. They revelled in what they did and loved to play their murderous game to the very end. Most importantly, they seemed to have no conscience, no awareness of sin, no guilt or reproach; except for one: they could not be baited themselves. If they were, that might well incite them to further killing. Athelstan was determined not to provoke Ambrose into a murderous rage.

'Friar, have you gone to sleep?'

'Oh no. I am just reflecting on your cunning as well as on the past. You had another henchman, Jacques Mornay, tavern master of La Chèvre Dansante – the Dancing Goat. Mornay was in fact mad, lunatic, moon-touched. He did not hide behind a disguise but he was certainly one of yours.'

'And?'

Athelstan noticed the sharpness in the question and renewed his resolve not to provoke his opponent too far. 'Well, of course you know.' Athelstan spread his hands. 'Mornay was keeper of that tavern. He could hide you and your disguises, provide you with everything you needed as you passed from being Ambrose Rookwood to the Oriflamme and then back to your own true self.'

'And you will come back to him by and by as well, eh friar? Oh, I do love this!' Ambrose crossed his arms. 'This is better than any game of hazard. You are correct, friar, about my many disguises. Do you remember that scene from the Gospels when Christ is supposed to have exorcized a man who was possessed? The good Lord, or whoever he was, asked the devil by what name was he called? The demoniac retorted that his name was Legion for there were many inside him.' Ambrose stroked the arbalest. 'That's what I feel, friar; all these different individuals inside me wanting to get out, knocking at the door of my soul, peering through the shutters of my mind. Sometimes at night I can hear them whispering, chattering to themselves as they gather in the darkness of this corner or that. Oh, I will lead them a merry dance.'

'Aren't you afraid that one day you will be caught and hanged either here or elsewhere?'

'Aye, and the moon could turn to blood and the sun might dance in the sky. But enough of this,' Ambrose's voice turned sharp. 'Do continue. And I mean continue. Time is passing, soon I must be gone.'

'The war ended. French commanders began to push the English

garrisons back to their coastal fortresses at Boulogne, Harfleur and Calais. The company of *Le Sans Dieu* disbanded. They returned to England to don the cloak of respectability and assume a trade. You, of course, presented yourself to a bishop here in London with the appropriate sheaf of letters. Heaven knows where you got them from, or how. I admit, there are pieces of this murderous mosaic I have not found. Nevertheless, you are glib and presentable. Church officials such as the archdeacon's clerk, Master Tuddenham, are desperate to appoint educated priests to London parishes. You charm your way in. You are given the parish you want, the benefice of St Olave's, only a short walk away from The Leviathan.' Athelstan held Ambrose's gaze. He thought he heard a sound outside different from the rest, but the moment passed.

'Once you were appointed, you did not return to your murderous ways. After all, you have a comfortable sinecure here in Queenhithe as well as the attentions of the comely Alice, now brutally slain. You probably assisted her in ridding herself of a sickly husband. She would cater for all your lustful desires, as well as your revenge for whatever part she played in that hideous house of foundlings on the corner of Slops Alley. Anyway, the years passed and the world's wheel turns again. You played the two-backed beast with Mistress Alice but you also continued to consort with whores, especially those managed by that queen of the night The Way of all Flesh in her House of Delights along Grope Alley. Through one of these, Mathilde, you learnt about a surprising and, to you, most dangerous occurrence. The French, their secret men the Luciferi, under their leader the Candlelight-Master Hugh Levigne, had arrived in England. They were searching for the Oriflamme, the perpetrator of dreadful crimes in Normandy and, in particular, the horrid abuse and murder of a French noblewoman Madeline de Clisson. The Luciferi were most eager to barter with the English Crown for their quarry to be unmasked, arrested and swiftly despatched to Paris. Once there, he would be tried, found guilty and condemned to die in the most gruesome way possible on the great scaffold at Montfaucon. They were looking for others, but I suspect the Oriflamme was their principal quarry. You must have been frightened, alarmed?'

'Not frightened.'

'No, no of course not,' Athelstan muttered. 'To be frightened you must have a conscience. You lack that in every way. You are arrogant, Ambrose. You wanted to be left alone. When you appeared in your nightmare form in my house you asked, you *demanded*, to be left alone, to let sleeping dogs lie. Such a question sprang from rage. The French had not done so. They were prepared to spend treasure and time in hunting you down. So you decided to turn your anger against them. You reverted to perpetrating the same atrocities you had along the Seine, choosing those whores favoured by the French. You used Mathilde to buy sacks of red wigs. I am sure they are stored somewhere in this benighted place. Mathilde was the first to die. She had to. She knew too much, didn't she?'

'They should have left me alone,' Ambrose, his eyes half closed, shifted the arbalest so Athelstan could clearly see it was primed: the wicked bolt with its small, sharp feather flight and jagged points was aimed directly at him. 'They should have left me alone,' Ambrose repeated. 'I was happy.' He lifted a hand. 'My house is comfortable, my parish small, I had all the joys of bed and board. Oh, by the way, friar, I know you haven't searched my house but there is nothing there. Do continue.'

'You were also furious at the way the English Crown was prepared to cooperate with the French. Such measures interfered with your well-laid plans to flee the kingdom for pastures new. But, of course, you need treasure for that. Now you are the parish priest but also the chaplain to the sept of the Worshipful Guild of Barge- and Watermen here in your parish. They are all former members of the war barge, *Le Sans Dieu*. You must have known Bramley, certainly met him, Dorset's henchman on the cog *The Knave of Hearts* and also a former member of that English free company. Somehow, you learnt of the rumours about Master Thibault wishing to send gold to Calais on board that war cog, so you and Roughkin plotted to steal it and flee.

'Why should Bramley cooperate? Dorset was the master.'

'No, no,' Athelstan corrected, 'you know the company of *Le Sans Dieu*, their memories, their fears, their remorse. You are, after all, a priest, a chaplain to the guild, a man they could confide in. I am sure Bramley did. He confessed to you, the two-headed Janus – ostensibly a caring priest, in truth a killer to the bone.'

'You do not know what fashioned me, friar. Not really. What truly formed me.'

'I agree, not entirely. But, I recognize the essence of your soul. You kill and you love to do so. You don masks and take them off whenever it so pleases you. The caring priest disappeared. The Oriflamme emerged to terrify Bramley and his family. Now,' Athelstan tapped the arms of his chair, 'what happened next truly intrigues me. I concede I can only indulge in guesswork.' Athelstan paused, still listening keenly, still hoping.

'Friar?'

'Heaven knows how you learnt about *The Knave of Hearts*: perhaps from Bramley, perhaps from the whores employed by The Way of all Flesh, maybe even from river gossip. Now, you were already alarmed by the determination of the French to hunt down and capture the Oriflamme and his henchmen. You resumed your evil alliance with the principal one, Master Roughkin. This villain had returned to London, pretending to be his own son. He would certainly realize the real danger posed by Levigne. He would definitely be greedy for that treasure allegedly aboard *The Knave of Hearts*. Both you and Roughkin are twins of evil. You can be the Oriflamme and, when it suits you, put as much distance as possible between your role as a caring priest and your secret life as an assassin. If the Oriflamme is needed but you are unavailable or unable to assume that guise, Roughkin would take up the mantle. After all, you had perfected that deadly game in Normandy. Your face and head hidden behind a mask and wig, your body beneath a woman's grey gown, whilst I suspect you altered your voice by inserting small sponges in your gums.' Athelstan waved a hand. 'You are well-versed in such trickery. Very cunning, very subtle. Two killers playing the same role, shifting the mask whenever it suits you, like actors in a mummers' play: that's what happened along the Seine, didn't it? By the way, how did you meet Roughkin?' Athelstan forced a smile. 'Though, there again, there is no need to tell me. Like attracts like, doesn't it?'

'Be careful, friar,' Ambrose touched the arbalest. 'You can leave whenever I decide.'

'Of course,' Athelstan soothed. 'But you were together in this venture, weren't you? You both decided to plunder *The Knave of Hearts*, utterly destroy it and flee. Bramley was the key. On your orders, Roughkin terrified that poor soul, his family, his wife and children. It must have been him, as Bramley would recognize you.' Athelstan stared at the priest. 'Well, never mind,' the friar continued, 'we know that Bramley, terrified by the Oriflamme, provided you with as much detail as possible, especially about the guard being despatched to the *The Knave of Hearts*, those two Tower archers. I do not know the precise details, though I can guess what happened. Through Bramley you learnt those archers' names, the time of their arrival at Queenhithe. Bramley may have even sent them coins to drink in The Prospect of Whitby. It's logical enough. The two archers were not members of the crew, just the guard. They would be eager for refreshment before they set sail, perhaps a stoup or blackjack of ale, then you and Roughkin, disguised as fellow bowmen, joined them.'

'Very good, friar,' Ambrose purred. 'Very clever. You have been busy.'

'You both play the role of veterans, an easy enough task with your past. You swaggered into The Prospect of Whitby, cowled and visored, faces almost hidden. You joined those archers, bought them drinks, told each other stories referring to this and that. You acted as two successful mercenaries with bulging purses ready to treat and honour fellow soldiers. The two Tower archers drank deeply. You then enticed them to leave with the prospect of further pleasure perhaps at The House of Delight. Whatever, you and Roughkin take both men to some desolate place. The archers are totally unprepared for death. They are fuddled with drink, tired and fully trusting these two benevolent comrades. Easy victims, killed by crossbow quarrels loosed close. You and Roughkin show no mercy, no compassion. Both archers are decapitated, their heads slung down the sewer in the garden of that dreadful house on the corner of Slops Alley: their corpses stripped naked and sent floating like rubbish into the river. You don their clothes, belts, boots and weapons. You may have concealed your faces with false beards or just used the felt cap such archers wear to cover their heads and the bottom half of their chins.' Athelstan pushed back his chair. Ambrose immediately straightened up in his, raising the arbalest directly at the friar. 'I have the cramps,' Athelstan confessed. 'I need to move.'

'Be careful,' Ambrose warned. 'Soon, you meddlesome little man, you will be past all care and pain. I must concede,' Ambrose lowered the arbalest, 'you are skilled, keen and sharp. Do continue.'

Athelstan stretched out his legs. Again, the arbalest was raised. 'You have now donned the guise of the two Tower archers.' Athelstan relaxed. 'Bramley, of course, allows you on board *The Knave of Hearts* and you go down into that dark hold: a sombre place where you and Roughkin squat, pretending – as ever – to be what you really are not.'

Athelstan stared into the dancing fire. He was sure he'd heard sounds different from the rest as the strengthening wind rattled the shutters. 'Two shadow men,' Athelstan retorted, 'both you and Roughkin. You pass the mask of the Oriflamme to each other: sometimes him, sometimes you. You did that when Roughkin visited us both in St Erconwald's disguised as the killer. You arranged such a visitation in an attempt to terrify me as well as to confuse and mislead. A devious ploy used on other occasions.'

'Your story,' Ambrose snapped, 'tell it.'

'Ah well, *The Knave of Hearts* sailed on the evening tide. A few hours later, the cog was obliterated from the face of God's earth.' Athelstan moved in his chair as if trying to rearrange his robe. In fact he was trying to catch any sound, a noise which could mean he was no longer alone with this demon.

'Come on friar, the hour passes.'

'On board *The Knave of Hearts* you both lurk in that dark hold, squatting outside the arca as the cog sailed downstream, aiming like an arrow for the estuary, its bum-boat, at your insistence with Bramley, still not hoisted aboard. You are going to need that.'

'Wouldn't Bramley object? I mean the cog is going to be destroyed?'

'Ah, but he didn't know that did he? He thought you were going to steal the gold and flee. Even in his darkest nightmare, he would never dream of what was truly going to happen. Anyway, the cog approaches the great sandbanks of Sodom and Gomorrah. Most of its crew are now forward. Bramley, terrified like a rabbit by two stoats, joins you in the hold. You kill him, open the arca and take out the hand-held coffer.' Athelstan paused and crossed himself, lips moving as if reciting a prayer for the dead. He just wanted to be sure about what he'd heard.

'Bramley dies,' Athelstan continued, 'as would any member of the crew if they were present in the hold. You don your grue-some costume, take the coffer and go up on deck. You are disguised just in case anyone did glimpse your face and survived. You and Roughkin intend to flee using the bum-boat. The crew are still forward, but Master Dorset confronts you. You deal with him and, helped by Roughkin, hurriedly leave. You have no choice, you have to. Before you left that hold, you broached the black cannon powder and lit a long fuse. Both you and Roughkin are former soldiers, skilled in such matters. The two of you clamber off the cog into the boat. You cut the rope and tie the cord above the tiller. You row as fast as you can. Again, you are experienced in that, former members of the crew of *Le Sans Dieu*.'

'And my henchman Roughkin? I heard that he was busy drinking in some tavern? You yourself said that.'

'Nonsense,' Athelstan retorted. 'People become confused, who was where and when. Roughkin haunted taverns. He would come and go even on that night he might have decided to hurry back and indulge in some drinking. Now both of you escape. *The Knave of Hearts* is destroyed in a hideous conflagration. You reach your hiding place. You open that coffer. Only then did you realize the truth. It held no treasure, only rusty nails or some other rubbish.' Athelstan smiled, he now decided to taunt his assassin. 'I would have paid good silver to see your faces when you discovered Master Thibault's trickery. How you must have railed and cursed!' Athelstan laughed, shaking his head as if deeply amused by what he'd said. The wind now seemed to have fallen. A river mist had swept in, a thick, cloying cloud which seeped through cracks and forced its way under doors and shut-ters. Athelstan, still smiling to himself, rocked backwards and forwards.

'Be careful friar.'

Athelstan glanced up. Ambrose had raised the arbalest again, no longer smiling, the devil priest glared at Athelstan.

'I knew I was tricked,' he rasped.

'So you decided to indulge in a little trickery of your own! You spread those rumours that the Oriflamme and his henchmen were hiding in that derelict mansion overlooking the Court of Thieves. You enjoyed that didn't you? Despatching both the Luciferi and Sir John on a wild goose chase, diverting their attention from other matters. There was something else.' Athelstan pointed at Ambrose. 'You wanted those Upright Men silenced, didn't you? One of them recalled a most bizarre incident during the Great Revolt. A shabby house, on the corner of Slops Alley where its inhabitants, two old women, were found hanging with red wigs pulled over their heads.' Ambrose smiled, nodding in approval. 'You know what that house once was? You went there. A foundling home for orphans or children abandoned by their parents. As I said, you Ambrose Rookwood, or whatever your real name, served some time there. The sheer cruelty of your guardians scarred your soul, we at least agree on that? The two sisters were eventually deprived of their living. They moved away but then returned. You learnt about this and used the great disturbance in the city to carry out your vengeance.'

Ambrose put the arbalest down in his lap and softly clapped in mockery. 'Very astute friar. I used to visit that house and yes I put those two old crones on trial for their crimes. I took my time because you can imagine how busy I was. I mean, I had to act as judge, prosecutor and jury. Of course, in the end I found them guilty. I thought of cutting their throats but, by then the city was in turmoil. In the end I sentenced them to hang. I became their executioner. I did enjoy their death struggles, watching those wizened, twisted faces turn purple, the life breath hissing from their wicked, filthy mouths.'

'You must have known the Upright Men would learn of this and be puzzled? You certainly thought about that when guildman Falaise informed you in confidence that Grindcobbe and his henchmen were in hiding, preparing to flee, waiting for former comrades to safely row them to some waiting ship. Falaise spoke to you, didn't he? After all, you were his priest and, I am sure, proved to be sympathetic to the Upright Men. Typical Ambrose, all things to all men. Falaise may have thought he was talking to you under the seal of the Sacrament, but in truth that means nothing to you. You simply used the Upright Men to deepen the confusion. Now Falaise was another matter.' Athelstan gestured with his hand. 'He must have wondered sooner or later, who betrayed his former comrades. Perhaps he never really considered it was you. Time would pass and he would reflect that you, the only other person who knew, might be the traitor. Falaise would certainly be troubled. Perhaps he approached you again to get to the truth and you priest, like the deadly beast you are, moved swiftly to the kill.

'Oh come, Brother Athelstan. You are greatly mistaken. Other people must have known about the Upright Men sheltering in the court of Thieves.'

'I disagree. Whatever you may think,' Athelstan pulled a face, 'you do not control everything. Sir John visited Grindcobbe in Newgate. The Upright Men were bartering for their lives and my Lord Coroner agreed. According to Grindcobbe, other members of the guild, your poor parishioners, may have the deepest of sympathy for their plight but only Falaise knew where they were hiding and what they intended to do. I understand the Upright Men maintained such secrecy so as to diminish the threat of betrayal. Only those who had to know would be informed. Monkshood told me the same. Falaise had sworn to Grindcobbe that he would share the information with no one. I suspect he kept his word, with one exception, his priest. It would take time for Falaise to realize this, so you murdered Falaise but you did so in a manner that would protect you.'

'How wrong you are!' Ambrose shook his head. 'I am sorry but, little meddler, you think you have the truth. I learnt about Falaise through that silly bitch.' He pointed at the dead Alice. 'The Upright Men needed feeding. Falaise hadn't the sense or time to secretly buy purveyance for a cohort of desperate hungry men. He approached the taverner of The Leviathan to purchase food under some stupid pretext or other. She told me. I followed Falaise when he pushed his wheelbarrow to Thieves' Square. Both the silly bitch and myself talked to Falaise: it became fairly obvious what mischief he was involved in and the rest was simple.'

'Very clever,' Athelstan agreed, 'you were most cunning even to the end when Falaise was murdered. After all, at the very moment the alarm was raised, you and your confidante Mistress

Alice were closeted with me and Sir John. Poor Falaise! Rendered
helpless by the drugged wine you probably forced him to drink,
he was trapped and bound, forced to stand on the step of that
bell tower, desperate to undo the clever knot which kept the
noose so tightly and securely around his throat.'

'Oh, you are sharp,' Ambrose interrupted. 'I really did think
I would fool you.'

'No you did not.' Athelstan retorted brusquely. 'Falaise would
pluck and pick at the knot, wary of making a mistake. Eventually
he did. He slips, loses his footing, the noose tightens and Falaise
is gone. And who could point the finger of suspicion at you
closeted with me in your sacristy?'

Athelstan smoothed down the folds of his robe. He had to
bait, taunt and challenge this killer, keep him absorbed in this
deadly game as the hour candle burnt lower and lower. He raised
his hand. 'In murdering Falaise, you made another stupid
mistake.' Athelstan steeled himself against the spasm of fury
which twisted Ambrose's face, but the mood passed. The priest's
arrogant curiosity was getting the better of him.

'I know, I know,' he breathed. 'That was a silly mistake.' He
laughed sharply. 'Being betrayed by a knot. I realized that later.
I watched you, like the little, nosy friar you are, sifting amongst
the chests and sacks brought by my dear parishioners. You
stopped when you came to mine, didn't you?'

'Of course. You had tied your coffer with rope. I glimpsed
a similar knot on your chancery satchel when I first visited
The Leviathan, the same again on that coffer and, of course, the
deadly knot on the noose around poor Falaise's throat. Finally,
I saw it on board the bum-boat which was found floating on the
Thames after *The Knave of Hearts* was obliterated. You'd tied
the tiller to a bench, hadn't you? Such knots, seaman's knots,
require a certain skill and you with your service as a bargeman
would be expert in fastening ropes and cords.'

'Someone else could do the same!'

'Yes, they could except that through elimination you become
the only suspect.' Athelstan leaned forward patronizingly. 'Why
don't you admit your terrible error?' Athelstan pointed at Alice's
sprawled corpse. 'I wonder, I truly do about her role in all of
this but she is past all caring and has to answer to a higher court.'

'You are playing for time friar but the hours burn away, soon you too will be despatched into nothingness. I don't believe there is anything there so it's futile to rage against the gathering dark. Do you know what it feels like friar to know there is nothing?'

'I believe you are in for a most unpleasant surprise as your accomplice Roughkin has surely discovered. Roughkin your accomplice . . .'

'Are you sure it was he, not his son?'

'It doesn't really matter does it? I think it's Roughkin. Only the angels know what truly happened to his son. Perhaps Senlac discovered the truth about his father and had to be silenced. However, in the final weaving of this terrible tapestry, Roughkin must be depicted as an assassin, a murderous soul who returned to St Erconwald's. Roughkin was your accomplice. He must have been furious to discover there was no treasure on board *The Knave of Hearts*. Desperate, he recalled his days as keeper of the mortuary at St Erconwald's. How he had murdered some of his guests who stayed at the miserable Piebald, burying both their corpses and their wealth beneath the old death house. He'd left himself a memorandum, a clumsy cipher to show where these corpses and their looted treasure lay hidden, a special mark on particular stones so he would know which ones to lift. After all, Roughkin had been forced to hurriedly flee St Erconwald's years ago when Sir John Cranston came investigating.' Athelstan paused. 'Roughkin ran the risk of being arrested for one felony or another: pretending to be his son Senlac was a clever disguise which gave him the freedom to wander St Erconwald's and The Piebald tavern.' Athelstan stared into the flames. He glimpsed the poker lying to one side and wondered if that could prove a suitable weapon. He picked it up and pushed it into the flames.

'I am waiting, friar.'

'Roughkin knew full well where the treasure chart was, but he couldn't go directly to it. He really had no right to wander the tavern. More importantly, the chamber on the top gallery, which I suspect was an old chancery, was locked, the key held by Master Joscelyn. Roughkin therefore pretended to be an honest searcher but, really and truly, like you he was a mummer, his mouth crammed with lies.' Athelstan pulled out the poker.

'Put it back, friar.'

Athelstan shrugged and dropped the iron bar, letting it clatter to the ground.

'I admit,' Athelstan decided to placate his opponent, 'there are gaps in the tapestry I weave, in the story I tell. I am not too sure who was the Oriflamme at any particular time. I do suspect that Roughkin terrified Bramley in ways and at certain times we don't even know about. He probably also sent the information regarding the Upright Men to both Cranston and the Luciferi. He must have broached with you a second possible source of treasure in my parish. I concede,' Athelstan raised his hands, 'you are very, very cunning but, there were obstacles. Roughkin's plans were seriously disrupted when he realized that the mad beggar Godbless lived in the old death house along with his pet goat. Now Godbless was completely moonstruck, but he was also very possessive. He regarded that mortuary as his home, as any lord would his manor house. But further shocks awaited.' Athelstan chewed the corner of his lip, even as he strained to hear any sound from the darkness around him.

'What shock, friar?'

'You know full well. Godbless was a lunatic, as mad as a box of baby frogs. He was an old wizened man with no brain, no wits and certainly no past. At least not until you and Roughkin arrived. Both of you realized that Godbless was no lesser person than Jacques Mornay, Master of La Chèvre Dansante, The Dancing Goat, a tavern on the banks of the Seine in Normandy, the former camp of the English free company, *Le Sans Dieu*. Mornay, lunatic and mad as a march hare, was also one of your henchmen. Over the years he'd slipped down the greasy pole of life, wandering England as a beggar, learning what he could of the tongue until he arrived at St Erconwald's, desperate for a place in our community, which we gave him. The poor soul never referred to his past. Indeed, except for the salutation 'Godbless', he hardly spoke sensibly to anyone.'

'You are sure it was Mornay?'

'To quote you back, don't play games, priest, this is the truth. Now Godbless was moon-touched in every sense of the word. However, I do suspect he recognized Roughkin from his days along the Seine; he may have also recognized you.'

'Recognise, recognize.' Ambrose retorted in a singsong voice.

'If Godbless was that tavern keeper, surely members of the guild would recognize him as he would recognize them?'

'You know the answer to that,' Athelstan retorted. 'It's almost twenty years ago since that free company left France. People change, they grow older, alter their appearance. Roughkin did that, and Godbless certainly did. The only description we have of the taverner at La Chèvre Dansante is that he had thick hair with a bushy moustache and beard. You know he did. Now the years passed. Godbless grew thinner. Bereft of hair on head or face, he was virtually unrecognizable. Of course, his wits wandered, though I don't think he would forget his fellow henchman Roughkin.'

'Godbless was mad.'

'On rare occasions he could be lucid enough. Godbless hadn't forgotten La Chèvre Dansante, which explained his keeping of a pet goat. I also suspect the poor madcap recognized faces from his past. The day before he was murdered, Godbless was heard shouting La Chèvre Dansante, repeating it time and time again in his usual lunatic style. In your eyes, Godbless had to be silenced. First, to shut his mouth, and secondly so that Roughkin could seize the plunder he'd hidden away beneath the paving stones of that sombre death house.'

'So Roughkin killed him?'

'No, you did. On that night Roughkin made great show of drinking and carousing in The Piebald tavern. He would not go into the cemetery and Godbless would definitely not open the door to him. He may have opened it to you, a priest, but there again, I suggest there were two keys to the death house. Godbless had one, the other was still held by Roughkin either on his person or hidden somewhere in God's Acre. You used such a key to enter the mortuary and murder Godbless. You then deepened the mystery by inserting the dead man's key in the lock, though not fully, then secured it from the outside taking the second key with you: that's your soul isn't it, Ambrose? You kill and kill again, but you love to cloak it in mystery, as if the game is the all-important thing. To you another person's life is like the flame of a candle, to be snuffed out without a second thought whenever it pleases you.' Athelstan paused. 'No one and nothing is sacred to you, be it

a poor widow-woman or a statue in my little chantry chapel!
You blight anything in your path.'

'They all deserved to die,' Ambrose replied dreamily. 'We
couldn't take that treasure and just row away. The French . . .
well, I did think of striking at Levigne, but the death of those
stupid whores was punishment enough. And the same is true of
the rest, be it Falaise or Godbless.'

'You must have worried about Roughkin?' Athelstan retorted.
'You did, didn't you? His wits aren't as sharp as yours. On the
morning we found Godbless, Roughkin arrived and made the
most curious remark. He didn't enter the death house, he couldn't
really see the corpse, yet he knew the beggar's throat had been
slit. I later deduced that he was either the murderer or was given
that information by the assassin responsible.'

'You are nearly finished, friar?'

'Your murder of Hornsby was cold and calculating, perpetrated
out of malicious spite more than anything else. There was no
real reason for slaying that bargeman. He may have entertained
his own suspicions. However, by the time you plotted his death,
you were totally immersed in your murderous game. You staged
a seemingly mysterious killing in a locked, bolted, sealed
chamber, fashioned out of the hardest rock, with no other entrance
except for a fortified door sealed from the inside.'

'And?'

'Oh, it is as obvious as it is logical. You are the parish priest
of St Olave's. You knew about the stone at the base of the rear of
that building, how it could be pushed in and out. Hornsby must
have mentioned he'd be working there that day. Or, better still,
did you tell him to go there at a certain time? Perhaps check
that all was well before he, like the others, joined you at St
Erconwald's? You entered that arca by the secret entrance and
you waited. Hornsby arrived. Now the arca is used to store
different goods. Hornsby was probably nervous, especially after
the death of Falaise, so he locks and bolts the door behind him.
In fact he has locked himself in with his assassin: you.'

'And the reason, friar?'

'As I have said, you love your murderous games. You enjoy
the power, baiting the likes of Sir John, proving yourself to be
superior to everyone and anyone, particularly those who oppose

you. You are a dyed-in-the-wool killer, a prowling malignant, desperate to protect yourself from the consequences of your sin. Falaise and Hornsby were murdered to silence them and you intended to do the same to all who might prove to be a threat.'

Athelstan cleared his throat. 'Sooner or later one of your former comrades may have stumbled onto the truth about their priest. You thought it was time to clear the field.' Athelstan sketched a cross in the direction of Mistress Alice's corpse. 'She had to go and so did Roughkin. I suspect your henchman's death was easy enough. He came to consult with you. You told him to meet you in that desolate part of St Erconwald's cemetery. He would shelter beneath a yew tree and you made that his tomb. A crossbow bolt to the forehead and another clacking tongue is silenced. Ah well.' Athelstan heard a click, a quite distinctive sound in the darkness at the far side of the taproom. He turned and glimpsed a bulky shadow move.

'What are you staring at, friar?'

Ambrose was also alarmed. On the hand he had to confront Athelstan, but he was now wary. He sensed something new, something very dangerous, was creeping through this hall of dancing shadows. The priest rose, his back to the fire, slightly turned so the crossbow was still aimed directly at Athelstan.

'What is it, friar?'

'The war in France.'

'Don't play games with me, you little shit,' Ambrose snarled.

'Sir John Cranston was once a knight of the royal household,' Athelstan replied forcefully. 'Despite his bulk, he could steal through the darkness like a slithering snake. He could penetrate the enemy camp and inflict grievous damage on his opponents. Sir John may be fat, bulky, gross in your eyes but, in truth, he is swift and silent as a shadow. And do know, priest, I believe he is here. Not too far from us . . .'

PART SEVEN

Dies Irae: *The Day of Wrath*

Ambrose turned. Athelstan lunged at him but the priest, lithe and swift as a lurcher, twisted away. He pulled at the catch on the arbalest but the bolt tumbled to the ground. Ambrose used the crossbow as a club, knocking Athelstan aside. He then fled across the darkened taproom into the buttery, slamming the door behind him. Athelstan, his shoulder bruised from the blow, struggled to his feet and almost collided with Cranston, who slipped – swift and soft as a hunting cat – from the shadows. The coroner resheathed both sword and dagger and swept the little friar into a crushing embrace, not releasing him until Athelstan gasped that he couldn't breathe and that his shoulder was hurting. The friar sat back in the chair as Cranston, now joined by Flaxwith and his bailiffs who'd forced a door, hurried across to the buttery, Athelstan shouting that the criminal had fled there. The door, however, had been locked and bolted from the inside and, by the time these clasps were prised loose, the buttery was empty. Ambrose had pulled back a wall bench as well as a strip of coarse floor matting to reveal a hidden passageway, the trapdoor to it resting against a stool. Cranston bellowed at Flaxwith and his company to go down in pursuit, as well as to take care of Alice's corpse. Once he'd imposed some sort of order, the coroner came back across the taproom, pulling a chair to face Athelstan squarely.

'Thank God,' the friar leaned over and grasped the back of Cranston's gauntleted hand. 'Thank God,' he repeated, sitting back, sketching a blessing in the direction of Alice's corpse, now sheeted and ready to be taken away.

'Satan's tits,' Cranston breathed. 'I heard a little of that, Athelstan. I realized you were confronting Ambrose. So what happened?'

The friar swiftly summarized what he called his bill of indictment against the priest. The coroner heard him out, shaking his head, cursing under his breath. For a while the coroner just sat, staring into the middle distance. Athelstan excused himself and, opening his chancery satchel, took out his holy phials. He rose and, pushing aside the makeshift shroud, hastily blessed and anointed the dead Alice. He pressed his fingers against her cold, hardening flesh, sketching crosses on her bloody face and gaping lips whilst he mouthed the requiem, pleading with Christ to shrive this woman of any sin. He'd hardly finished when Flaxwith came stomping in with Samson his mastiff, all excited after his journey along the secret passageway.

'Sir John,' the chief bailiff pulled back the hood of his cloak. 'We went down and followed the tunnel. It leads into nave of St Olave's, just before the rood screen.'

'And?' Cranston demanded tersely.

'Sir John, Brother Athelstan, you won't believe this. The fugitive priest Father Ambrose is already claiming benefit of clergy, that he is a cleric, not subject to the King's justice but that of the church. More importantly,' Flaxwith added lugubriously, 'he is also claiming sanctuary. Apparently, St Olave's has that right for someone being pursued by royal or city officials. There were a few parishioners in the church. The priest is already protesting his innocence, his privileges as a cleric . . .' Flaxwith paused. 'Don't be angry, Sir John. We couldn't do anything to stop this, but the fugitive has already despatched two of his parishioners to Lambeth to speak to the archdeacon's man Master Tuddenham. Remember what you told me, Sir John? We never cross swords with the Holy Mother Church, especially in a church. In a word, there is bugger-all we can do about him.'

Cranston groaned, putting his face in his hands, even as he shoved Samson away with the toe of his boot.

'Finally Sir John,' Flaxwith snapped his fingers at the mastiff, who reluctantly left the coroner to squat beside his master, 'when we entered the tunnel, we passed a hidden enclave. One of my men stumbled and his hand hit a wooden barrier – an aumbry built into a wall cleft. We opened it and . . .' Flaxwith turned and bellowed into the darkness. One of his men hurried forward and gave Flaxwith a sack, which was promptly emptied onto the floor. Athelstan and Cranston stared at the pile of coarse hair wigs dyed a deep, sinister red.

'Satan's tits,' Cranston whispered. 'The devil's handiwork. Well done, Flaxwith. Clear them away. Take that woman's corpse to the death house of another church. Oh, and mount a strong guard on both St Olave's and our sanctuary, man. Do this now. Despatch your swiftest courier to the constable at the Tower. I need twenty Cheshires down here as soon as possible.' Cranston clapped his hands. 'Swiftness is of the essence. Oh Flaxwith, one of your comitatus is called the Badger?'

'True, Sir John, he can dig anything out.'

'Good. Ask him to search the priest's house, turn everything over and give it a good shake. Knowing the little I do about that cunning bastard, I doubt very much if you will find anything suspicious, but you and your lads have done well. The priest's possessions and belongings are not covered by sanctuary, they are forfeit to the Crown. I want you and your lovely boys to make an honest list and I will give you a share.'

'That's very kind, Sir John.'

'It's my middle name, my friend, so off you go.'

Cranston and Athelstan sat in silence whilst Flaxwith and his cohort clattered about, removing Alice's corpse as well as bringing the coroner and friar freshly brewed ale and a platter of food from the kitchen. Both men ate and drank whilst the taproom emptied. Once it had, Athelstan blessed himself and pushed the platter away.

'Sir John, my friend, once again I thank you. You suspected something was wrong, yes? Ambrose made a terrible mistake. No one, apart from Benedicta, ever sends messages on my behalf across river to you, especially a courier you do not know.'

'Precisely, my little monk.'

'Friar, Sir John.'

'Precisely,' Cranston repeated. 'Why should Ambrose act on your behalf? Why tell me to wait in Southwark and not travel as swiftly as God's angels permit to meet you here if it were so important. No, no.' Cranston shook his head. 'The courier, some ordinary parishioner, seemed innocent enough. He just repeated what he'd been told, adding that you were now with the priest when the message was delivered. Moleskin then arrived. He told me what he knew and I suspected something was very wrong. Deeply suspicious, I hastened across, ordering Flaxwith and his

comitatus to follow. Now,' Cranston's face broke into a grin,
'during my long and not-so-glorious career, I have done business
with some of the most skilled picklocks, naps and foists in this
kingdom. They taught me their tricks as well as one incontrovert-
ible truth.'

'Sir John?'

'In every dwelling place, there's always a downstairs shutter
or door which can be breached, picked or prised open. I found
a window with shutters begging to be forced and so here I am.'
The coroner sighed deeply. 'I wish I could have seized that
murderous soul. Now he is going to use the King's law and that
of the church to protect himself and walk scot-free. Come,
Brother. Let us at least confront the bastard.'

They both rose. Cranston adjusted his warbelt and cloak and
helped Athelstan collect his chancery satchel. The friar was still
weak and tired after his baleful confrontation with the Oriflamme,
but he also felt a growing determination that such a sinister sinner
did not elude God's justice or the King's. They crossed to the
buttery and went down the secret passageway. The dark, freezing
tunnel was hollowed through the rock, reinforced with stout
timbers and carefully constructed pillars. Athelstan reckoned that
the needle-thin passageway had once been some form of escape
from either church or tavern during those hurling times which
often swept London. Torches fixed in crevices and sconces had
been lit, the flames hungrily licking the tar and pitch, the darting
fire creating wide pools of light. The air was musty but not too
uncomfortable, whilst the ground underfoot was dry and hard.
Two of Flaxwith's bailiffs patrolled the tunnel and, when they
climbed the steps into the nave, more bailiffs were guarding the
entrance through the ancient rood screen.

Athelstan and Cranston went up the steps into the sanctuary,
the icy coldness of the old church wrapping itself around them.
Braziers had been lit. Bailiffs, together with a group of curious
parishioners, were busy warming themselves. The hour was very
late but the news that something was wrong in St Olave's had
spread along the runnels and narrow alleys of the parish. Flaxwith
hurried over, he whispered to Cranston, and led both coroner and
friar across the sanctuary. Every candle, lantern and cresset had
been lit. Flaxwith pointed towards the sacristy door.

'Two of my lads are within. They will guard the prisoner should he want to use the jakes' hole.'

Athelstan glimpsed a wall painting on a pillar to the right of the sanctuary, its brilliant colours catching the light.

'That's freshly done,' he observed. 'Sir John, just let me have a look.'

Intrigued, Athelstan walked across and stared at the fresco. The scene was one of Hell, with sinners bound to fiery pillars with a sea of flame lapping around them up to their chins, red-hot chains in the form of snakes circling their waists. The faces of the damned blazed in torment; hosts of demons gathered around them, armed with fiery clubs.

'What's the matter, little friar?' Cranston whispered.

'A vision of Hell,' Athelstan replied. 'Common enough in old churches. At first glance nothing suspicious.'

'But?' the coroner asked.

'There's usually some form of deliverance, a harrowing by the good Lord, his angels being closely present, to demonstrate that Hell itself is part of his dominion. Look, Sir John, there is no such reference here. If I had come to this church a month ago, I would have made nothing of it but now, knowing what I do . . .' Athelstan plucked at the coroner's sleeve and led him back. 'Where is the prisoner?' Athelstan asked.

Flaxwith led them into the apse behind the high altar, a narrow passageway which ran past an enclave where Ambrose slouched on the mercy chair as if he hadn't a care in the world. On the small table beside him stood a jug of wine, a goblet and a platter of dried fruit, along with a small lantern and a pot of candles. Nearby glowed two wheeled braziers providing both light and warmth. Ambrose hardly moved, except to point at the blanket-covered paillasse on the floor behind him.

'I shall be retiring soon,' he declared.

'It's a wonder that you can sleep,' Athelstan rasped.

'I do hope you are not here to threaten?' Ambrose rose swiftly to his feet. 'I have appealed to all my parishioners.' The priest's powerful voice echoed around the sanctuary and two parishioners appeared, coming round the far end of the high altar, almost as if they'd expected such a summons. They walked towards the enclave to join their priest but Cranston thundered at them to go no further.

'Our priest,' one of the parishioners, an old man in faded, stained clothes bleated, 'our priest has been falsely accused. He—'

'That is not a matter for you,' Cranston boomed.

'Stay,' Ambrose shouted. 'Stay near to the entrance to the rood screen. If my sanctuary is violated, cry "Harrow" and raise the alarm. Do you understand?' The parishioners chorused they would before allowing Flaxwith to shoo them away. Ambrose watched them go, then sat down on the mercy chair, crossed his legs and smiled up at his two visitors. 'The chickens,' he murmured, 'still don't believe that the fox is deep in the hen coop. They still regard me with their usual stupid devotion, as if I was the cock Chaunticleer, not Reynaud but,' he sighed noisily, 'this fox will soon be gone.' His smile faded as he glared up at Cranston and Athelstan. 'Need I remind you that I am Ambrose Rookwood, a true cleric, a priest validly and legally ordained by Richard Bishop of London, and formally assigned to the parish of St Olave's here in Queenhithe?' He tapped his wallet. 'I have the necessary letters. Accordingly, I am not subject to royal justice, be it English or French. Arrest me and arraign me before any justice in this kingdom and I will plead benefit of clergy. Master Tuddenham and his archdeacon will have me surrendered to the jurisdiction of Holy Mother Church.' Again the smile. 'I know what you are thinking.' He stared at Cranston. 'Church courts do not have the power of life and death. I will get my bottom smacked and sent on my way. I will dance away free and innocent as any maypole maiden.'

'You are a false priest,' Cranston crouched down, peering close at Ambrose. 'You are a drinker of human blood. You feast on death.'

'Sir John, I agree with you. But who cares about that? Concentrate on the problem in hand. I have claimed sanctuary here at St Olave's, my own church, which extends the ancient right to those fleeing from royal justice, of safe and secure sanctuary. You know the law, Sir John. In forty days' time, I, Ambrose Rookwood, a recognized cleric, will leave this church. I will be protected by the sheriff's men, not to forget Master Tuddenham's escort. On a cold winter's day, dressed, cloaked and booted, food in my sack and money in my wallet, I will trot down to the nearest port which is,' Ambrose raised his eyes, 'Queenhithe.

Once there, I will board a ship for foreign parts. I will escape. Though,' he pointed at Athelstan, 'you never know when I might return. Oh, it could be a year, two years; perhaps I will return as a monk.' His face grew serious. 'A monk, a soldier or merchant, and I will lurk deep in the shadows around your pathetic little priest house or that dark, cold church of yours. You will get a surprise shared only by you and me.' Ambrose began to laugh, fingers fluttering to his face as he stared up at his two visitors.

Athelstan restrained his anger, plucking at Cranston's sleeve. 'Let us leave this demon,' he muttered, 'to the darkness of his kind.'

Ambrose appeared to find that funny. 'I shall return,' Ambrose sang out. 'I have unfinished business with all of you. Sir John, how is the Lady Maude and the two poppets?'

Athelstan grabbed Cranston's sleeve. 'Don't,' he hissed, 'don't even think of it.'

'I must thank you,' the coroner stepped closer.

'Thank me?' Ambrose jibed.

'For killing Roughkin and sparing me the trouble of arranging his hanging. Now I must only concentrate on you. Tell me,' Cranston cocked his head to one side, holding the priest's gaze, 'Brother Athelstan has told me all about you. Why did you kill Roughkin, your alter ego? I mean, you were twins united in evil. He was with you, wasn't he, when you attacked and abused that French noblewoman, Madeline de Clisson? From what I learnt, there were three which, I suspect, were you, Roughkin, and that lunatic Godbless?'

'Why do you mention that?'

'Well,' Cranston took a deep breath, 'you know the French are hunting you. It's a long walk down to Queenhithe. Oh, you will board a cog, but the French will know. So don't talk about being scot-free. The ship you board will not be the first to be stopped and searched by our good friends from France.'

'Oh, don't worry,' Ambrose replied, 'I have already thought of that and I will make the usual preparations. I will escape. I will come back, Fat Jack, little friar, and you can give the same warning to the likes of measly Moleskin and those other fools in the guild. But thank you for the warning.' He began to laugh, falsely yet loudly.

'Let us leave,' Athelstan hissed.

Cranston agreed and both coroner and friar crossed the sanctuary, hurrying down the nave to be free of that killer's ridicule.

They left St Olave's. The church was now ringed by Cheshire archers who, like professional soldiers, had swiftly set up camp with makeshift tents. Cooking fires had been lit. Food seized from The Leviathan was being shared out amongst those not on watch. Cranston had a few words with their captain and returned to the tavern where Flaxwith and his cohort had prepared chambers on the second-floor gallery, whilst one of the bailiffs, a former cook, had broached a cask of Bordeaux and grilled strips of chicken and ham in a mushroom sauce. Cranston and Athelstan sat at one of the taproom tables. The friar blessed the food and both men quietly ate and drank, lost in their own thoughts. Athelstan felt a deep apprehension about what might happen. He knew all about the rigour of church law, especially in London with the likes of Master Tuddenham.

'He cannot escape.' Cranston put his horn spoon down. He leaned closer. 'Brother Athelstan, you heard that villain. He intends to escape. He plans to return and he is already plotting murder. He threatened Lady Maude. I tell you, little friar, if he leaves this church for Queenhithe, I will personally take his head.'

'No, no Sir John.' Athelstan grasped Cranston's arm. 'Then you would be guilty of murder. You would go on trial whilst Holy Mother Church would excommunicate you. A tragic end to your days of glory, Jack, and, in his own perverted way, that priest hopes you might commit such a crime. So, even in death he causes more mayhem. Believe me, my friend, some souls are possessed by demons. He certainly is and they are legion. He is a man who would love to see the world on fire and merrily dance as the flames roared up. Be patient, wait . . .'

Cranston and Athelstan adjourned for the night and rose early to break their fast in the taproom. Athelstan declared he did not wish to celebrate Mass in a church which housed and protected such an assassin, adding that he would celebrate the mysteries on his return to St Erconwald's. They were still sitting at table discussing this when Master Tuddenham and an escort of church beadles, garbed in the livery of the Archbishop of Canterbury, swept into the tavern. At first there was some confusion. Athelstan gently pointed out that he and Sir John were not the felons but the perjured priest Ambrose now sheltering in sanctuary. Athelstan clearly explained what had happened and Tuddenham's harsh, pale face relaxed. The archdeacon's man undid his cloak and handed it to his chief bailiff, telling him to take his escort and join the others guarding the church. Once he'd left, Tuddenham accepted a tankard of morning ale and sipped it as Athelstan once again summarized the indictment against Ambrose. Tuddenham's face visibly blanched, his air of harsh officialdom being replaced with a deeply worried expression.

'This is an abomination,' he said. 'Nevertheless, the archdeacon who speaks for my Lord of Canterbury is most insistent. A sanctuary man is always sacred, even more so when he is a legitimately ordained cleric. All hell,' he clasped his hands as if in prayer, 'and I mean the very furies, will descend if you violate those privileges won by Thomas Becket and defended by Holy Mother Church both here and abroad.'

'So this demon incarnate will . . .' Cranston broke off as Flaxwith hurried in and whispered heatedly in the coroner's ear.

'Satan's tits,' Cranston breathed. 'My happiness is complete. Show him in . . . Hugh Levigne,' he added, turning back to his companions, 'the French envoy has arrived demanding an audience.' He paused at the sound of booted footsteps and the clink of steel. 'Ah well,' he whispered, 'and here he is.'

Levigne came striding across the taproom, two of his Luciferi trailing behind. Levigne stopped and whispered over his shoulder at his escort; pushing back the hood of his blood-red cloak, Levigne picked up a stool and joined them at table. He placed his chancery satchel beside him and smiled dazzlingly at Cranston, who hastily introduced Master Tuddenham. They clasped hands, Tuddenham murmuring a benediction.

'I am welcome am I not, Sir John?'

'The honourable envoy of the French court is always welcome,' Cranston's tone was soft though menacing, 'though I must ask why you are here?'

'Why indeed,' Levigne replied, unbuckling the chancery satchel. 'You do realize I pay for information so I know what has happened here. How the Oriflamme might well be Ambrose

Rookwood, parish priest of St Olave's and the former member of an English free company. Now,' Levigne drew out a faded parchment page, 'according to the records of the Bishop of Beauvais, Ambrose Rookwood, a former scholar from the halls of Cambridge and the Sorbonne in Paris was an ordained priest, but then moved to the Archdiocese of Rouen. Once he'd arrived there, he was given a benefice at Moyaux.' Levigne pulled a face. 'Our chancery clerks ruthlessly searched and investigated the entire *Le Sans Dieu* company. We learnt scraps about Rookwood and a few others such as your Moleskin.'

'And?' Athelstan asked. 'I am intrigued by that parishioner.'

'No, Moleskin was just a follower, a common mercenary, who seemed eager for plunder and nothing else. In one village that *Le Sans Dieu* raided, Moleskin proved to be chivalrous towards a small convent of nuns. He gave them his name and assured them that they would not be troubled.' Levigne lifted the parchment page. 'One further item is now truly significant.'

'What is it?' Athelstan tried to curb his excitement.

'Well, the Bishop of Beauvais wrote a memorandum. How he was visited by a distant kinswoman of Rookwood. She had gone to Moyaux to visit a member of her family, namely the priest Father Ambrose, but the person she saw celebrating Mass was not her kinsman. Perplexed and confused, this woman did not do anything there, but travelled back to Beauvais and gave the bishop's people a description of the man serving as curé in the parish of St Simon at Moyaux. She had gone there for Sunday Mass and intended to visit him in the sacristy afterwards. But, of course, she was so mystified that she decided not to. Now, she admitted that she may have made a mistake and that any changes might be due to the passage of time. They asked the woman to return to Moyaux to be certain. She left but never returned. Now,' Levigne waved a hand, 'the war in Normandy was raging. Chaos, carnage and confusion caused by the Goddams.' Levigne gave a wry smile as Cranston stiffened. 'My friend,' Levigne went on, 'you English turned Normandy into a battlefield. Anyway, the Bishop of Beauvais also concluded that perhaps the woman had been mistaken, recognized her error and let the matter drop. He certainly did for a while.'

'Flimsy evidence,' Tuddenham intervened.

'It might be,' Levigne countered, 'if there wasn't a second memorandum which gave the kinswoman's description of her distant cousin Rookwood compared to that of this mysterious priest she saw in Moyaux. In a word, her description of this village curé certainly fits the criminal now sheltering in St Olave's church. Read for yourself.'

Levigne passed the document to Tuddenham, who exclaimed in surprise before handing it to Cranston and Athelstan. Both coroner and friar read the elegant, cursive script, murmuring their agreement: the priest at Moyaux was certainly Ambrose Rookwood now sheltering in sanctuary.

'I believe,' Levigne declared, 'that somewhere between Beauvais, Rouen and Moyaux, the real Ambrose Rookwood was murdered, his corpse hidden, and the malefactor we now hunt took his name and identity. He was probably a scholar and would find such a disguise as easy as pulling on a pair of gloves cut to his liking.'

'You mention the Bishop of Beauvais let the matter drop for a while?'

'Yes, yes he did. But what is quite significant is that, though the priest at Moyaux later disappeared, the kinswoman also vanished. There were petitions to the bishop concerning her whereabouts. Of course, all he could say was that she had visited him twice and left it at that.'

'I suspect I know what happened.' Athelstan replied grimly. 'That poor kinswoman of the true Rookwood returned to Moyaux and confronted our demon. He would be charming, give some lie, but then silence her for good. Somewhere in the cemetery of Moyaux or the woods around it and, in my service as a soldier, I marched through that part of Normandy . . .'

'Did you now?' Levigne asked.

'Yes, yes I did. I believe that somewhere in that densely wooded countryside lies the corpse of a poor woman who went looking for a kinsman and met a demon incarnate.'

'Possible,' Levigne conceded.

'I am sure it happened,' Athelstan replied. 'Chaos devastated Normandy, its people were attacked and harassed. Communities were shattered. People thrown out onto the roads to wander where they wanted. Priests, religious, peasants and, of course, the tribe

of beggars, confidence tricksters and, above all, murderers looking
for fresh prey.'

'Tell me, my friend,' Cranston asked, 'were there any murders
such as here? Young women with their throats cut, heads decorated with those disgusting wigs? Brother Athelstan is correct,
Normandy provided a good hunting run for the likes of our
assassin.'

'No, no,' Levigne retorted. 'We did the most thorough search
but discovered nothing, except of course victims such as Madeline
de Clisson, murders directly attributed to the Oriflamme.'

'Of course, of course,' Athelstan mused. 'There wouldn't be.
Our fugitive can control both himself and his dreadful desires,
as he did in London until a few weeks ago. He kept his preda-
tory ways well hidden.'

'But eventually he gave in,' Cranston asserted. 'Normandy
presented so many opportunities for the killer, the assassin, the
rapist and the marauder. The malignant who now calls himself
Rookwood grew tired of his parish, of being a priest; he drifted
south and joined that free company now known as *Le Sans Dieu*.
Once there, this demon priest could don his disguise and, having
served in Normandy, he would know the land; which communities to attack, which places to plunder.'

'One final matter we did not share with you,' Levigne declared,
'but will do now, were purported names of the Oriflamme and
his henchmen. I tell you this now because it could well account
for the rumours that we were searching for other members of
that mercenary free company.'

'What names?' Cranston demanded.

'Oh, the self-proclaimed identities of the Oriflamme and his
henchmen.'

'What!' Cranston declared.

'Patience, my Lord Coroner. Madeline de Clisson was tortured
and abused by the Oriflamme and two of his followers. They
fled at the approach of Madeline's kinsmen to the château. These
three criminals had already locked and barred all the doors to
the house, leaving one open for their escape. By the time
Madeline's kinsmen broke in and stumbled on the horrors
awaiting them, the malignants responsible had fled. That area is
thickly wooded, an army could hide deep amongst its trees. Now,'

Levigne tapped the parchment before him, 'Madeline de Clisson lingered for a few days before she died. She haltingly informed those caring for her about her attackers, their assault and the abominable way they disguised themselves. She also whispered about three visitors who claimed to be Scottish mercenaries fighting for the French; these arrived at the château the night before. Of course these visitors must have been the assailants.'

'And they gave their names?'

'Yes. According to Madeline, Samuel Moleskin was their leader, Matthew Hornsby and John Falaise his two companions.'

'Never!'

'Of course, Brother Athelstan, we did not believe such misinformation. No villain would give their real name, and the same is true of Madeline's visitors. Nevertheless, whoever they really were, they certainly knew all about the company of *Le Sans Dieu* and the names of its members.'

'Yet we all hold for certain that the man calling himself Ambrose Rookwood is and was the Oriflamme. He led the assault on that hapless châtelaine.'

'I agree, Sir John. The attack on Madeline was Rookwood's handiwork. He was guilty of similar outrages against other individuals who fell into his power, be they woman or priest. Now Madeline's three assailants arrived in the evening. On that same day, according to the evidence received, they attacked and murdered a lonely old curé Father Ricard, who held the benefice of a small woodland church. Ricard was a retired priest seeing out his days, caring for those who worked in the forest around the château: peasants, farmers, charcoal-burners and hunters. Ricard was murdered and his cottage ransacked. In fact the Oriflamme seized a seal used by Madeline's father to forge a letter declaring that Madeline's three visitors had been despatched by himself.'

'Of course,' Athelstan reflected, 'Rookwood would know a great deal about the Normandy countryside. He is also skilled in chancery matters. He would steal a document kept by the priest, remove the seal and place it on another piece of parchment.' Athelstan glanced up at Levigne. 'But why didn't you inform us about this at the beginning?'

'Because there were other similar outrages, weren't there?'

'Sir John, you have it. The Oriflamme and his henchmen were now following the coffin roads, woodland tracks and forest paths north to the coast. They passed through hamlets and villages where the menfolk had been called to the banners and standards of their lords. The Oriflamme and his fellow demons could writhe and slither, like the serpents they were, into these undefended communities, using the same names as they had at the château. We learnt this from another witness. Apparently the Oriflamme and his henchmen stopped at a local tavern, The Heron, where they slaughtered two chapmen, then brutally abused and murdered two women. What they did not know was that a spit-boy, Gaspard, hiding in the cellar, watched the hideous masque unfold. They played the same treacherous tricks as they did on the Lady Madeline, giving the names of other members of *Le Sans Dieu* free company.'

'In other words,' Athelstan declared, 'the Oriflamme was indulging in his heinous pastimes whilst protecting his true identity even further?'

'Of course, Brother, and what use would such lies be?' Levigne spread his hands. 'We could not arrive in England demanding the seizure of this person or that without any real proof. Your masters at Westminster would certainly object. More importantly, we did not wish the Oriflamme to make fools of us all. He would have been delighted to see the wrong person arrested and carted off to Montfaucon. We had to be prudent, cunning.' The French envoy joined his hands together as if in prayer and sketched a slight bow. 'We decided to wait and our patience was rewarded. We could not have asked for swifter or more cunning hunters than yourself and Sir John.'

'Flattery, my friend,' Athelstan smiled, 'soothes many a sore.'

'Brother Athelstan, Sir John,' Levigne's handsome, swarthy face turned sombre, 'please, on behalf of my royal master and the other seigneurs of the Secret Chancery at the Louvre, accept our most profound thanks. Monseigneur Pierre de Clisson will be satisfied. Madeline was his sole beloved daughter and she was horribly abused. They stripped both her and her maid naked, before hanging them from the ceiling beams. The malignants spent the entire night inflicting every possible degradation on their victims. They grew tired of Béatrice and slit her from throat to crotch as if she were a pig. Madeline was a mass of welts, bruises and wounds. She survived only a few days, but her description of what happened scarred the souls of all who knew and loved her. She was a gifted young woman . . .' Levigne paused to draw in breath. 'Accordingly, we will, at the appropriate time and in the appropriate place, demand that the Oriflamme be handed over to us. Lord Pierre has taken a solemn oath that he will gibbet the Oriflamme's corpse before the gateway to his château. Once again, accept all our thanks for the capture of this demon incarnate.'

'Rookwood is a criminal,' Cranston growled, watching Levigne leave, 'and certainly worthy of death.'

'I agree.' Tuddenham spread his hands. 'But our sanctuary man is a priest, a lawfully ordained cleric. He has served as a priest and he could certainly confuse any court if he has the necessary documents, warrants and licences to prove it. I suspect that – at the very least – he has all these so he will insist on being protected by canon law and the full power of the church. More importantly, he is also in sanctuary and, as you well know, Sir John, as long as he stays there for forty days, he can then leave, walk to the nearest quayside, which is Queenhithe, and take ship abroad. Until that happens, I must insist on a guard being mounted both within and without St Olave's. At night these guards must be withdrawn, except for two who will lock and bolt the church from the inside. I demand that such a guard be those of my retinue. Remember, the only way such a fugitive can be lawfully seized is if he leaves sanctuary of his own free will. Brother Athelstan, Sir John,' Tuddenham rose to his feet, 'I will set my own guard then I will be gone.'

Athelstan also made his farewells and, lost in his own deep thoughts, made his way absent-mindedly back across the river to St Erconwald's where he celebrated a late Mass. He then had words with Benedicta about parish business and declared that he would appreciate fresh food and a good sleep. Afterwards he would become a hermit and, for a while, withdraw from the hustle and bustle of parish life. Once he had assured Benedicta that all was well and that he just needed to be alone, Athelstan closeted himself in his priest's house. He sat at his table, staring down at the smooth square of parchment before him.

'This will become my world,' he whispered, 'here, I will try and resolve this problem.'

The friar felt coldly furious. He regarded the man calling himself Ambrose Rookwood as probably the most evil soul he had ever encountered. The friar also realized that this demon might very well take wing and fly away to fresh meadows of murder.

'I cannot allow that,' Athelstan observed to Bonaventure, who had joined him at the table. 'I cannot and I will not leave here until I have resolved this.'

Athelstan kept to his word, only leaving to celebrate morning mass. For three full days he sat reflecting on that hideous sanctuary man, gloating and gleeful in St Olave's. How could he be lured out? Athelstan turned this question over time and again as he kept in constant touch with Cranston, sending messages through Tiptoft or Benedicta.

On the fourth day after his return, Athelstan decided to go for a walk in God's Acre. He visited the old death house. All of its flagstones had been lifted. Any treasure found had been placed in a sack and sent to Cranston, whilst the mortal remains of Roughkin's victims had been coffered and taken to the death house at St Mary's Overy where the parish priest had promised to give them honourable burial. Athelstan stared down into one of the pits. Cranston had seized Roughkin's corpse and carted it off to the cellars of Newgate. The friar closed his eyes and whispered a prayer for the dead. He was about to walk away, making sure he kept clear of the pits, when he remembered something at St Olave's and stood stock still in surprise.

'I wonder,' he murmured, 'I truly do.'

He returned to the priest's house and sat for a while, scribbling on that piece of parchment. Once he'd finished, he made sure all was well, collected his cloak and chancery satchel and hurried down to the quayside, where he ordered a grim-faced Moleskin to row him across to Queenhithe. The bargeman wanted to question him, but the friar put a finger to his lips.

'Not here,' he declared gently, 'and certainly not now.'

Moleskin nodded and, once his barge reached the quayside, Athelstan hastened up the steps and through the rabbit-warren of lanes and arrow-thin alleyways to The Leviathan, where Sir

John had set up camp. They clasped hands and exchanged the kiss of peace. Athelstan had a few words with the coroner then both hurried into St Olave's. They walked down the nave and Athelstan heaved a sigh of relief as he scrutinized the battered paving stones in front of the ancient rood screen.

'Very good, Sir John, very good.' Athelstan rubbed his hands. 'Are you sure Master Tuddenham does not know?

'Brother, I am certain of it. The trapdoor was closed, sealed, and I made no mention of it. The church beadles,' Cranston pointed at a knot of liveried ruffians squatting on the floor near the ancient baptismal font, 'never mention it. They keep an eye on the criminal and one on us. Brother, they are over-confident and, more especially, they love their drink.'

'Good, good, Sir John, so let us prepare our Trojan horse. This is what I suggest . . .'

Later that day, when the bells of other churches were tolling the end of Compline, the last great prayer of the day, Athelstan slipped into St Olave's with a basket of food and a jug of The Leviathan's best Bordeaux. He was immediately confronted by the two church beadles assigned to stand on guard inside the church that night. They acted all officious, holding their hands up as Athelstan made to go towards the rood screen.

'No, Brother,' one of them warned, 'the bell has tolled. This church is to be emptied except for us and the fugitive we guard.'

Athelstan nodded understandingly, placing the food basket and wine jug on the floor. He blessed the beadles and left to rejoin Sir John in The Leviathan. The coroner greeted him merrily and they made the final preparations, organizing Flaxwith and his bailiffs, gathered in the large kitchen, where everything was laid out for them. Athelstan scrutinized the hour candle and, when two rings had been burnt off, he opened the trapdoor.

'We are ready, Sir John. God be with us.'

Carrying a lanternhorn, Athelstan led Sir John down along the secret passageway and up into the church. They moved silently, bracing themselves against the icy coldness of the nave. Athelstan crouched cautiously. He stared around before stealing across the nave to where the two beadles lay sprawled fast asleep. He collected the wine jug and goblets.

'As we thought,' he said, handing the cup and jug to Sir John who carried a sack containing identical goblets and a flagon from the tavern kitchen. The coroner used his miraculous wineskin to pour a little into the fresh jug as well as into the two cups. Athelstan took these back to where the bailiffs lay sprawled. He strained his hearing, listening to any sound from Ambrose sheltering in the mercy enclave which was concealed by both the rood screen and high altar; he could detect nothing amiss. Athelstan returned to the raised trapdoor.

'Very good, Sir John, summon up the ghosts.'

The coroner, grinning from ear to ear, put a finger to his lips and went down the passageway. A short while later, a macabre procession made its way up. Flaxwith and his bailiffs were now garbed in grey gowns, faces covered by ghostly white masks, their heads crowned with fiery red horsehair wigs. This nightmare cohort made their way up the steps to gather outside the rood screen. There were twelve in number. At Athelstan's direction, they entered the sanctuary and parted to go either side of the high altar. Athelstan, now hiding in the shadows, watched the masque unfold. The cleverly disguised bailiffs were armed with metal-tipped staves and they beat these on the ground as they entered the apse, six from one side, six from the other. Athelstan heard Ambrose's screams as he woke and stared at the hideous vision facing him, his yells echoing eerily through the church.

Athelstan heard the sound of a struggle, more screams and curses then, as planned, Ambrose came hurrying around the altar, pursued by the grotesquely garbed figures of the night. Holding his cloak and belt, Ambrose fled across the sanctuary and into the nave where Cranston, similarly garbed as the bailiffs, stood on guard. Ambrose had no choice; he was given little time to think. Roused from his sleep, confronted with his own macabre nightmare, Ambrose had lost all that arrogant sheen which cloaked his personality and actions. There was no escape. Confronted and blocked by another dreadful apparition, Ambrose fled down into the secret passageway, Cranston and his bailiffs following in hot pursuit. Athelstan carefully checked the sanctuary and nave before moving back to the beadles, but these still lay snoring after drinking the heavy Bordeaux generously laced with a strong opiate. The friar decided all was well and went down into the secret passageway, making sure the trapdoor was securely closed behind him. By the time he reached the taproom in The Leviathan, Ambrose – roped and shackled – lay slumped on a stool guarded by bailiffs.

'Very well, very well,' Athelstan beckoned Flaxwith and Cranston to follow him into the shadows.

'So what happened here?' the friar demanded.

'As you planned, Brother,' the chief bailiff replied. 'The fugitive was not caught by those you sent into the sanctuary but the small cohort we left here.'

'And Ambrose never saw you remove your disguises?'

'No, by the time we reached here, the small comitatus waiting in the taproom had seized him and pulled a hood across his head so he never actually realized who was pursuing him.'

'Good, good,' Athelstan mused, 'so the trap has been sprung. The nightmares which created Ambrose's soul are also responsible for his downfall and capture. Sir John, the prisoner is yours.'

'In which case my happiness is complete.' Cranston led them across to the prisoner, the coroner pulling the hood from the fugitive's head.

'Ambrose Rookwood,' the coroner intoned, 'or whoever you are, false priest and outlaw, have been apprehended whilst fleeing sanctuary.' He clasped the prisoner on the shoulder. 'So I arrest you in the King's name for sentencing before the royal justices.'

Ambrose just moaned to himself, not even bothering to look up. Cranston snapped his fingers. 'Master Flaxwith, lodge the prisoner deep in Newgate's pit.'

Once the bailiffs and their prisoner had left, Cranston insisted on broaching a small cask and served both himself and the friar generous goblets of winking red wine. Athelstan sipped at his whilst Cranston, ushering the friar to a table, slurped his noisily, raising the cup in toast to his companion.

'A good night's work, little friar,' Cranston leaned across the table. 'Ambrose is a ruthless, cold-hearted assassin, a killer to his very marrow, but how did you know he would panic? He might have stayed, resisted?'

'I told you this before, my friend,' Athelstan replied. 'My guiding light is St Augustine, who lived in the twilight years of Ancient Rome. A bishop in North Africa, Augustine proved to be a brilliant theologian and the most astute observer of human

208 Paul Doherty

nature. He argued that we human beings are a mixture of both the divine and the demonic. Deep inside us we house phantasms, deep fears and sharp frustrations. Even if we try to ignore them, these emotions play a vital role in our lives.' Athelstan sipped at his wine. 'So it is with our killer. Try Sir John, for a short while, to forget his murderous ways, difficult though that might be. Think of a small boy in that bleak house on the corner of Slops Alley. Imagine those hideous harridans garbed in grey, their heads festooned with dreadful wigs. They had the likes of our prisoner to torture and abuse over the years. A mere boy, already bereft of his parents or any kin. Such cruelty inflicted a deep and dire deadly soul wound that was never healed. Indeed, it festered and produced its own poison. Over the years Rookwood, or whatever his true name is, tried to forget, to ignore what had happened, but the humours of his soul were cracked and the infection broke out. He could indulge his phantasms, vomit the poison by turning on his tormentors, namely women. He did this in France and, when he returned here, he chose his victims from amongst the most vulnerable, the whores and prostitutes of London.'

'And yet he acted as a priest?'

'Sir John, the perfect disguise. Rookwood loved disguises. We know that, switching between the caring devoted priest and the hideous monster known as the Oriflamme. He indulged his murderous passions in Normandy both before and after he joined *Le Sans Dieu* company. However, once the war was over, he again tried to restrain himself, but the news about the French hunting him stirred up a violent tempest within him. He wanted revenge, so he returned to his killing days: seizing whores, murdering them, stripping their bodies, ridiculing them with those wigs before they were sent floating along the Thames for all the world to see.' Athelstan sipped his wine. 'Ambrose indulged his murderous fantasies, he never dreamed they would turn on him. Sweep out of the darkness to seize him, as happened tonight. When they did, he reverted to being a small boy and tried to flee.' Athelstan sighed and pushed away the cup. 'And so it is,' he whispered, 'and so it was.'

Ten days later, Athelstan joined Cranston on the great execution scaffold overlooking Smithfield. On that particular morning, execution day, the broad stretch of common land used for fairs, markets and horse-trading, teemed with London citizens. The crowds thronged, flocking in their thousands to watch a felon, now proclaimed as Satan's own assassin, receive just punishment for treason, murder and robbery. Ambrose Rookwood, condemned under the name he had assumed before royal justices at the Guildhall, had been spared the full rigour of the penalty for treason: his sentence was not reduced on any compassionate grounds. Thibault, Gaunt's Master of Secrets, had insisted that the criminal be subject to English courts and English law. In a sense, Thibault had added wryly, there should be no problem. After all, the kings of England also styled themselves kings of France, so it didn't really matter where the felon was actually executed. Monseigneur Levigne, present at the meeting held in the Jerusalem chamber at Westminster, had just smiled, shrugged and murmured the usual French diplomatic response to such an outrageous claim.

Cranston and Athelstan had also been present to receive the regent's thanks, as well as listen to what was decided. In the end, a compromise had been reached. The Oriflamme would be executed at Smithfield; his accomplice Roughkin would hang gibbeted beside him. After execution, both corpses, suitably prepared, would be handed over to Levigne. He could transport these to Paris to decorate the majestic but macabre gibbet at Montfaucon. Levigne also insisted that Godbless's remains should be handed over, but Athelstan pleaded that the beggar man had been truly lunatic whilst his corpse, mangled and corrupted, was in no fit condition to be transported anywhere, so it should be left deep in the soil in God's Acre at St Erconwald's. Levigne had promptly agreed, pleased at the outcome.

Roughkin's corpse, sheeted and bound, already hung from one branch of the great Smithfield gallows. The main arm of the scaffold was now being carefully prepared for the Oriflamme. Athelstan watched as the Hangman of Rochester, garbed from head to toe in his black leather costume, busied himself with the ladder and the dangling noose. The Oriflamme, Ambrose Rookwood as he was proclaimed, stood manacled and chained, staring dully out before him. Master Thibault had ordered that the condemned man be garbed as he had his victims, with a blood-red wig on his head, his body draped in a grey gown. The city mob, with their mordant sense of humour, had responded in kind. Many of them had turned up wearing red wigs with white linen masks over their faces, so it seemed a veritable army of Oriflammes had assembled to watch this gruesome pageant.

Athelstan wondered why so many citizens were so fascinated by public executions. Sudden death was no stranger to London. The poor were dying by their hundreds along the narrow, filthy alleyways and runnels of both the city and Southwark. Perhaps, Athelstan quietly concluded, it was the sombre, grisly ritual, yet there was no denying the fascination. Certainly the city had emptied. The good burgesses and their portly wives, garbed in samite and fur, rubbed shoulders with the denizens of the underworld, the twilight-dwellers who robbed, tricked and murdered, fearful of ending up being part of the ritual they had flocked to watch. Athelstan stared out over the crowd. Pimps in their garish clothes milled about, snouting for business for their cohort of ladies. Minstrels, troubadours and chanteurs offered lurid descriptions of the condemned and his crimes. Others were present to offer comfort, be it the Guild of the Hanged or the Society of the Condemned. Friars of the Sack intoned hymns of mourning whilst a guild calling itself 'The Good Women of Jerusalem' pattered aves for the repose of the souls of both the killers and their victims.

The noise rolled constantly and, despite the frosty morning, the crowd were patient, suitable customers for the itinerant cooks with their moveable ovens, grills and stoves. The air reeked of sweat, dung and different roasting smells, both sweet and foul. Athelstan glanced back at the Oriflamme. The condemned man had grown visibly agitated by the prospect of impending violent death, his eyes writhing in a face like that of a demon's sick of sin. The hangman was now ready; everything was in place. The executioner lifted a hand and nodded at the Lord High Coroner. Cranston moved to the edge of the scaffold, ringed on all four sides by Cheshire archers. The coroner signalled to the trumpeters who blew a long, shrill fanfare, which was greeted by the blare of horns from the milling mob. Again, the powerful trumpet blasts, one after another. Silence descended and the tambours began to beat, a rolling, menacing sound which grew louder and louder. Athelstan felt someone come up beside him. He turned and smiled at Master Tuddenham.

'That was very clever, Brother Athelstan.'

'The ways of God are truly marvellous.' Athelstan whispered back.

'They talk of a secret passageway beneath St Olave's?'

'Do they now?' Athelstan shrugged.

'Did you want to take this man's life so much, Brother?'

Athelstan did not reply but pointed at the scaffold. The Hangman of Rochester had now hustled the pinioned Oriflamme up to the top of the ladder. He secured the noose round the condemned man's neck and scrambled back down, staring across at Cranston who stood, hand raised. The drumbeat stopped. The coroner let his hand drop and the hangman twisted the ladder. The Oriflamme fell like a stone, the sound of his breaking neck, a sharp snap, echoing loudly across the platform. Athelstan turned back to the archdeacon's man.

'Master Tuddenham, I did not want this man's life. God did, and now he has him!'

AUTHOR'S NOTE

The Hundred Years' War in France was sharp and cruel. France was ravaged by English chevauchées out of Gascony, or from the English fortified camps along the Channel coast such as Calais and Boulogne. The devastation inflicted was widespread and grievous. Some historians maintain that the English occupation was more horrific than that of the Nazis during World War II. We tend to think of knights in shining armour riding forth to do battle, and so they did, but their main aim was plunder, booty and ransoms. A high-ranking nobleman such as Charles of Orléans spent years languishing in the Tower while his ransom was raised. Many great English lords literally made their fortune at the expense of the French. The soldiers these knights led might well be skilled archers or bowmen. However, they also included a fair proportion of jailbirds, murderers, thieves and other outlaws who, in return for a pardon, would agree to serve in the King's array. Shakespeare captures this very cleverly in his play *Henry V*. Here we meet the followers of fat Sir John Falstaff, felons such as Nym, Pistol and Bardolph. If you have read the play, you will recall that Bardolph was hanged for stealing a pyx from a church.

Nevertheless, these fictional figures pale in comparison to the grim reality. The French chronicles talk of écorcheurs, literally 'flayers', who would peel the skin off their victims. Indeed, the English occupation was so pernicious that the chronicles point out that only God could resolve the situation, which he did by raising Joan of Arc who initiated the French recovery and the eventual English withdrawal. Joan had no time for the free companies, those mercenaries who wandered Northern France bent on murderous mischief. It was Joan who actually told the English to either go home in their ships or she would ship them home in their coffins. Despite her saintly ways, Joan was ruthless towards the captains of these companies. On one occasion, whilst attacking an English-held fortress, Joan approached the walls and screamed at its commander, 'Glasdale, come out, so I can send your soul to Hell.'

One historian maintains that the English army was made up of sweepings of this country's jails. There's more than a dash of truth to this. Homicidal criminals, psychopaths, the mad and the bad could wander to their heart's content, inflicting whatever damage and mischief they could.

The macabre figure of the serial killer is not just a modern invention. The forces of law and order became aware of this phenomenon through the use of computers and other modes of modern communication, so the police could learn that a murder committed in one area had been replicated in another. During the medieval era such facilities were non-existent, but it does not mean that these assassins did not exist. We can imagine the solitary rider, well-armed, passing through isolated small villages, farmsteads, or – as in this novel – châteaux and churches, with no real defence.

Ambrose Rookwood is not just a figment of my imagination. Indeed, wandering clerics were a constant thorn in the side of both church and Crown. 'Criminous clerks' were one of the great unresolved issues of the medieval era. If a man could demonstrate that he was a cleric by reciting the opening verses of the 'Miserere' psalm, then he could plead to be handed over to the church courts, which were much more lenient in their sentencing. The right of sanctuary was also a sacred one. Different churches throughout the city and kingdom enjoyed these privileges, to the absolute fury of officers of the crown.

The seizure of Rookwood is based on a true incident which occurred in 1305. Richard Puddlicot was a merchant who turned to crime. He organized the most brilliant robbery in medieval history: the seizure and theft of the Crown jewels, stored in the crypt at Westminster Abbey. The monks of Westminster were also involved, but that didn't deter the royal clerk, John Drokensford, who was sent to investigate. He tore into the abbey claiming he was looking for something else and found treasure hidden beneath the monks' beds. Richard Puddlicot was also tracked down, hiding in sanctuary. Drokensford, however, persuaded some city bailiffs to break into the church and seize him. They did so and were suitably rewarded, given every assurance that the excommunication levelled against them would be lifted. Richard Puddlicot was flung into the Tower, then taken down in a wheelbarrow to hang on the gallows at Westminster. The King ordered Puddlicot's corpse be flayed and the skin nailed to a door in Westminster Abbey as a warning to the monks. In medieval London, life could be hard, but so was justice!